SHUBNUM KHAN

The Djinn Waits a Hundred Years

MAGPIE
BOOKS

A Magpie Book

First published in the United Kingdom, Republic of Ireland and Australia
by Magpie, an imprint of Oneworld Publications, 2024

Copyright © Shubnum Khan, 2024

The moral right of Shubnum Khan to be identified as the Author of
this work has been asserted by her in accordance with the Copyright,
Designs, and Patents Act 1988

All rights reserved
Copyright under Berne Convention
A CIP record for this title is available from the British Library

ISBN 978-0-86154-626-8 (hardback)
ISBN 978-0-86154-828-6 (trade paperback)
eISBN 978-0-86154-625-1

Design by Meighan Cavanaugh
Printed and bound in Great Britain by Clays Ltd, Elcograf S.p.A

This book is a work of fiction. Names, characters, businesses,
organisations, places and events are either the product of the author's
imagination or are used fictitiously. Any resemblance to actual persons,
living or dead, events or locales is entirely coincidental.

Grateful acknowledgment is made for permission to reprint the following:
Rumi poems from the book *Rumi: The Beloved is You* by Shahram Shiva
Translation of Iqbal's *The Bird's Lament* from Urdu to English by Taahir Umar

Oneworld Publications
10 Bloomsbury Street
London WC1B 3SR
England

Stay up to date with the latest books,
special offers, and exclusive content from
Oneworld with our newsletter

Sign up on our website
oneworld-publications.com

ADVANCE PRAISE FOR *THE DJINN WAITS A HUNDRED YEARS*

'A cracking novel. I loved getting to know Sana, a curious but lonely girl dealing with loss, and Akbar Manzil, an old mansion groaning with memories and secrets. As girl and house connect, Shubnum Khan unfolds a devastating history woven into the present with mastery and poise.'

Jennifer Nansubuga Makumbi, author of *The First Woman*

'Haunting and healing, *The Djinn Waits a Hundred Years*, with its shades of *The House of Spirits* and *Rebecca*, is one of the best books I've read this year... Khan's gorgeous writing lays bare what it means to love, grieve, haunt and, ultimately, let go.'

Sarah Addison Allen, author of *Garden Spells*

'Filled with wonder and colour, the secrets of the dilapidated mansion Akbar Manzil come to life in this rich tale of loss and love. The arrival of fifteen-year-old Sana, who is herself haunted, is the catalyst that revives long-forgotten memories, as well as the spirit that still lingers in the empty rooms. I was enthralled and completely swept away by Khan's masterful unspooling of family secrets, fatal jealousy, and a love that endures after death.'

Yangsze Choo, author of *The Night Tiger*

'Shubnum's magical storytelling creates a dark and luscious mood, where every character is expertly given life. Rich with family and community, this is a novel full of redemptive love.'

Melody Razak, author of *Moth*

'A dark and heady dream of a book, which reveals itself in layers as a gothic horror, a tragic romance, and a classic coming-of-age tale. Hauntingly gorgeous.'

Alix E. Harrow, author of *The Ten Thousand Doors of January*

'*The Djinn Waits a Hundred Years* is an utterly intoxicating novel that hums with life. The labyrinthine corridors of the Akbar Manzil mansion swallowed me whole, left me sacrificed to the mercy of its vengeful lovers and desperate spirits. This is a story with two faces, at once a romance and a horror, full of mirth and full of gore. Its pages will leave you breathless, haunted.'
Karina Lickorish Quinn, author of *The Dust Never Settles*

'South African novelist Khan blends gothic tropes with Indian mythology in her poignant [UK] debut… Playful and evocative.'
Publishers Weekly

'Beautiful, just beautiful. A story – a history really – elegiacally written and filled with everything that makes for an absorbing read: love, intrigue, conflict, mystique, and so much character. Shubnum Khan's *The Djinn Waits a Hundred Years* invites us to examine South Africa's issues of race, class and gender through a refreshingly unique lens. A revelation!'
Siphiwe Gloria Ndlovu, author of the City of Kings trilogy

'*The Djinn Waits a Hundred Years* is a cinematic spectacular, rife with doomed love and vengeful spirits and a lurking violence always waiting to pounce. Shubnum Khan has written a gorgeous gothic mystery, a fascinating meditation on the nature of forgiveness and time.'
Julia Fine, author of *Maddalena and the Dark*

'Beautifully written with intriguing characters and a storyline that spans time, this subtle fantasy novel mixes historical fiction with dark fairy tales.'
Booklist

'Shubnum Khan is a spellbinding storyteller. Her subtly spooky debut is a marvelous literary tableau.' *Shelf Awareness*

'Khan's prose is lush and lovely, her pacing skilful, and she successfully weaves a complex plot with a large cast. A ghost story, a love story, a mystery – this seductive novel has it all.'
Kirkus

In memory of Abbajaan,

our first storyteller

The Djinn Waits
a Hundred Years

Part One

Prologue

1932

In an old wardrobe a djinn sits weeping.

It whimpers and murmurs small words of complaint. It sucks its teeth and berates the heavens for its fate. It curses the day it ever entered this damned house. It closes its eyes and tries to imagine a time before it came here, before it followed the sound of stars from the shore, before the world turned dark and empty.

Something thuds somewhere and the djinn is drawn from its misery by a commotion happening outside. It stops to listen and sounds begin to emerge; doors bang, windows shut, and things are thrown about. There are shouts as orders are given and people hurry through passages. They run up and down and bump heavy things along the stairs.

The djinn pauses, then it uncurls its limbs, swings open the cupboard, and steps out.

There is the patter of footsteps, then the front door slams downstairs and everything is suddenly still.

The djinn steps into the passage and looks around curiously. The floor is scattered with clothing and bedding. It wanders into the rooms; in a child's bedroom, next to a smoking fireplace, twenty-seven plastic soldiers wait for a French army to advance. In a woman's bedroom, a silk camisole slips off a swinging hanger in a closet.

The djinn creeps downstairs. In the kitchen, a dish of potatoes soaks beneath a dripping tap. Steam rises from a set-aside kettle. A basket of fresh laundry waits to be ironed.

The djinn wanders into the long dining room, among the high-backed chairs, and peers into the entrance hall where a grandfather clock ticks loudly. It pulls open the heavy front doors and looks into the bright, clear light of early morning. The stone stairs are strewn with opened trunks and scattered books. The driveway lies empty. The djinn steps outside into the pale pink light and looks to the still, shimmering ocean.

It turns to the looming house behind and wails.

One

2014

No one in Durban remembers a Christmas as hot as this.

The heat is a living breathing thing that climbs through windows and creeps into kitchens. It follows people to work and at queues in the bank and on trains home. It crouches in bedrooms, growing restless until at night in fury it throttles those sleeping, leaving them gasping for breath. It sweeps through the streets and bursts open pipes, smashes open green guavas, and splits apart driveways. It burns off fingerprints and scorches hair and makes people forget what they are doing and where they are going so that they wander around beating their heads.

At the taxi rank in town people wave newspapers under their arms and wipe their foreheads with pamphlets that promise to bring back lost lovers. Witch doctors' phone numbers drip down their temples and into their pockets in inky-blue puddles. Bananas blacken in the sun on pavement tables. The humidity grows and strangers are drawn to one another without meaning to and they cling together in a sweaty unhappy mess.

Out in the suburbs people sit in their inflatable pools with party hats and sip cheap wine from plastic cups. They eat bunches of litchis and hunks of watermelon and burn meat black on the braai. Maidless madams push hair out of their eyes as they hang up washing and count down to the end of the holidays. Dirty dishes pile up in sinks, garbage bags burst open with maggots.

At the coast the sky opens wide and burns the sea white. Little children in multicolored swimsuits skip across the hot sand and shriek in thrilled agony. Families with pots of biryani and lukewarm Coke sit under small umbrellas fanning themselves with Tupperware lids as they dish rice onto paper plates.

The pier stretches on to eternity like a foreboding finger.

SANA MALEK WINDS DOWN her window and searches for a breeze. The dark curtain of hair flies off her neck to reveal her mother's chin, and she turns this way and that as she struggles to make it her own. She is neither girl nor woman, hovering in that space between the two, where at the edge of her thoughts, curling at the eaves, is the glimpse of a fluttering light that promises something wonderful: a knowledge that the world is going to change.

She carries it close to her chest like a secret box.

She is going Home. It is not really home, but her father says it is because he believes it. He says Home can be many places, even places you haven't been before. He says Home can also be a memory if you return to it enough. Sana wants to know exactly how many times you have to return to make a memory Home and her father says you will know when it happens.

Which isn't really an answer but she accepts it anyway.

She accepts many things about him, like the fact that he lives by a collection of axioms of his making: Home can be a memory, rivers are more reliable than roads, and the ground keeps problems in. She accepts he will never be like the fathers she reads about, strong-minded and determined, wearing suits and cracking knuckles. She accepts that without her mother he has lost some anchor and like a ship he has strayed off into uncharted waters. And so when he announces one morning that he has finally found Home, she is not surprised and simply packs up and leaves with him in their Isuzu.

Since her mother's death four years ago her father has become obsessed with coastal towns, marking cities along maps. He studies weather graphs and learns about the histories of towns along the South African coast. The west coast, he says, has many good things, like mussels and otters and small, wild roads, but it is cold and windy and there are too many white people. You can't trust a place with too many white people, he says. The east coast has warmer waters, smoother stones, and a brighter sun—and warm places help you forget the past. They help you leave behind the painful things, he adds.

When they enter the city, the salt hits the air and a streak of blue skims the horizon. They work their way toward the ocean, passing little shops, conference centers, and brick buildings, and come to a knot of streets filled with graffiti, the smells of cooking food, and blaring foreign music. As they move past Nigerian pawnshops and Somali haberdasheries, African immigrants give way to Asian ones as Pakistani chicken tikka stalls emerge between Chinese fashion outlets. Farther down, Indian immigrants adjust the signs of their small spice stores, shift uneasily away from the crowds of new foreigners, trying to make it clear they are not as fresh off the boat. They tack signs onto their storefronts that say ESTIMATED 1918 and mutter about the good old days when everything did not come from China, when customers filled their stores searching for quality cloth and spices.

The secret box in Sana's chest throbs. She is on the brink of womanhood and everything feels full and heavy with expectation; there are

Discoveries That Are Waiting and Experiences to Be Had, and for a moment she allows herself the pleasure of wondering what a new life will be like.

Everything feels shivery and waiting.

"I think we're close," her father says, pointing to the small mosque with a green dome on the side of the street. He turns down a narrow road between apartment buildings that press so close together people can pass notes or pots between the windows, if they like. After a moment the tight buildings fall away and the land opens up around them.

They are driving up a hill along the ocean.

At the top they find a rusting gate, which she swings open for the Isuzu to pass. Ahead of them, in front of the driveway, stands a large house distorted by the shadows of the setting sun. Its windows seem to turn like empty eyes to watch them as they drive up.

Sana wonders if Home can be something that swallows you up.

They turn into a gravel driveway, and in the last of the light Sana sees that the entrance has the crumbling stone letters "Akbar Manzil" above it. She looks up and on the top floor she sees a figure: a girl outlined in the arched window above, watching them. Sana's breath catches and she closes her eyes quickly. She tells herself she is imagining things, that she is just tired from the journey. That nothing can follow her here. She counts to ten and opens her eyes.

The window is empty.

She sighs in relief and jumps out of the car and begins helping her father off-load the luggage. As she heaves out bags, she hears the front door open. In a pool of yellow light in the doorway stands an old man leaning on a cane. He smiles, limping as he comes toward them.

"Welcome!" he calls out.

Behind him the lights in the house stutter and go off.

Two

Sana opens one eye slowly.

The whole world creeps in through a hazy light. The room is bare except for her mattress, a cupboard, and an open suitcase on the floor. Dust sits quietly on everything. The windows hold tattered curtains that sunshine passes through easily.

She tries to lie still, but she's forgotten how. On the farm everything had been still. The silence was a complete thing. She could touch it with her fingers, taste it with her mouth, and sit in it like bathwater. Things took time on the farm; they gathered and grew. You sat and drank tea on the stoep and didn't think about whether it was day or night. But here she feels life being *lived*; outside the curtains people are shouting, children are laughing, trains are running, and buses are leaving.

The world is no longer a quiet place. Like unpicking stitching, she has to slowly undo the thread that keeps the sound in.

Sana comes from a quiet world and so she is a quiet girl. Words are obtrusive things that are too heavy, too solid for her mouth. She sidesteps and maneuvers them like furniture in a room. In a way she has forgotten how to speak; her language has turned into a collection of gestures and nods and whispers. Her quietness unnerves people; they speak more when they are around her to make up for her silence, eventually raising their voices, straining their necks, laughing loudly, using excessive gestures, and becoming exhausted from the effort. Then, suddenly conscious of their behavior, they turn nervous, string their hands into their necklaces or agitate rings around their fingers; they tap their feet and begin to sweat and they blame her for their discomfort, the fear she unexpectedly elicits in them. They begin to despise her for her quiet instigation, feel brutish and uncouth and eventually avoid her altogether, making circles around her at family functions, pretending that she does not exist.

Eventually she begins to disappear into furniture, against walls, her bare ends blending into things like the end of a brushstroke. Perhaps this is the reason they begin to forget that she is there; they cannot find her edges, the parts of her to pull out from the background to identify her by. They walk past her, talk through her, and are surprised when she stands up too suddenly.

Or perhaps it is simply that they refuse to see her because they cannot understand the way she holds herself—so composedly, still as water, unperturbed by such bare edges.

Unaffected by her tragedies.

In a world devoid of sound, she embraces one of shapes. She wonders how letters fit into words and words fit into mouths and mouths fit into other mouths without letting go of the words. She wonders about in-between parts like bridges, ears, and tongues, places that forever remain journeys and never destinations.

In her new room she spreads herself across the floor and against the walls and tries to gauge how much of her fits where:

She is half the length of her bedroom windows. She makes up a third of her doorway. She is eight size-seven steps away from the bathroom. If she lies on the floor, she is the length of the space between her bedroom door and her father's. She can do three somersaults from her bedroom to the kitchen. She fits in the cupboard below the sink.

Just.

The sound of life being lived outside the curtains becomes unbearable and Sana throws open the windows. The air outside is hot and muggy and the day is just beginning.

At the bottom of the hill a knot of streets begin that lead into the heart of the town: here people leave their flats and turn onto the main road with bags and documents and other important things to catch buses and taxis. Those left behind—toddlers, mothers, men who limp, and the elderly—shuffle across their rooms behind thin curtains. The women in their gowns cook smoky breakfasts, dye their hair a streaky brown with the tint running down the sides, and occasionally cry into toilet paper in the bathroom.

She leaves the window and digs through clothes in the open suitcase; she locates a crumpled kurti, too big in the shoulders, something passed down from some distant family member; yellow embroidered cotton with cloth-covered buttons that run down the front. She slips on the long tunic, then puts on a pair of jeans and pulls on her shoes, plastic gum boots that somehow make her feel prepared. She brushes her hair, clips it to one side, and adjusts her mother's chin. She holds a particular roughness, a looseness to her gait and clumsiness to her manners that comes from being an unmothered daughter. She tries to smooth down the creases in her shirt with her hand and for a moment through the thin material she brushes the uneven skin of the scar running above her right hip. She stops suddenly then, and cautiously looks around, but nothing happens and, relieved, she leaves the room and enters the kitchen.

Her father, Bilal Malek, is standing on a stool in the middle of the kitchen and screwing in a light bulb.

"Ah, you're awake. I have good news and bad news. Which do you want first?" he asks as she comes in.

"Bad," she says as she leans against the doorframe and watches him.

"Doctor says the electricity is uh—not entirely stable. He says it can be a little . . . moody. But the good news," he rubs his hands together, "is that I changed some bulbs so it won't be so dark in here anymore," he says, smiling.

The night before, the electricity that fled on their arrival abruptly returned as they were carrying boxes upstairs and they discovered the only light that worked in their apartment was a dim bulb in the kitchen that shuddered every few minutes. They lit stubby candles they found rolling in kitchen drawers and had to feel their way to their rooms, where they dusted sheets and emptied boxes, using their fingers to feel for toothbrushes, towels, and pajamas.

"You know Doctor stopped taking tenants for years? He says he'd been meaning to put that ad in the paper for so long but just never got down to it. I told you—it all works out in the end. This was just waiting for us—I mean no one's lived here for years."

"I can't imagine why," says Sana to herself as she steps over a number of pots that are scattered on the floor to collect dripping water from the ceiling.

"It's not so bad," Bilal says, catching her words. "Look, already one light is fixed," he says as he climbs down and hits the switch. The new bulb in the grimy light fitting remains dead.

He frowns. "Ha! That's strange. It must be something else, maybe a fuse," he says as he scratches his head. "I'll have to check it again later when I find my toolbox." He wipes his hands on a dishcloth. "I'm going to buy some groceries from town—you want to come?"

She shakes her head.

He nods and walks to the crooked door and then turns.

"I think she would have liked this place. She would have said it has . . . character."

Sana pauses. Says nothing.

As he shuts the door behind him, Sana looks around and thinks: She would have hated this place. She would have said it was filthy and falling apart. She would have said he was out of his mind for coming here.

Three

For a long time Akbar Manzil was the grandest house on the east coast of Africa.

When ships from Europe came into the harbor, those on board caught sight of the outrageous manor with its Palladian windows, marble parapets, Romanesque towers, and golden domes. The astonished travelers pointed to the strange structure on the hill and declared among themselves that there was indeed hope for the Dark Continent if such development existed right at the bottom.

It was a sign that civilization (however bizarre) was possible.

But as with many great ambitions in the world, the house was abandoned and soon fell into neglect and began to deteriorate. With an overwhelming responsibility the house passed hands from auction to auction until the local municipality made the financial decision to convert the giant structure to house tenants. The contractor, a cheap draftsman, was called in because no architect would agree to a project involving such mutilation.

After thirty-seven years of lying abandoned, the house was reopened and a group of municipal workers with hammers, tape measures, and pencils made their way up the hill. The designs of the new apartments were awkward, flimsy, and downright peculiar. Trembling rooms were hacked into, misshapen bathrooms were pushed into corners, kitchens rose up inside of bedrooms, walls were broken into to make way for plumbing, and passages were squeezed between rooms like struggling arteries. Smoke rose from the windows and the walls began to stretch, then crack.

Outside on the hill, the house began to swell slightly, like a mouth after treatment at the dentist.

The project was a failure. Those who moved in quickly moved out. People complained; the electricity was unpredictable, the water unreliable, there was damp in the walls, pipes leaked, doorways were too narrow, rooms were unfinished, and the designs were absurd, but mostly, they said, mostly it was just that the place didn't *feel* right. Someone said they had seen a shadow moving across the walls. Another complained of scratching at the doors.

It felt, one tenant ventured to say, like the house was *watching*.

IN THEIR APARTMENT Sana feels squashed and caught in corners. Walls present themselves to her suddenly and thrust her into the bedroom or toss her into the kitchen, or sometimes she finds herself being pushed and pushed until she is out of the apartment completely and standing in the original house.

It is there that the pushing and pulling abruptly stops and everything turns quiet. The silence is heavy, broken only by the groan of pipes and the occasional trickle of water. Sana has the sense that things are moving around her quietly, but if she turns around everything is still.

Of course, such places have secrets. Sana knows it. She knows it from the day she enters, even *before* she enters, such intuition arising with other unknowable knowings, like sensing when a phone will ring or a dog will die; she knows there are all sorts of things to discover.

They wait in the house like keys inside couches.

A mahogany staircase runs beneath a worn carpet and lands on the ground floor at the entrance foyer. Grimy skylights provide patches of light, but for the main part the house remains dark and this makes distances indistinguishable so that passages seem to go on forever.

On the stairway landing Sana passes ragged curtains that throws out speckled light. She peers behind and finds a tall stained-glass window that overlooks a courtyard. In the early morning light, she sees the old man known as Doctor standing outside, throwing seeds to pigeons. Suddenly he pauses, then looks up directly at her. Unsure why, she quickly pushes herself away from the wall. When she looks again, edging slowly around the corner, he is gone. She peers through the curtains, and as she pushes the material, it gives way and falls on her in an explosion of dust and moths. In a tangle of cloth, the sun rushes into the house in a blaze of blue, red, and green.

There is a screech and a voice calls out, "Ya Rabb! Save me. Save me. She's come to kill me. I'm going to die!"

Sana looks around bewildered and is blinded for a moment by the dazzling rays. Then someone laughs manically. As her eyes settle from the flashing light, Sana sees a thin woman with hunched shoulders and narrow hips drift out of the shadows at the foot of the stairs. She has a black scarf draped loosely over her graying hair. Her face comes into the light; her skin is soft and creased like an old map that has been opened many times. Her eyes are bright and wet beneath her eyelids.

"Acha, so you find our little friend. Or did he find you?" the woman asks. Her voice crackles like a radio that wavers between stations.

"W-what?" Sana asks as she untangles herself from the curtains.

The woman gestures toward a dark corner on the landing. In the dim light Sana makes out a metal cage half covered in black cloth housing a small green creature watching her with beady eyes. It gives a small squawk, almost mechanical.

"Our jaan, our beloved, our light of our eyes, don't you know? Our baby . . ." the woman coos mockingly.

"That's enough," snaps a voice. A small, rotund woman wrapped in a sari and a big jersey appears at the top of the stairs. Her thinning hair, parted down the middle, is held in a tiny bun and her red lips are turned down in distress. Bangles clatter around her wrists as she marches downstairs.

"Arreh wah, look at that. Our queen has arrived. Her majesty has come from the Great Upstairs. Welcome!" says the thin woman at the bottom, as she bows, sweeping her arms to the floor.

"That's enough," the small woman says. Her voice is soft, almost squeaky, like new shoes on polished floors. "I told you to leave him alone, Razia Bibi. Tum takleef kyu de rahe hain?"

The woman at the bottom of the stairs crosses her arms over her chest.

"How! I'm just introducing him to our new neighbor. I was saying how sweet he is"—she turns to Sana and continues—"tell her, tell her, how I was saying how sweet he is. So cute. So bechara." She scrunches up her face in an expression of seemingly being unable to bear the cuteness.

The small woman lifts her hand and shakes her bangles as she speaks.

"Bas, Razia Bibi. Bas. Don't making fun of him. He understands everything. You know he's sensitive."

"Sensitive? *Sensitive?*" The thin woman uncrosses her arms. "Ha! Please. That thing is not sensitive. Did you hear him? Arreh bapre, he called God's name in vain. How he can say like that? Even a deaf thing like you must have heard. It's . . . outrageous, *outrageous* I tell you," she says, clinging to the dramatic English word she has unexpectedly discovered in her vocabulary. "I won't have God's name taken in vain by a Hindu bird in a decent Muslim house like this."

"Oh shut up, shut up, shut up, I said that's enough. You're upsetting him," says the other woman. Her lips tremble. "Mr. Patel doesn't know what he's saying. Obviously he must have heard you. You know he repeats things."

The woman at the bottom of the stairs strides forward and thrusts out her neck. "Me? You're blaming me? Everyone knows that good-for-nothing bird keeps screaming for everything! We can't get any work done with all the racket."

Fancy trembles. She moves toward the bird. "I'm taking him upstairs."

"Yes! And keep him there. Until he dies. I hate him on the bloody stairs. I hate seeing his stupid face. Woh jara kabuthar thera jaisa lagtha hai. Just like you he is."

Fancy looks tearful. "You know he likes to look out the window at the pigeons. You know he doesn't like being cooped up in my small room. It's bad for his confidence. And the damp gets in his lungs!" And with that she grabs the big cage and marches up. A few seconds later a door slams somewhere upstairs.

Razia Bibi scowls.

"Sensitive as her bird that one." She turns to Sana now and appraises her. "So, you're the new girl. They told me you're a child—but you're almost a woman. Father-daughter combo, eh? How old, fifteen? Sixteen?" She clicks her tongue and snorts. "I don't know what Doctor was thinking," she says, beginning to mutter to herself. "Thinks he can make all the big-big decisions here without even asking us. I told him nowadays you can't trust anyone. If we take any Tom, Dick, or Harry off the street, what will happen?" She turns to Sana as if *she* has asked *her* the question. "I'll tell you what will happen—this place will become a drug den!" she spits out. "It starts with just letting in some new tenants but pretty soon the drunk down the street is knocking at the door and next thing you know those good-for-nothings from Sydenham are selling ganja out of the parlor. I know trouble when I see it." She looks at the pile of curtains on the landing. "Already you are breaking things in this house, eh? As if enough things are not broken already? Tell me, who leaves a whole farm in Jo'burg to work in an office canteen in Durban? Which man works in an office canteen? And how can you have no mother?"

"Well . . . my mother died," says Sana reasonably.

"So what? Whose mother doesn't die? Which man doesn't get married again? From what I heard it's been *years*. You can't trust a man who chooses to be without a woman. And why did he move *here*? Who in their right mind will move here?" she says, raising her hands in the air. "It's fishy." She climbs the first few stairs and brings her face close to Sana's. "Tell me, are you up to something fishy?"

Sana shakes her head.

"Well," Razia Bibi says, moving back to the foot of the stairs, "you just remember that I may look old but I'm the sharpest one here. You and your father get up to anything and I'll know it. I have the nose, you know," she says, tapping her undeniably well-defined nose. "Carried down from the Pathans, this. GoolamHussein ancestry. You should know we have rules: one, your father is not allowed to bring any strange women here and you're not allowed to bring any boys. We're very strict about that sort of thing. It's a decent house. Two, you call me Razia Bibi, none of that Aunty Razia or Razia Khala business. Am I your aunty? No. Three, if you light a candle or stove in this house, you watch it until it goes out." She lowers her voice and says more to herself, "I shouldn't worry, you'll leave soon enough. This is a crazy place. With crazy people." She raises her voice in the direction of the stairs. "Especially that old one upstairs!" She continues, "Anyone who comes here, leaves. Trust me. This place does funny things to you."

"What sort of things?" Sana finds herself asking.

Razia Bibi pauses, then continues, "You'll see for yourself. Just don't get too comfortable—you'll be packing to leave soon. I would leave if I could! Everything is a problem. The damp! The electricity! The leaks! Why, the other day I swear I could even hear mice in the roof, running around, scratching about." She shudders and continues, "Even that bird is crazy. Did you hear him? Imagine! Tell me, where you come from, do birds say such things?"

"No," Sana answers truthfully.

"Of course not! We should get rid of it. A caged bird is bad luck. My

Goramamoo, he was eighty-five—fit as a fiddle, not a single problem, not even arthritis and you know how much that runs in the Goolam-Hussein family—his bloody grandson, that damned Nafeesa's boy, brought a parrot in the house and just like that," she snaps her fingers, "the next day, Goramamoo had a heart attack and died."

At this point the grandfather clock begins to chime loudly in the foyer. Razia Bibi throws up her arms in the air.

"And *that* thing! Loud enough to wake the dead. It sets that bloody bird off every morning. I can't get any peace here. All I want is some peace. Is that too much to ask for?" she wails. Before Sana can answer, she continues, "You'll find out soon enough. This is a mad place. And you'll leave like everyone else."

And with that she scowls and walks away, disappearing around a corner, leaving Sana standing in bewilderment amid the crumpled curtains.

Four

That night Sana unpacks clothes into the empty cupboard in her room. There is not much: a few dresses, some kurtis, and a pair of jeans that are too short. Most of her clothes are gifts or hand-me-downs from family. She has never been shopping; her mother and father have never told her how to dress so she wears anything that comes by, secondhand dresses and gum boots and her father's old shirts. She keeps her hair short enough to feel full of possibility but long enough to hide her chin.

The only light in her room comes from a lamp next to her bed; it throws shadows over the mottled wallpaper. Her window is open and the gauzy curtains ripple from a sea breeze outside. Sana, grateful for the slight coolness in the room, pauses to wipe the sweat from her top lip before continuing to unpack. As she bends to push her muddy sneakers into the bottom shelf, the lamp flickers, then goes out. She sighs and stumbles in the dark toward her bedside, where she keeps candles and matches. Then from the side of her eye, she catches a small movement across the darkened room. It's slight but so certain that she stops.

Her heart begins to beat fast.

It's nothing. It's nothing. It's nothing, she thinks.

There it is again—a seamless flutter along the side of her eye. In a sudden frenzy, Sana scrambles for where the matches lie. A deep dread has risen in her. With shaking fingers she locates the matchbox and yanks it open; she strikes the flint, and when the flame erupts she holds it up to the darkness like a weapon; in the gloom she makes out a ghostly shape charging toward her across the room. It writhes and twists, reaching for her. She yells, dropping the match that goes out, and leaps backward. On the floor, she braces herself. When nothing happens, she opens her shut eyes and realizes what she was looking at; the sheer curtains have picked up in the wind and are dancing wildly in the darkened room.

It's nothing. It's nothing. It's nothing.

She almost weeps in relief.

Her father appears at the door with a gas lamp.

"Are you okay? I thought you called," he says, looking around.

"No, sorry. I just fell over getting the matches. I'm okay," she says as she picks herself up and looks around, feeling embarrassed.

"You sure?" he says.

She nods.

He brings his lamp to her bedside to help as she lights the candle. The wick catches and she blows out the match.

He studies her. "Are you sure you're not hurt?" He gestures to her.

She looks down and finds she is clutching her hip tightly. She drops it quickly.

"I'm fine, I told you. Don't worry," she says with a wan smile.

"Sana," he hesitates. "You don't hate it here, right? This could be Home?"

Sana looks around the empty room. "This could be Home."

He smiles then retreats, the light of the lamp following him.

When he is gone, Sana raises her candle to the room but the darkness seems impenetrable.

"There's nothing here," she says quietly. "Nothing can follow you Home."

She gets under the covers. She closes her eyes and pictures herself in the bed, within the room, within the apartment, within the house.

It calms her.

Five

Doctor sits on the veranda soaking up the sun. Every morning he makes himself a cup of Five Roses tea, brewed extra strong, and sits in a chair facing the sea. His habit is to sit here after Fajr prayers to watch the sun rise. It is one of the reasons he loves this city so: being able to watch the darkness turn to light over the water.

Occasionally he falls asleep on the veranda, and when he wakes up to see the sun high in the sky, he looks at his wrinkled hands and his whole history rushes up to remind him of what has passed, the important parts building like a jigsaw puzzle, filling out gradually until he finally sees the part he is in.

This afternoon when he wakes, it seems to him that he is still married, that his leg still exists, and that he is waiting for something, perhaps his wife to bring him some tea. He nearly calls out for her, her name already on his lips, but when he tries to stand up on a nonexistent leg, an even older forgotten space, he loses his balance and sits down abruptly.

He remembers: he is living in this house now, his wife is dead, and he is an *old man*.

It astonishes him every time.

"Asalaamwa'alaikum, Doctor!" someone calls out to him from the stairs at the front of the house.

"Walaikumsalaam," Doctor says, turning his head to see who is talking as he pushes himself out of that other time, sets his mind like someone adjusting his watch to the current time zone. "Oho, Bilal!" he exclaims as he spots the tenant standing on the stairs, his arms full of shopping bags. "How nice to see our new member of the party out and about. How are you, beta?"

"Alhamdulilah. Enjoying some sun, I see," says Bilal, smiling as he shades his eyes with his hand.

Doctor brightens and adjusts himself so he can face the new tenant properly. "Yes, it's my favorite thing to do. Such lovely sun here—the weather is good even in winter. You appreciate these things after living in a place like Dublin," he says.

"Is that where you studied, Doctor?"

"Haan. Studied and then lived there for fourteen years. Fourteen freezing winters. But tell me, how are you settling in? Not too many problems, I hope?"

"No, it's been wonderful. Fascinating place, really. I like to fix things—so it's perfect for me. The electricity is very interesting—the house was wired for electricity *after* it was built so you have to really search for the wiring."

"Don't worry yourself, beta, some of the things here are too old to fix. Especially the people!"

They laugh together. Then Bilal says, "You know what happened earlier? A bat nearly attacked me in the big kitchen."

"A bat? Ha!" Doctor sits up and adjusts himself. "That's the least of your troubles, my boy. Have you met the women who live here?"

Bilal chuckles.

"A lot of shopping you're doing," Doctor observes, looking to the bags in Bilal's hands, which strain with tomatoes, potatoes, and packets of spices.

He raises a grizzled eyebrow. "So much food, beta?"

Bilal looks down at the packets in his hands and grins. "I find nothing feeds the soul as well as food. Don't you?" He hesitates. "My wife—cooking reminds me of her."

Doctor smiles. "She was a good cook, beta?"

Bilal looks sheepish. "Not exactly."

"Well, you must teach me how," says Doctor. "I've always wanted to learn."

"Of course," says Bilal amiably. "In fact, I was thinking of having a dinner for everyone. You can help me."

LATER, UPSTAIRS IN HIS KITCHEN as Bilal unloads packets of spices into the cupboards, he considers the bag of coriander seeds in his hands; just a few years ago he wouldn't have known what this was and yet now he knows how to clean it, roast it gently in a pan, and grind it with cumin to get the most out of its flavor. This learning process was how he had managed his grief.

He had been widowed at a young age from a distant wife, left with a daughter on the cusp of puberty. The loss had overwhelmed him with an unbearable feeling he had not known what to do with. Immediately after her burial, he threw himself in his wife's study and locked the door. Surprised at this passionate display of emotion from their usually docile relative, his family had attempted to break the door down. It was while he was sitting among her papers and complicated books—works that even in her death mocked him with their serious titles and dull covers—that he saw a heavy red book planted on top of one of the shelves. While his relatives banged at the door, he climbed up a small stepladder, pulled the book down, and blew dust off the cover. It was *Indian Delights*, the legendary local Indian cookbook his mother had bequeathed them for their wedding, that his wife had never used. Curious, he opened the book and turned the pages slowly. He muttered the words to himself under his breath, rolling his tongue over each pronunciation: paratha, korma, jalebi, papadums, and ras malai.

He ran his finger under each word and wondered what they would taste like.

When they finally broke the door down, that was how his family found him; perched upon the stepladder with the heavy book on his lap, his head bent low. He calmly climbed down the ladder and walked past them muttering, "Gulab jamuns."

And that was how Bilal Malek ended up cooking.

He spent much of his mourning period in the kitchen, whisking bowls of cream in the crook of one arm while inspecting a recipe with the other, then ladling rich curries onto visitors' plates. For hours in the day he read cookbooks and at night he tossed and turned in bed as he dreamed about beating egg whites to stiff peaks and braising fresh garlic in curry leaves. Now, over pots of boiling water, he steams rice and potatoes, sifts through pans of cumin as they toast on the stove.

It softens the blow somehow, makes something come alive again.

SANA SITS CROUCHED in the cupboard below the kitchen sink.

It makes her feel safe to be surrounded by something that fits her exactly. As if she is enclosed in an egg, waiting to hatch. As if this space were meant for her only. She can hear her father walking about the kitchen, opening cabinets and closing them, whistling to himself. She stays quiet.

When her father whistles, he changes shape; he becomes a fuller, clearer thing, like an image coming into focus in a pair of binoculars.

When her father whistles like this he is remembering her mother. And when he remembers her mother, he turns so crisp and so clear, her eyes almost hurt.

When she was nine, Sana made a discovery at a family wedding that would change the way she saw shapes in the world. A newlywed couple holding hands onstage were laughing together and the man briefly reached over and placed his mouth lightly to the woman's mouth. Some of the guests laughed and looked away shyly, but Sana stared in amazement. She had never seen such a thing. It seemed to her that in that precise moment, the moment the man and the woman's eyes met in some understanding, two separate people suddenly transformed into one person with one shape and all their ends and trailing edges joined to form a single perfect outline. The woman *was* the man and the man *was* the woman and there were no halves, only wholes with no beginnings or endings.

To see two human beings merge seamlessly into one distinct shape left her breathless.

From then on, she has tried to discover how love affects the shape of things.

She watched how the faces of the workers on the farm changed when they talked about their loved ones; how a divorced uncle of hers talked about his ex-wife; listens to how her father whistles when he remembers her mother. She sees that the signs of love exist in small and quiet ways, from how people look at each other (or don't), from the way they speak to each other (or don't), how they touch each other's shoulders carelessly or search for someone in a crowded room. She scribbles notes, trying to capture it all.

In a history class she learns about the Grecian myth of half humans, how human beings originally had four arms, four legs, and a single head made of two faces. With such great strength, her teacher had told them, these beings threatened to conquer the gods. To punish humanity for their pride, Zeus split them in half into separate beings.

These halves are said to be in constant search for each other in the world, Sana writes. *And that when the two find each other, there is an unspoken understanding between them, they will feel unified and lie with each other in unity for eternity.*

It is a passage she keeps returning to.

Six

In the courtyard stands an empty stone fountain crowned with a statue of a lion's head.

It had been a magnificent thing once, gushing water from its open maw into the vasques below, drawing the courtyard's attention with its roaring water, shimmering fish, and bathing birds. But time has worn away the edges, rubbed raw the rims and corbels, and the fountain looks somber now, more mournful than mighty.

Sana traces canals that run from the fountain out of the courtyard beyond an archway of the house. She passes into a garden filled with trees and overgrown hedges and in the distance she can see a crumbling stone wall that breaks off where the coast drops into a cliff. As she wanders through the trees she finds a swath of mesh half strung and fallen in what she recognizes to be a giant aviary by the birdhouses and baths. Despite the disarray, the remains still house a number of birds that peck in basins or call from the trees. Some are common like Indian mynahs, and others more exotic like ring-necks and bulbuls. As she wanders through the tangled mesh, she hears a rhythmic clicking coming from deep inside and she follows the sound until she rounds a guava tree and comes in view of a sea of pink roses. Fancy is standing in its flowery midst wearing earmuffs, an oversize coat, a large pair of sunglasses, and a floppy hat. In her gloved hands she holds a pair of pruning shears. She pauses to dab her sweaty brow with a facecloth she untucks from the waist of her sari and then stops as if she senses something. She swings around and tilts her head to see beyond her hat, then gives a shriek.

"Arreh! You gave me a shock," she shouts at Sana as she drops her facecloth. "I almost had a heart attack." She pulls off her muffs and bends down to pick up her facecloth and dusts it.

"I'm sorry," says Sana as she steps forward. "I was just . . . taking a walk."

Fancy shakes her head and tuts. "Oh no, don't apologize dear. *I* should be apologizing to *you*." She takes a deep breath and drops her head. "I'm so sorry about yesterday. I was going to welcome you properly but that Razia Bibi put me in *such* a bad mood—I stayed in my room the whole day. She's so mean sometimes! Mr. Patel—he's such a bechara. Poor thing. What he knows what he says? He doesn't like my flat—it's damp you see and there's no view. At least on the landing he gets to see what's happening in the courtyard. But Razia Bibi hates him—she says he's noisy but tell me how one *small* bird can be so noisy?" Fancy suddenly drops her pruning shears. "Anyway, dear, welcome to our house!" She grabs Sana in a tight embrace. Sana, unable to recall the last time someone hugged her, holds herself stiffly. "When Doctor told us we were getting new tenants I was over the moon! We haven't had anyone new in *years*. Razia Bibi was always against it. This time Doctor put his foot down—he said we needed new life in this old place. But Razia Bibi made him promise that if he brought anyone in, they must be *our* people—or else she said she was going to pack up and leave. I don't know *what* she's talking about because she has nowhere else to go." Fancy pulls off her hat and fans herself as she talks. "Do you like my roses? I thought I'll give them a trim while it's cloudy."

Sana steps into the plot and looks around. "They're very nice." Then she looks at Fancy curiously and asks, "Why do you trim them when it's cloudy?"

"I'm allergic to the sun, you see," Fancy says, as if it were the most natural thing in the world.

Sana considers this. "I've never met anyone allergic to the sun," she says.

"It's very rare," replies Fancy matter-of-factly. "I mostly work in the garden in the evenings. When I first moved here, this was all dead, but now look how wonderful it is," she says, waving to the flowers.

"How long have you lived here?" asks Sana.

"Let's see . . ." she says, drawing her fingers up. "Doctor got the place in 1988. I came in 1990, the same time as Razia Bibi. Then came Pinky, and then Zuleikha a few years later." She turns to Sana. "And you? You lived in Jo'burg all your life?"

Sana nods.

"And it's just you and your father, haan? No brothers or sisters?"

Sana looks down and clears her throat. "Just the two of us."

Fancy looks at Sana sympathetically. "You must be missing home, dear."

Sana shakes her head. "Not really."

"Yes, that Jo'burg is too fast." Fancy nods her head knowingly. "You'll love it in Durban, trust me—and soon enough this house is going to be home."

Sana pauses, then says, "Razia Bibi said funny things happen here. What did she mean?"

"Oh, don't worry about her. She's full of nonsense, that one," says Fancy dismissively. "Who knows what she's talking about half the time."

Sana turns to look at the house. "Who lived here before?"

"Ah, nobody knows. They say it was empty for decades before the first tenants came, and then they left too," says Fancy. She looks up at the sky and tuts. "Look at that. It's getting sunny again. Let me get back inside," she says as she pulls her hat back on firmly.

The garden is better at keeping secrets than the house. Whereas the house has grown stiff and slow and occasionally drops a piece of history from the rafters, the garden is nimble; it grows and climbs and peers. It is alert enough to ensure it keeps its secrets.

Sana tramps through it in her rubber boots, her fingers grazing the long grass that oftentimes rises to her calves. She closes her eyes, feels the coruscating sunlight on her lids. She walks along a section of the west wall and trails her fingers through the wild tickey creeper. The stone behind the vines is rough against her fingertips.

The garden bristles. Calculates. Tries to distract with rustles in the grass. But she doesn't notice, continues to move her hand through the creepers, until quite suddenly the wall beneath gives way.

Sana stops. Curiously, she pushes her hand in and it disappears up to her shoulder into a cool space. She opens and closes her fingers in the space beyond. She digs through the vines, wrestling with knotted layers until she pulls apart the foliage and finds herself looking at metal bars. She tears away the creepers and finds a small door.

She is looking into a low cage that runs under the house.

She unbolts the door and the gate squeaks open shrilly. She steps in and her eyes take time to adjust to the darkness beyond. It smells of damp earth and dead leaves. The quietness inside is a crouching thing ready to spring.

Despite the heat, Sana shivers. She walks around but there is nothing inside but leaves and sawdust on the floor. The brick is covered in a creeping moss. At the exit, she notices something next to the door.

Along the wall are deep scratches.

She crouches on the ground and runs her fingers into the sharp grooves.

Outside, the sparrows titter.

Seven

For eighty-two years something has been happening upstairs in the east wing of Akbar Manzil. Like the start of a rash, one can never say exactly when it began, except to say that it always seemed this way.

At first glance it seems as if one section of the upstairs hall is painted darker than the rest. On closer inspection it is revealed to be a passage crammed with objects that run down the length of the east wing. It is a mesmerizing tower of ruined items that have been dumped over the years; broken wardrobes, cracked mirrors, damaged paintings, and rusting bathtubs balance on one another in an unabashed display of abandonment.

On the surface it seems quiet and still but underneath, in the gaps between chair leg and clawfoot, a frenzied air lurks as things clamber, cling, and crawl, each trying to escape a forgotten fate. Spiders spin webs and scuttle across bottles, their delicate legs dancing in shafts of light. Mice shuffle in nests made of pages from old books while silverfish slip between waterlogged carpets.

The passage becomes a no-man's-land that most of the rooms have been emptied into during renovation and where tenants over the years have quietly crept to at night to abandon their unwanted possessions. When morning dawns they feign ignorance at the growing collection in the east wing.

For the people themselves who come to Akbar Manzil come to forget or be forgotten. If they could, they would insert themselves in that passage like stone statues and close their eyes forever.

It is there between the discarded shapes of discarded peoples' lives that Sana feels most comfortable. She spends her afternoons in the passage peering, prodding, and pulling open things. She shines her torch into boxes, unrolls carpets, and empties glass bottles, trying to revive the forgotten by acknowledging them. She pushes her fingers into their chests, pumps gently.

She leans in and whispers, *"Are you still alive?"*

When she asks questions about the house no one seems to have answers; they do not know who lived here before, they do not know why there are cages in the garden, they do not know who built this place. They just say it was always this way.

ONE RAINY AFTERNOON, Sana sits under a damaged dressing table inspecting objects in the passage. She is used to the sounds of the house now—the creak of the floorboards, a drip from a pipe, the wind whistling through a crack in a window. And then sometimes there are sudden deep silences. It is as if the house had its own language, constantly whispering or turning stonily quiet.

She pulls a box toward her and opens it; inside is a collection of plastic army men, and as she reaches her hand in, she hears something down the passage: a rattle, like a door being tried.

She moves the box aside and sits upright on her knees to look into the packed east wing; she squints her eyes and it seems to her there is something moving down there, a shifting of shadows. She picks the saucer with her candle from the floor and lifts it in the air. The flickering flame throws light on the junk and something flashes in the distance, or perhaps the light throws itself too forward, farther than intended, slips on a broken lamp, landing for a moment too far in the passage, too close to where it shouldn't be. The light quickly dances back through the objects, dusts itself off, and waits on the walls, pretending it has not behaved so carelessly.

But Sana sees it.

Her skin prickles. At the end of the passage a white face grins at her from among a mix of mops and brooms.

She gasps and scrambles off the floor, her heart beating madly. She turns but then pauses as something occurs to her. Something about the face, the caught grin, the peculiar inanimation of it strikes her.

She turns back.

She raises the light and squints into the darkness ahead. The face is still there. It does not move. Her light falls on the objects ahead and she realizes she is looking at the face of a doll. She climbs through the pile, stepping over broken chairs and boxes to get a closer look. When she finally reaches the end, she finds a porcelain doll tucked deep among the brooms. She slips her hand into the jumble all the way to her elbow, searching for the doll's body until her hand touches something smooth, round, and heavy. She wraps her fingers around it. She feels the weight and the texture of it in her palm; she tries to pull it out but can't.

She realizes what it is.

A *doorknob*.

She slips her hand deeper and twists the knob but it does not yield. She fishes in the pile again and manages to pull out the doll. The white face with black-painted eyes is cracked across one side and its heavy porcelain body is covered in a frilly faded satin. The break runs from the left eye down over the cheek into the smiling mouth, where a crack reveals the hollow inside.

She slips the doll into her dress pocket and leaves.

The house had shifted uneasily when the girl waded toward the end of the passage. In the rafters a mutter had risen and the cockroaches had scurried to find darker places. The spiders had spun their threads faster and the little mice hearts beat harder, *boom, boom, boom.* When the girl reached for the door handle, the house had held its breath.

The spiders had stopped midspin, the cockroaches had frozen, and the mice had trembled.

When the girl finally climbs out of the pile and leaves the passage with the doll tucked away, the house exhales a shaky breath. The creatures calm down and the house, relieved, becomes drowsy and nods off.

Everything turns quiet.

Except the door behind the mops and brooms, which jostles in its frame.

Eight

The next morning Sana wakes up to the sound of a child laughing. She sits up and looks around warily. Dawn is just breaking outside and already the air is hot and heavy in the room. She closes her eyes and counts to ten. She hears it again; a girlish giggle echoes through the corridors. She slips on her boots and follows the sound to the main house.

It's nothing. It's nothing. It's nothing.

At the bottom of the stairs sits a girl.

Sana closes her eyes. She counts to ten again. When she opens them, the girl is still there.

Sana holds the balustrade and takes an unsteady step forward and the girl turns back to look at her accusatorially.

"Took you long enough."

Sana feels bile rise in her throat.

It is not nothing.

"When did you come?" she asks wearily.

"That's not a very nice way to welcome someone," the girl says, crossing her arms over her chest.

"You aren't supposed to be here," says Sana, shaking her head.

"You *left* me," the girl says, her face growing dark. "You left me *alone* on the farm. Do you know how scary it is there at night? There are *jackals* there."

"I had to go," Sana says quietly, as she finally reaches the figure.

"You can't go anywhere without me, silly. I'll always find you."

Sana sits down on a step and puts her head in her hands.

The girl inches closer toward her and puts her arm around her. She whispers, "There, there. I'm here now."

When Sana was born, she was born as two. A Two-for-One special, her father had said. Like two bottles of Sunlight Soap for the price of one at Checkers.

In reality, it was more than that. If truth be told, its true name was something far more terrible than a Two-for-One special.

It was the Maleks' First Tragedy.

She and her sister came into the world as one person. When the doctor pulled them out from the slice in their mother's stomach, a nurse had to help the doctor hold the struggling mess. They were joined at the hip. Literally. When they slept, her father said, it looked like they were two babies lying side by side. They were exactly the same, except the other girl had gray eyes, a gift from some ancestor high up in the lineage. Her mother was very tired, had become a very tired woman after their birth. The marriage was not ready for a child, let alone two sick children.

Conjoined twins were for white people in soap operas and medical dramas. It wasn't for people in the real world who had real lives with real problems.

You must understand, her father had said, they loved them very much but it was strange to have babies like that, children who had not learned to let go of each other in the womb. People who visited grimaced and her mother stopped visitors from coming to the farm. Her mother sometimes wondered if it was her fault, he said. She wondered if she had eaten something wrong or had taken too many walks. She sometimes blamed an apricot she had eaten from an orchard; she said it had looked bad but she had eaten it anyway. Other days she would stop for a moment and say, "Ah, it must have been the chicken that day. I saw the way the hen looked at me—her eyes were hard."

Given to bouts of melancholy, her mother had always thought of herself as a damaged person. Often she felt that she had spread her brokenness to her children at some point. After all, they had been inside her; they of all people were closest to whatever was wrong.

At six months the pair were deemed strong enough to have the simple operation to separate them. But soon after they were separated, her sister became sick; the day after the operation, her heart began failing, she shrieked and jerked her tiny feet furiously, as if she had suddenly realized that she had lost a part of herself. She left the world screaming and kicking in an angry frenzy and it seemed to doctors that her breath had just been pulled out of her midscream; in the middle of her struggle, she just simply stopped.

Her hands fell limp and her gray eyes froze.

SOMETIMES SANA THINKS she remembers it; the pain of being separated. She remembers the scalpel, the cut, and the blood. Sometimes she thinks she remembers everything. It comes to her in such a vivid ache she draws a hand to her waist. She thinks she remembers the other face beside her on the bed, even vaguely as a warm haze in the womb.

She feels her sister's space around her the way some feel a phantom limb, except this is a phantom sister.

She learns in madressah that souls leave the body when a person sleeps. That a sleeping person is practically dead. Souls wander the earth or other worlds or the future or the past until they are called back to their bodies. Those that don't return or cannot find their way back leave their bodies to die in their sleep. She wonders then perhaps when the pair of them were unconscious on the operating table if their soul had left, and when it returned to find them separated, had chosen her to enter.

It seems to her that she has been the coward, the one who let her sister down, as if they made some pact in the womb that if they cannot be together then they will leave together. Sometimes she feels the remains of her sister still in her blood or caught in the stitches of her scar.

A part the doctor missed, or the part that belongs to neither but both.

She once read of an American physician named Duncan MacDougall, who sought to measure the mass lost by a human when a soul departs the body at death. He weighed those in the final stages of death and revealed that when they died they lost twenty-one grams. According to him, the weight of a human soul was twenty-one grams.

She wonders then if her soul is heavier or lighter than twenty-one grams. Perhaps the soul that returned still carried bits of her sister, like pulp at the bottom of juice.

HER SISTER SITS WITH HER on the stairs in the early morning light.

She moves closer and pulls Sana tighter toward her as she gently pats her head, smoothing down her hair. Then she brings her face close to Sana and whispers in her ear. "If you feel so bad, you should kill yourself."

Her sister's fingers dig slowly into her scalp.

Sana tries to move. The floor beneath her seems to fall away and she feels herself descending into a familiar hopelessness. She tries to pick her head up, to look for the light at the eaves, but everything is dim. She closes her eyes and tries to imagine her shape in the house, in her apartment, in her bedroom. Then from under her eyelids she sees a flutter at the edge, just a flicker of light, barely perceptible. She takes a breath and stands up suddenly so that the other girl falls off her.

Her sister scowls and leaps to her feet.

"You wretched girl! You thought you could leave me? *Me?* You thought you could come to this house and I wouldn't know? *I know everything!*" she yells.

Sana walks down, ignores her.

"You're wrong, you know. *She* would have loved this place!" her sister calls out.

Despite herself, Sana turns.

"Yes. She would have loved it. It's exactly like her. Broken and ruined. She would have been right at home here."

Sana looks around at the murky windows and worn carpets.

Her sister descends the last few stairs. "Do you know *why* she would love it especially?" Her sister looks around, then lowers her voice. "There's something here. Something dark."

Sana finally looks at her.

A twisted smile lights up her sister's face. "Something darker than her." She starts to chuckle. "The *irony*! You thought you escaped but all you did was end up in another broken place."

"I wasn't trying to escape *her*," says Sana suddenly.

Her sister stops smiling. "Why are you so cruel? Am I not your blood?"

"I don't know what you are," says Sana as she turns and leaves.

"Oh, don't be like that! Let's be friends again," her sister wails and reaches for her hand. "Like the good old days."

Sana shakes it off and continues walking away.

"I'm the only one you have to protect you!" her sister shouts after her.

Sana steps into the black-and-white-tiled foyer, her heart beating hard in her chest. She thought she had escaped. She thought her sister would leave her when she finally found Home. Hadn't her father said the sea washed everything away? She thought they had a new beginning. She should have realized there was no such thing.

She pulls open the front door and steps out. The day is just starting and a faint red lines the ocean. She looks away. Her edges ache and she wraps her arms around herself to contain what she can; to stop herself from spilling over. She hears someone calling her name and she closes her eyes and counts to ten, but she hears it again and this time she turns.

Nine

Doctor had called from the veranda.
His apartment is filled with various things—piles of books, travel souvenirs, towers of videocassettes, and pots with plants.

He sets a cup of tea before Sana. He sits down and pours the steaming brown liquid from his cup into a saucer and blows. "Looks like we're both early birds, hai na?"

Sana nods as she picks up her tea and sips. It warms her insides and comforts her. Blunts the sting of her edges. She takes one of the chocolate biscuits he offers.

He also takes one and says guiltily, "I'm not supposed to have them but I've always had a sweet tooth." He chuckles. "They couldn't keep me away from the sweetmeats as a child!"

Sana laughs then, finding it hard to picture the old man as a small boy. She leans back into the sofa and looks around.

"How do you like living here, beti?" he asks as he lifts his saucer and slurps.

"It's different," Sana replies. She thinks about her encounter a few minutes ago. "And also, the same."

"It must be boring for you. All these old aunties and uncles everywhere. I'm sorry we don't have young people for you here," says Doctor.

"Oh, it's okay. I'm used to being by myself most of the time." She puts down her cup and picks up a black-and-white photo of a couple on the table next to her. The young man in the picture wears a suit and looks seriously into the camera.

"Wow, is this you?" she asks, unable to hide her surprise.

"Yes. Back when I was a serious young man," says Doctor, smiling as he returns his cup to the saucer. "I was born in South Africa but I grew up in India, you know? But it's only when I went to Ireland to study that I really felt alive. Ah, it was a new world to behold! The landscape, the buildings, the people. And no mother always telling me what to do. It felt like I was my own person suddenly. It felt like I was . . . real." Doctor falls suddenly silent.

Sana waits but Doctor does not say more. He picks his cup up again and brings it to his lips and blows over the surface. The clock ticks. Sana sits in her words, wallowing in them, and then slowly, gently, she steps over the line she usually waits behind and says, "But didn't you miss home?"

Doctor leans back in his chair. "No, beti. I wanted to be Irish. Some days I almost thought I was." He chuckles then shakes his head.

"Why?"

"Why did I want to be Irish?"

Sana nods.

He looks down. "I think—I think I was ashamed of who I was. I so badly wanted to be someone else and in Dublin I could be anyone. I felt like I could make myself into someone new, you know?"

Sana, who knows all about this feeling, looks down at the biscuit she is holding. She watches crumbs fall to the carpet.

"And, could you?" she asks softly.

Doctor sips his tea. "I learned a new place doesn't mean you get to start over," he says, sounding a little bitter. There is a pause before he continues. "Still, I stayed. After I became a doctor, I called Ireland my new home and vowed never to return to India again. My mother wrote me letters but I stopped replying. I thought I was my own person and I thought it was enough. But the past will always follow you, no matter how hard you try to leave it behind." He puts down his cup and sighs.

"Beti, when you're away from your family and everything you know for so long, it eats you up. I did not understand this then. I stopped talking so much or going anywhere. I stopped sleeping. I just sat with my books and pretended to read." His wrinkled face turns creased as he frowns at the memory. Sana leans forward in her seat, feeling an urge to reach out and touch his hand in some way. It is such an unusual feeling for her that she coughs and shifts in her seat to distract herself.

Doctor continues in a gravelly voice. "And then news of my mother's death arrived." He closes his eyes. "I regret—but it's too late now." He lowers his voice. "Even then it was too late." He trails off and turns quiet.

A moment passes before Sana asks tentatively, "So you never went back to India?"

"No." He sits back. "I tried to live my new life in Ireland. But I don't know, somehow it always felt like a lie. Something didn't feel right about it."

"Is that how you ended up back here?" asks Sana, picking up her cup and wrapping her hands around it. "Because it didn't feel right there?"

"No. It was war," Doctor says grimly. "War brought me back."

Sana's eyes widen. "War?"

"In fifty-eight. Africa was bleeding, civil war erupting everywhere. Medical volunteers were urgently needed, they said, and I don't know why, perhaps I needed to escape . . ." Doctor sighs. "I just signed up and left for Algeria."

"What was it like?" asks Sana, holding her cup tight.

"It was another world," Doctor says shaking his head. "People"—he shifts uncomfortably—"people were fighting for freedom, for the right to live, to *exist*." He looks into the distance and continues in a soft voice. "It was like nothing I had ever known. *Nothing* could have prepared me. There was . . . so much blood. Sickness. Disease. We were working with so little—such limited supplies. And there was always noise: crying, screaming, explosions. I don't ever remember it being quiet." He looks into his hands. "But you know, I preferred it that way." He nods to himself. "I know it sounds terrible, but—the noise was better than the quietness. It meant we were still alive. It meant there was work to be done. All I knew was I had to work as hard as I could, everything else was forgotten."

Doctor's eyes cloud over and it seems as if he has suddenly found himself back at camp, among the passing stretchers, the distant gunfire, and the calls for him to come quickly. Sana watches him raise a hand as if waving away smoke, almost mumble something to someone as if giving an instruction.

"Doctor?" Sana says uncertainly.

Doctor drops his hand and laughs self-consciously. He takes a shaky breath. "Forgive me, I haven't spoken about this in a long time." He sits back and continues. "I kept moving. I didn't want to stay in one place for too long."

"Why not?" asks Sana.

"I—I wanted to forget. Who I was. I didn't even want to know my own name anymore. And some days I didn't. The longer hours I worked, the less I slept, the less I remembered. And then it was 1960 and the continent was exploding. I moved with an aid organization from Congo to Somalia, then Sierra Leone. My colleagues, my fellow doctors, they told me to slow down, to go home and rest, but where was home? Where could I rest? I didn't know."

Sana nods. She knows about Home; she knows it is not a simple place to find.

Doctor leans forward suddenly, his eyes slightly glazed. "I still remember this one day . . . I was sitting with a sick child in a refugee camp and someone switched on a radio and there was a Bembe song playing. The sudden beat in the quiet camp made one of the nurses smile and she started to sway her hips and one of the other nurses started laughing and joined her and soon the whole camp was clapping and smiling with the swaying nurses as the crackle of the radio went on. I started clapping along, too, and I was smiling, then laughing, and then— then I was crying and I didn't even know it until I felt the tears and brought my fingers to my face. And then I was sobbing and I thought in the commotion no one had noticed, but after a moment I felt the arms of the child whose bed I was sitting at rise up around me and this child— this child with his little body was comforting me over a sorrow even I couldn't explain." Doctor takes a deep breath. "It's the last thing I remember properly about that time. The next day the explosion hit the camp. The shrapnel sliced my leg almost clean off. And—and I don't know how to explain it but when it happened it was almost as if I had been *waiting* for it. That everything had been building to that moment."

He sits back then, as if relieved to be here in this room, now.

Sana looks at his leg curiously. "Is that when you—lost it?"

He almost laughs at her brusqueness. "Yes. The very next day."

"Do you . . . *feel* it? They say when you lose a part of yourself, it can feel like it's still there. Like a . . . phantom." She looks around the room. "But it's not real. It's just your imagination playing tricks."

Doctor nods. "Oh, yes. That feeling never really goes away. In fact, I kept opening my stitches by falling over because I kept trying to stand up. I forgot that it was gone. That early period was a hard time," he says, sighing. "I became very quiet, you know? I stopped eating or doing anything. I would just stare at the walls. I would even throw my food at the hospital staff. My sister thought I was dead. She sent telegrams but I never replied. They took me to Kenya then; the facilities were better there. Then, for me, the war was over, because I couldn't run away from myself any longer. It felt like my life was over."

Sana looks at the photo next to her. "But your life wasn't over. You got married, right? This was your wife?" she asks and points to the woman in the frame. "How did you meet?"

Doctor smiles. He picks up the photo and looks at it fondly.

Sana watches him and sees something shift in his shape. It is just a shudder, but something in him lifts and softens like the first light at dawn. Sana takes out her notebook. As Doctor begins to speak, she writes.

"She was my nurse. She was strong and kind, even when I was stubborn, even when I was rude. She was the one who forced me to eat and took me out in the wheelchair. She knew how to talk to me. That's a rare thing you know, knowing how to talk to another person." He leans back. "She would run ahead of me on the path, calling for me to catch up." He closes his eyes. "She had this scent, you know? I never knew what it was at first. It was floral, but also like coconut." He sniffs the air as if breathing it in. "Later, I found out it was gardenias. She smelled of gardenias." He opens his eyes and smiles.

Sana watches as Doctor changes shape in front of her as he speaks. The dawn breaks and he is no longer a lonely man with frail hands; he is a strong, young man with wild hair and bright eyes, and she realizes then *a memory can make you whole.*

"She would take me to the bioscope in Mombasa every Saturday," he continues. "Oh, she *loved* going to the pictures. Sometimes she would see the same film five or six times! She liked the Hollywood films but her favorites were always the Indian ones." He points to the videocassettes stacked on the floor. "She's the one who got me started."

He clears his throat and puts the photo back down. He finds that he is suddenly overwhelmed. He is quiet, then he says, "I hardly speak about her. No one really asks me these questions." He looks up to find Sana waiting with pen in hand. He smiles. "Have you been writing this down?" he asks.

Sana, embarrassed, says, "Sorry . . . I hope you don't mind. I just write things down to remember later. The parts that feel . . . important."

Doctor nods. "That's clever. I wish I wrote down more things."

Sana smiles gratefully. Then asks, "What was she like?"

"Cheeky!" Doctor says immediately and laughs. "She was a no-nonsense person! She had to be with her sort of job. I never wanted to go anywhere, but she kept forcing me until she got her way. I still remember the first time she took me; I said I didn't want to go but she turned up at seven, her curls brushed out, smelling of gardenias, and I found myself being wheeled by her to the bioscope. The cinema hall was dark and there were people around us and I remember thinking I was going to leave; I was going to wave for the usher and ask him to help me get back into my chair and I was going to leave on my own. I didn't have time for this nonsense. But just then the curtains opened and the projector came alive and then—then I forgot everything. There on the screen was a man walking through the sand with such a pained expression, and behind him was a convoy of elephants dressed in splendor. And I was caught up in the story of kings and courtesans. It was one of the greatest films ever made—*Mughal-e-Azam*. Of course, she made sure we went for one of the greatest films ever made!" He laughs. "And you know, for one moment during 'Pyar Kiya to Darna Kya,' while Madhubala was whirling in front of the prince, I turned to her and she was smiling, the scene reflected in her eyes, and it was in that precise moment I knew I would marry her."

Sana is quiet. She takes in the moment. She tries to remember what it feels like to hear this, how the morning light passes through the window onto the plants around her. How she can hear the seagulls in the distance. This is how love sounds: *it was in that precise moment I knew I would marry her.* When one human being recognizes another. She treads in the feeling. She asks, even though she already knows the answer, "Do you miss her?"

"Every day, always," he says.

Every day, always.

The light at the eaves tremble, begin to fill with a warm glow.

Doctor picks up his cup and pours the last of the tea out gently. "Do you miss your mother, beti?"

The light flees. Everything becomes still. Sana knows what she is expected to say.

"She was very sick at the end. It was better it happened," is all she manages. She stands up and gathers the empty cups. "I'll take these to the kitchen."

She steps through the piles of cassettes. Her chest feels like a cage with something aflutter inside.

Ten

The old kitchen is busy after a long time; onions are chopped, tomatoes are diced, and a pot of rice boils and bubbles.

The commotion troubles the sleepy house; it creaks and groans and shifts in its foundation as the new smells climb excitedly into the eaves. The older smells, annoyed, move higher up, away from the jostling young scents.

The bats shift their sticky wings and fall asleep into an onion-scented stupor.

There was a time, the kitchen remembers, when there were smells like these, of food and people and life; when Grand Ammi with her silver shalwar kameez marched down the stairs and ordered servants to peel mounds of potatoes, grate piles of carrots, and wash buckets of chicken in preparation for a feast. The kitchen remembers how the servants scurried about, balancing porcelain tureens of vichyssoise, trays of fish, and crystal bowls of custard.

This was of course before *she* arrived. The little factory sweeper. The kitchen sniffs disdainfully at the memory.

Now the fish smells and the custard smells look down drowsily from the rafters and observe the scene below. It is nothing like they remember from years ago. It's a sad sight to be sure—no servants, no great platters of spiced meat and goblets of pink sharbat, just a few people milling about in an empty kitchen.

The old smells whisper to one another and creep higher, distancing themselves from such shameful antics below.

DOWN ON THE GROUND, Bilal Malek masalas two chickens carefully. They have moved into the main kitchen simply out of convenience, his kitchen being too small for the preparations. The air is tinged with the smell of something burned and despite the open back door and a single yellow bulb, the room remains dank. Next to a shut small fireplace sits a gas stove against a smoke-stained wall. Cracked teacups, moldy plates, and unrinsed glasses are scattered on the kitchen surfaces. Guiltily, Pinky, the maid at Akbar Manzil, tries to push some of them into cupboards and drawers, which are already stuffed with various unclean objects, from ruddy tablecloths to oily frying pans.

When Pinky was first hired to clean at Akbar Manzil, she spent hours lifting tables and vacuuming behind sofas, climbing stairs and dusting rooms. But eventually it became clear that the work was overwhelming; there was too much house and too little woman, and she gradually began to clean less and less until she somehow stopped altogether. In fact, as the years progressed, she learned the art of giving the impression that things *seem* clean. She sweeps dust under mats, pushes dirty dishes into drawers, and only wipes visible surfaces.

"Pinky!" Doctor calls. Pinky jumps in shock and abandons her attempt to wrestle a saucepan into a drawer.

"Sit, my dear. No need to stand on our account."

If anyone but Doctor had asked, she would not have listened. But then, no one but Doctor would ever ask.

Pinky sits with a thump.

Doctor is grating carrots and across from him sits Fancy, cutting triangles of cucumber. In her excitement at the prospect of a social event Fancy has weighed herself down with so many necklaces that every time she leans forward she topples slightly on her stool until she rights herself.

"We've never had a party before! I asked Bilal to try and fix the old gramophone. I thought it will be fun if we have music."

Just then Bilal comes into the kitchen with a small pot. "Ah good, you're done," he says. "Now we can heat the ghee and braise the carrots."

While Doctor and Bilal busy themselves, Fancy begins again. "You know, I would have brought Mr. Patel—he just *loves* to be where the action is—but I'm worried that Razia Bibi will try to cook him with the rest of the food after what happened the other day. Poor baby," she says as she shakes her head sadly and nearly tumbles off the chair.

Bilal pours a dish of rice into boiling water and the steam rises into the rafters.

Burned crab smells scuttle along the walls, and in their hurry, some fall down and scurry under the stove.

But no one notices.

"You know, Bilal, beta. I'm *so* impressed. You've only been here a few weeks and already you're shaking things up! We should do this every month. Next time I'll do the cooking," announces Fancy.

Razia Bibi, who pops her head in at this moment, bursts into a peal of laughter. "You! Ha. That will be the day. What will our rani cook? Boiled eggs? Oh yes, that will be a feast that everyone will be *dying* to attend."

"Bilal will help me," replies Fancy sulkily. "See how good he is."

"First, you mix the ginger-garlic into the spices until you get a paste like this," Bilal instructs Doctor as he opens a box of yogurt and pours it into the mixing bowl. "Then you add yogurt and mix it into the chicken." He slips his fingers between the joints of a wing and smears the masala into a crevice. "It's important to get it everywhere. If you don't, it will have no taste, and if food has no taste, there is no meaning to life."

At the kitchen entrance, Razia Bibi rolls her eyes and Pinky, despite her dislike of the other woman, sniggers.

MUCH LIKE THE MAIN KITCHEN, the dining room is left to ruin. No one takes responsibility for the original sections of the house that seemingly belong to no one and nowhere. The dining room is large and regal-looking, decorated with a colonnade of columns with ornate capitals and flanked by long Georgian windows that face the front yard. The walls, covered in heavy blue wallpaper, bulge with dampness and disappear into corners where the light doesn't reach.

Sana adjusts the candelabra that she found in the upstairs passage and assesses her work; she has set the long table in a paisley curtain and a mix-match of dishes donated by the tenants. She fetches the gramophone, and when she returns, she finds Pinky and Razia Bibi in the dining room. They are walking around looking at the table curiously.

"Like one bloody funeral party," Razia Bibi mutters to herself. Pinky, who overhears this, giggles then stuffs her fingers into her mouth so that she will not guffaw loudly.

"My father says he think it works now," Sana announces as she lugs the box inside. Fancy comes around the corner and clasps her hands together in delight. She opens the box of records sitting next to the gramophone and fingers the layers of chains around her neck until she locates the one with her glasses and pushes them on as she inspects the records.

"These are before our time, Razia Bibi," she complains as she rifles through them. "I don't know half of them."

"Our time? You mean your time," grumbles Razia Bibi. "You keep acting like we're the same age."

Fancy's bangles clatter as she digs through the box and blows dust off the titles. Finally, she pulls out a crinkled jacket.

"I think Doctor will like this one," she says as she pulls the record out and sets it on the turntable. "Oh, I can't believe this is happening, I'm so excited!"

Pinky lets out a strangled squeal, an exaggerated laugh of someone who is unused to acting thus in company. She is seated at the far end of the table closest to the exit in the manner of someone who expects at any moment to be asked to get up.

Razia Bibi scowls at the sound, turning her chair the slightest breath away. Her unhappiness stems from two sources, the first being the more troubling one.

She knows the new tenant is trouble when she discovers he abandoned a farm to move here and become a cook. She has never known a man who cooked for a living and this makes her wary. Why were these men trying to do things they weren't supposed to? The world must be kept in balance. Girls must marry at eighteen and men must have stable jobs as doctors or accountants. Everyone knows it. The way they know *never* to paint their fingernails with polish or shake hands with a Shia (especially in Johannesburg, where she hears they are congregating in droves). She isn't asking for much—she doesn't expect girls to marry boys from the same village in India as them, the same region would be acceptable—she just wishes people would follow the rules. She feels like the constant keeper of balance in the house. If that modern Doctor and that deaf Fancy had their way they would be living with Black people, or worse, white people.

And now this strange new tenant who has barely been there a month offers to *cook* for them? It's very suspicious. Maybe he's an undercover Shia trying to convert them all. You never know. You just never know. Or maybe he's just one of those modernists who think women and men can do the same things. That poor child, no wonder she wanders around in those dreadful clothes.

What Razia Bibi doesn't realize, what she hasn't put her well-worn pointing finger on, is that she resents Bilal simply because he seems happy. Human beings are not supposed to be happy, she believes; they are a sorry lot who have to endure life with all its disappointments. But someone like Bilal Malek, someone like him ought to be downright miserable. His wife dead, a good farm lost to debt, and to top it all he has to move to this rotting house with rotting people and his only child looks like a delinquent walking around in pants that are too short.

And yet here he is, smiling, cracking jokes as if life had bestowed on him the sweetest of blessings. It's so . . . *distressing*. She feels she has to remind him that his life is in tatters. He shouldn't be trying to fix things, having big suppers, and changing the way things are done.

He is one of them now and he ought to behave the part.

Her second source of agitation stems from the presence of the maid at the dinner table. How has she been allowed to eat with them? This crazy Doctor and deranged Bilal have no understanding of how domestic matters work. Servants are supposed to eat in their own quarters, but now suddenly the maid is here, eating from the same mismatched plates as them. This will make her think she is as good as them and a false sense of entitlement is a dangerous thing. What if she starts to think she is an equal? What if she asks for a raise? *What if she asks to move out of the pantry into one of the rooms?*

She turns to look at the maid, who is seemingly attempting to push her fingers into her mouth before retching. The little woman yaks and wheezes and the new girl quickly gets up to knock her on the back. Razia Bibi turns away in disgust. This is exactly why you don't invite servants to share the table with you; they have no sense of decorum.

On her side of the table, Pinky takes a shaky breath and stops coughing. What she had been trying to do was stop from speaking to herself aloud, but much to her dismay, an errant sentence had tried to escape and she found herself reeling in the string of words before pushing her fingers in her throat to keep them down. She keeps a hand over her mouth, but can't help making small gasping sounds that are beyond her control.

The loneliness of this big house often provokes such strange behavior in its inhabitants. Years with only oneself for company can loosen things deeply buried in a person. Mainly forgotten and mostly ignored, Pinky had unconsciously grown into the habit of talking to herself. She whispers as she watches films or complains when she is occasionally cajoled into cleaning someone's apartment. She starts a habit of referring to herself in the third person. As if she and her are two different people. The Pinky that she is and the Pinky that she watches. She separates the two like the white and the yolk.

FANCY CHIRPS, "I wonder if Zuleikha will join. We hardly see her."

"Why will she come? That one thinks she's better than us," snaps Razia Bibi.

"She told Doctor she was going to try to come," says Fancy as she flaps open an embroidered handkerchief and lays it on her lap.

"*Try*. Hmph! That's just like her. Never gives a straight answer. Who she thinks she is? I told you a long time ago, Fancy, she's got something up her arse, that one. Someone should tell her, her looks faded a long time ago and she has nothing to be proud of. So what, she was famous before? Those days are long gone. You know, I heard she had *so many* proposals? But she didn't accept any of them. She thought no one was good enough for her and look how it turned out—now she's not good enough for anyone!"

"Razia!" chastises Fancy as she shifts in her seat. "Don't start, please."

"Who's starting? Who's starting? It's just the truth. If you get a good man, you hold on to him. You won't have your good looks forever. In this life you have to be realistic. When my family brought a proposal, we checked if the boy had a decent job and I got married. Khalas! At least I had a husband, huh! At least *I* know what it's like to have a child."

"And tell me, Razia Bibi, how did *that* turn out for you?" says a deep voice. Everyone turns; a slender woman stands leaning in the entrance in a cloud of smoke. She is draped in an elaborate silk shawl, wearing an array of mismatched bangles that tinkle slightly as she steps forward out of the shadows. "Where's that husband *now*?" the woman says as she raises a hand to her lips to suck elegantly on a cigarette between her fingers. "Where's that son?" she asks throatily before sweeping into the dining room. She passes close to Razia Bibi and pauses, "Wonder what happened to him." She continues to an empty chair and seats herself opposite the older woman, who glowers, and gently blows a stream of smoke in her direction. "Seems to me you're just as alone," she says as she leans back in her seat. "Such a shame."

The table goes quiet.

Sana has seen many shapes that people can take: broken and whole, full and empty, but she has never seen anything quite like this. The woman who seats herself before them seems to have a shattered quality to her, as if she is glass; you look hard enough, and a thousand reflections look back.

The woman turns to the table and smiles coquettishly. "Apologies for my tardiness, ladies. It takes a long time to get ready when your looks have faded."

Pinky laughs nervously and Fancy glances anxiously between the two women. Razia Bibi looks livid, and just as she begins to say something, Doctor enters the dining room carrying a steaming bowl in his hands.

"I hope you're not fighting again. I won't have any of that today," says Doctor as he sets a shiny dish of gajar ka halwa down on the table. "Oh Zuleikha! You made it! I'm so glad," he says, beaming at the woman who has just arrived.

"Wouldn't have missed it for the world, Doc," Zuleikha says as she turns to smirk at Razia Bibi, leaning over to pop a piece of crispy papad into her mouth.

"We don't allow smoking in the house, Zuleikha. You better put that out," Razia Bibi says between gritted teeth.

"Oh of course!" says Zuleikha smacking a hand to her forehead. "Silly me, I always forget the rules. It's hard to keep track of the ways you pretend to be important here."

"Now, Zuleikha," warns Doctor, just as Bilal arrives behind him and puts down a heavily scented rice dish.

Doctor looks at the table and smiles. "Alhamdulilah. Look how lucky we are. And more importantly, how lucky we are to *have one another.*"

"Yes, *so* lucky," says Razia Bibi, rolling her eyes.

"Our family is growing. This is going to be a good year," says Doctor happily as he pulls a chair and sits down.

"I don't know about that," Zuleikha says, arching an eyebrow skeptically. "Can we *really* top last year?"

"What do you mean?" asks Doctor.

Razia Bibi narrows her eyes suddenly, sensing trouble.

"Oh, you know, after Razia Bibi's tamasha last year. I'm not sure anything better can happen after that."

"What tamasha?" asks Bilal as he pulls the halwa toward him.

"You didn't hear?" Zuleikha asks, feigning innocence with a hand to her chest. "Last winter we heard a positively blood-curdling scream in the middle of the night. Fancy even heard it, didn't you, Fancy? We rushed out of our rooms and found our Razia Bibi at the foot of the stairs, white as a sheet. She was screaming and pointing at the landing, saying she had seen a ghost. We couldn't get her to calm down. I thought finally something exciting is happening in this house."

"Come now, she was scared. That's normal," Doctor chides.

Razia Bibi snaps, "I wasn't scared. And I wasn't screaming like how you're saying. Don't make up stories, Zuleikha. I thought I saw a burglar and I shouted for help. That's all. No need to thank me for raising the alarm and saving your lives."

"Oh Razia Bibi, let's be honest; you were hysterical. I never knew you had a set of lungs like that on you. Thought you were all skin and bones. Doctor nearly called an ambulance, didn't you, Doctor? Even Fancy wanted to call Preeti," Zuleikha goes on, a smile playing in the corner of her lips.

"Preeti?" Razia Bibi asks through gritted teeth. "That fool? For what? She's a pharmacist. Not a paramedic! What's she going to do—prescribe antibiotics?"

"Well, it just shows how worried everyone was about you, *including* Fancy," Doctor adds.

Razia Bibi ignores this and continues. "I don't know why you all make such a big deal about that night. I heard a noise on the stairs; I went to see and I thought I saw . . . someone. So I screamed. It could have been a thief, a rapist, a serial killer! Who knows? This country is not safe anymore!" Suddenly she looks at Bilal and continues, "Everything is changing for the worse these days! You know, even the Shias are opening mosques in this country? You think I don't know? I know everything." She taps her nose. "But they won't last here, mark my words. We won't stand for it. You hear?"

Bilal, confused, nods back at her.

Just then Fancy takes a bite of the biryani and exclaims, "Oh, Bilal, beta. This is delicious. Really. I haven't tasted food this good in years."

"Really? Even better than Razia Bibi's?" asks Zuleikha with a wry grin.

"Don't be so ridiculous, Zuleikha," interrupts Razia Bibi. "How can a man's food be better than a woman's, eh?" Just then she dislodges something from her mouth. She inspects it for a moment then shouts, "Aha! Look, elachi," she says, holding up the offending cardamom seed triumphantly. "Any woman would have removed that before she served the food. Didn't your wife teach you how to cook properly?"

"Oh, I'm sorry—I forgot. Actually, Razia Bibi, my wife didn't teach me how to cook . . . I sort of learned by myself," replies Bilal.

"By yourself? What nonsense. It's bad enough you cook, but let's not lie about it. Only a woman could have taught you to cook like this," says Razia Bibi.

Doctor chuckles. "That's as close to a compliment you're going to get from her. I think you should just take it."

"Oh, the music," says Fancy suddenly as she wakens with a clatter and rushes to the gramophone. "We forgot the music."

"*Oh, the music,*" mocks Razia Bibi. "What—now we are white people, we listen to music while we eat? What next? You will give us knives and forks and say bon appétit?"

Fancy winds the little handle on the box, then carefully sets the steel needle down. Soon the scratchy voice of Krishna Chandra Dey fills the house as he begins to sing "Na Aaya Man Ka Meet."

The kitchen, despite its intention to stoically ignore the happenings below, cannot help glancing curiously into the dim dining room as the song fills the house. The beams shiver a little as the heavy voice strings through the air like cobwebs from rafter to rafter. The kitchen remembers the last time music from the record player filled the house; how the crabs had burned and the end had come so quickly.

Doctor stops chewing. He closes his eyes for a moment.

"Arreh wah," he says. "*Devdas.* Nineteen thirties, I think. Yes, it's Saigal. What an actor! No one could top him as Devdas."

Pinky squirms in her seat, a hand cupped over her mouth. Then suddenly she blurts, "Pinky doesn't think so, sir! Shah Rukh Khan was too good."

Doctor smiles. "How many times must I tell you to call me Doctor? Don't worry what Razia Bibi says."

Razia Bibi scowls into her plate, but refuses to directly confront Doctor.

"As for what you say about *Devdas,*" he continues. "Does your, er—"

"Shah Rukh Khan," pipes Pinky.

"Thank you. Does he make you feel like his pain is real? Like he is truly living through the heartache of losing his Paro?"

"Oh yes, sir, er, Doctor. He's a top-top actor," says Pinky earnestly.

"Excellent." Doctor turns to look at Fancy, who is dabbing her eyes with her handkerchief. "My dear, what's wrong?"

"Oh, it's just too sad, Doctor," replies Fancy. "This song is too sad. I don't like these sad songs. I thought it was going to be something happy."

"You picked *Devdas* and you thought it was going to be something happy?" Razia Bibi asks incredulously.

"But don't you know? The best songs are the sad ones. It's like love—the best love stories are the painful ones," Doctor responds. He cocks his ear to the music and continues, "Ah! Sana, you must know this song, no? Come, come, you must add this to your book."

"What is he saying?" Sana's voice is as soft as a whisper.

"He's singing that his beloved did not come to him. A lifetime has passed and people tell him his beloved is coming, and he swears he can hear her footsteps—but he is being fooled again and again." Doctor claps his hands together suddenly. "Kya baat hai! Such sweetness in pain. Don't you agree, Bilal?"

Bilal nods his head vigorously. Fancy blows her nose noisily.

Zuleikha snorts. "You're all crazy."

"Arreh, I told you that long time ago. All mad people here!" interjects Razia Bibi.

There is a pause and then at the same time their faces soften, then break, and they burst out laughing. And for a small moment they don't even know what they are laughing about, and it is so loud and so sudden that even the rafters vibrate and the haughty smells look around in alarm.

That night in Akbar Manzil an unexpected thing happens. As everyone tucks into their plates of saffron-stained rice in the candlelit room filled with the crackle of music, they fall into a silence that the house has not seen for a long time: a comfortable one.

The buttery potatoes melt in their mouth, the tender chicken falls off the bone, and for a moment they each understand their place in the world. For a moment the food brings them together and they are no longer forgotten people.

Then the gramophone needle catches in its groove and gives out a harsh crackle before coming to an end, and like a curtain on a play, the moment passes. Pinky gulps, Razia Bibi scowls, and Zuleikha begins to cough.

As Sana puts out mangoes, the lights go out in the house and they are left with just flickering candles. They sit in the sputtering light, the yellow fruit wet between their fingers, pondering their place in the canvas of life.

In the rafters above, among the sleeping bats the echo of the music continues.

It fills their dreams with footsteps that promise the return of one beloved.

That night, Sana sits writing in her bed trying to describe what the woman who joined them at the dinner table looked like. Every time she begins to try to explain it, she changes her mind and starts over until eventually she begins to nod off.

She closes her eyes and dreams of cats running across the skies, leaping over clouds and landing on the roof of the house with softs thuds as their paws hit the tiles. They begin to cry until the sound fills the city like rain. Their tears run down their faces and into the rooms and water begins to fill the house. There are not enough buckets to catch all the water, and soon the whole house is full and everyone is swimming, including a giant china doll who moves her arms stiffly over her head. Soon the water engulfs Sana and the world becomes dark and she tries to breathe but she can't. Every time she tries to get a breath in, something stops the air from entering her lungs and she feels like she is disappearing into blackness filled only with the sound of cats.

She gasps and wakes up with a start.

She sits up on the mattress and adjusts her eyes to the room with its long windows and bare walls. It seems to her as if someone has just called her name.

She listens for a moment, and when nothing happens, she gets ready to go back to sleep. Then she hears it. A faraway noise, too far to be in the apartment but too close to be outside. She tilts her head and listens closely.

Somewhere in the house, someone is wailing.

"It's not me," her sister, sitting in the dark next to her, says.

Eleven

So far, Sana has managed to ignore the ocean. She looks to the west, not the east, she pretends the sound of the surf is part of the general noise coming from the town, and she never looks down the cliff. Her mother's dying wish had been for her father to move near the sea. Sana suspects it was to torment her because she has always been afraid of water. The only time Sana glances accidentally in the direction of the ocean is in the minibus taxi on the way to school when the sea appears as slices of blue between the buildings, aquamarine strips interspersed with running brown bricks.

She enjoys the rides to and from school. It is as if life is exploding around her during these drives. The packed minibus with the driver shouting for customers runs through the crowded streets filled with the sound of women wailing their wares, rap music screeching from speakers, and people talking in a number of languages. Once, a man with a live chicken in his hand ran alongside them negotiating the price of the bird with the passenger next to her through the window.

One day, as is normal in Durban, the minibuses go on strike and Sana is left without transportation home from school. She considers her options: It is dangerous to walk through the interior of the town; pimps, drug peddlers, and gangs lurk in the area, a mishmash of disgruntled locals and refugees who rule the city center, drawing boundaries with their own set of rules. The younger gangs, restless and turfless, wander the streets dipping their hands into people's pockets with knives held against chests while bystanders push past and pretend not to see.

She chooses to walk in the direction of the sea, hoping the coast will eventually take her to the house. She prepares by telling herself that the sea is nothing; it is merely a mirror reflecting the sky. She tells herself that she will not give her dead mother the satisfaction. She untucks her hair from behind her ears so that it covers her chin and she begins to walk.

AT FIRST, THE SHORE is quiet except for a few fishermen standing in waders flinging out long lines of silver near the abandoned Life Saving Club. As she trudges along, the beach opens out to a mass of mangrove that sprawls across the sand. This continues for some time before she reaches the popular beaches, with ice cream parlors, piers, and long hotels that cast shadows over the sea. Tired and hot, she pulls off her shoes and socks and sits where the tide comes to touch the sand. She turns her eyes up and watches the sea now for the first time. It makes her wary, all that water, all that unknown space with no definite way to understand how it fits into anything.

She swallows.

She will not let her mother win. She stands, hikes her bag higher onto her shoulders, and walks toward the shore. When the foam touches her feet she finds that the water is surprisingly warm, and as she wades deeper it reaches her calves and brushes the bottom of her school dress. She stands there for some time, with her shoes in her hand, feeling the sensation of the water flowing around her. The sand sinks below her heels as each wave breaks gently across her legs and she has the sense that she is moving even though she is still.

She closes her eyes.

When she reopens them, a wave, bigger than any of the others, is almost upon her. She turns quickly to retreat, but by the time she takes a step, it has already hit her, soaking her back. She gasps. She wades to the shore and shakes off her dripping backpack. She holds her bag away from her and pulls out her books and examines them.

A boy's voice breaks behind her. "That one came out of nowhere."

She looks up to see a boy, probably her age or younger; he is wearing pants folded at his knees. He has floppy hair and a smile that begins in his eyes.

She flushes.

"Yes. Uh . . . yes," she mumbles.

"Are you okay?" He sounds concerned.

"I'm okay. Just some of my books . . . are wet." She feels incredibly awkward. She digs in her bag to give her something to do. Pushes books this way and that way and holds on to a pencil at the bottom of her bag for a moment. The recognition of its place and shape makes her feel less uncertain. Words have never come to her easily. They always seem too big and bulky to get out. But she is finding in this house that she is beginning to move them a little around in her mouth. That she can taste them better now that she has questions to ask and things to explore. She clears her throat. "I'll put them out in the sun to dry when I get home."

The boy nods. "I haven't seen you here before," he says gesturing to the beach.

"I've never been here before," she says. "I just moved to Durban." She feels emboldened by her own bravery, by the words coming out of her mouth.

"Oh cool," he nods. "Do you like it?"

"I guess so," she replies.

He smiles then. "You don't like it?"

"I've never really liked the sea," she admits.

"What?" The boy seems genuinely shocked. "That's the first time I've heard that." He hesitates, then, "Why?"

She turns to look out at the water.

The day her mother died Sana filled a bathtub full of cold water. She looked at it for a long time, then closed her eyes and stepped inside with her clothes on. Then she slipped under the water and stayed there. Her sister whispered that this was the right thing to do. That it was better to go like this, less messy for everyone.

But then she changed her mind. She wasn't sure why. Perhaps because she remembered her father. Or perhaps because she wanted to live. But when she tried to come up for air, tried to pull oxygen into her lungs, her sister grabbed her head and pushed it down and held her there, screaming that they would be together. She struggled wildly, grabbing the edges of the tub and trying to heave herself up. There was splashing and fighting and slipping until her sister suddenly stopped and she pulled herself out of the water with a loud gasp. As she tried to get the air back in, her sister brought her face close to her dripping one and said that she could wait until she was ready.

BUT OF COURSE, she doesn't tell the boy this. She shrugs and tells him the sea just seems too rough here. And when he asks her if she wants to have ice cream with his friends nearby, she shakes her head and says no.

She has known for a long time that she cannot make friends. That when she tells others about her mother and her death, or how the world is full of shapes and ghosts and stories, they become afraid. Or worse, feel sorry for her. They are mothered children and she is an unmothered child. Even her father, despite his best attempts, is barely there; he is a man who has given too much of himself to another and there is not much left behind. Other children know how to behave. They are polite and say "hello" and "excuse me" and know to invite new people to join their friends for ice cream. They don't quite understand her. They think she is strange; they do not understand the types of questions she asks when she finally finds the words; things like what their bedrooms look like at home, what their parents talk to each other about, whether they ever feel like they're disappearing. She resigns herself to a life without company.

The boy asks if she is coming back again tomorrow. She feels an old ache for all the things she will never have. The secret box in her chest shifts. The lid flutters. Then she looks over and sees her sister, scowling at them in the sun. She sighs.

"I have to go," she says as she hikes her bag up and leaves.

Twelve

Sana wakes with a start.

Someone is crying again. She blinks in the dark, then sits up and listens intently. The wind outside rattles her windows, but gradually she makes out the sound of sobbing coming from deep inside the house.

She climbs out of bed, and as she slips on her shoes, she thinks she hears a door creak.

She steps into the shadows of the main passage, which is lit with a murky light from the moon. She hears nothing for a moment and then almost indiscernibly there is the sound of what seems to her like heavy objects moving around in the distance. She calls out a small "Hello?" and the sound stops immediately. She moves cautiously down the passage past the east wing that spills its contents like oil in the moonlight. From the stairwell, she hears a strange sound, like something dragging raggedly. She heads for the stairs and hesitates at the top, recalling Razia Bibi's encounter with the "burglar," and she wonders if she should wake someone first. Before she can decide, the noise grows louder and it seems to her as if it is almost coming from the tapestry along the staircase, a vibrating grate, like nails running along the wall. Sana peers down but sees nothing, and after a moment's hesitation she follows the sound. It seems to be moving. She reaches the stained-glass window at the landing and Mr. Patel ruffles his feathers in his sleep as she passes. The noise stops in the entrance foyer, and Sana looks around but sees nothing. She glances at the front door and thinks she hears something beyond—a kind of whispering or muttering. She crosses the tiles of the foyer and presses her ear against the front door and listens carefully. It almost sounds like the wind is saying something.

She reaches for the handle.

"What are you doing?" a voice breaks out behind her.

She swings around in shock.

Doctor stands there.

"What are you doing?" he repeats gently.

Sana steps back and looks up into Doctor's inquiring face.

"I heard something—a noise." She hesitates then. Wondering suddenly if her sister is playing tricks on her.

"Oh? What did you hear?"

"N-nothing. It's probably the wind."

Doctor smiles at her quizzically. "Haan, it is windy tonight. But don't worry, this house can take a battering. It's been through enough to see itself through." He motions her toward his apartment. "Now I have company for tea." He limps with his cane into the apartment and puts water on to boil.

Sana looks back at the door then follows him.

"This is an old house, you know," he continues. "You hear all sorts of things if you listen hard enough. When I moved here I used to sit up listening to the creaks and groans every night—I thought it was trying to tell me something. That's when I knew I had to get people to stay here. I would have gone crazy by myself." He looks around his room. "I got used to the sounds eventually. Or at least," he laughs, "I stopped hearing them so well."

He pours the boiling water into cups. The tea bags rise, full and heavy like unanswered questions. Lightning flashes in the distance over the sea. He stirs milk and sugar into the water, then says, "Come, I want to show you something. Bring the tea." He picks up his cane and walks out of the apartment.

They climb the staircase. Sana follows Doctor as he passes through the dim corridors, past Fancy's room, through an empty living room, and around the east wing. He continues down and takes a left into a dark passage Sana has never seen before. They come to a door at the end.

He turns to her. "Have you seen this room?"

She shakes her head.

He turns the knob and the door swings open. The room is flooded with moonlight. When she looks up, she can see the night sky through a shattered glass dome. As her eyes adjust between the light and dark, she sees the walls are lined with bookshelves. The mosaicked floor is covered in debris; broken glass and damaged books sit in pools of blackened water.

Doctor limps in, his cane dragging through the remains on the floor. "I tried to save what I could but most of it was ruined. I used to come here when I couldn't sleep but it's getting harder with this." He gestures to his leg. He goes to a desk at the end of the room and clears away leaves and papers. He motions for Sana to set down the tea and sits heavily on a worn armchair.

"I thought you might like it. Most of the books are damaged but there are still some worth perusing. I saved them there," he says pointing to a few shelves that are covered in plastic sheets.

The moonlight pools into the room, making it feel like they are underwater, swaying in a sunken ship. The sky lights up again, the storm moves closer.

"It's beautiful," says Sana softly, as she walks to the shelves, running her fingers over the spines. She picks up a book and skims through it. "My mother had a lot of books. She kept them in her study."

"Did she read a lot to you?" asks Doctor, sipping his tea.

Sana turns slowly, keeping her mother's chin in the shadows. "No."

"I suppose she must have been very busy. A farm is a lot of work," says Doctor.

Sana keeps her head low. She turns back to the shelves and picks another book to look through. "She wasn't busy. I *wanted* her to read to me. I wanted her to tell me stories," she says softly.

"Then why didn't she?"

Sana shuts the book. "My mother loved her books better than us."

IT'S WHAT HER SISTER would whisper. Back when they were children. Trailing alongside her, whispering in her ear, *Our mother loves her books better than us. She wishes you dead so that she can have more time with her books.*

It was hard to defend a mother so disinterested, so simply uninvolved in the rearing process of her own child. She would put Sana in a bath and forget about her and Sana would sit crying in the cold water until her father came home from the fields and picked her up. She sometimes wondered if this was where her fear of water emerged. Other times, her mother would disappear in the fields for hours and Sana would try to feed herself, standing on a chair trying to open a can of beans.

Sometimes Sana wondered if she had made her mother sick, if her years of resentment had grown into a ball that entered her mother's mouth and traveled inside her to rot away.

"Ah," says Doctor, looking into his teacup. "My mother, too, was a difficult woman. She was complicated; selfish and proud. We didn't have the best relationship. In her last letter, she begged me to visit. She asked me to come so we could put the past right. Even she had not guessed she would die so soon after sending that letter." He looks down at his hands. "Maybe I should have gone to see her."

They are both quiet.

The moon moves behind a cloud and the room is engulfed in darkness.

Sana tenses. Recognizes an old familiar feeling. She can feel someone walking, picking their small bare feet through the glass toward her. She closes her eyes and tries to ignore it. Her skin prickles.

The cloud passes and the moon suddenly slides back into the room.

"Sana?" Doctor's voice sounds far away.

Sana opens her eyes, the shadow retreating.

"You didn't seem to hear me anymore."

"I'm sorry," says Sana. She pauses. Then, "I have a question, Doctor."

"Haan?"

"Do you think . . ." She lowers her voice. "Do you think ghosts are real?"

In the shadows her sister pricks up her ears, turns her mournful eyes toward them. Sana feels it, closes her eyes tight. Tries to concentrate on the moment she is in.

Doctor nods as if understanding. "When we lose someone, it's hard to shake the feeling that they're really gone. Sometimes you even think you can hear them in the other room, coughing or laughing. It feels very real."

He pauses, then looks out the window near him. "You know why I studied medicine? Because it made everything clear. At medical school they told me everything had a scientific reason for why and how it happened. There were no secrets and hidden messages and unknowable things to fear. There were only clean lines and cuts and facts of the matter. It's easier to live in a world like that." He puts down his cup and leans toward her, his face grizzled in the moonlight. "The older you get, the more the lines blur. Sometimes something from twenty years ago can be happening right in front of you." He lowers his voice, almost whispering. "Sometimes . . . I think my wife is right next to me. And you can tell me she's not, you can tell me it's not physically possible, but for that moment it's the most real thing in the world." He stops whispering and clears his throat. "So are ghosts real? I think ghosts are as real as we make them."

Sana looks at the shadow of her sister next to her. Her sister hisses; shows teeth, turns around, and wanders through the bookshelves.

Doctor peers outside again. "The storm seems to have died down. Maybe we'll get some sleep now."

They leave the library. Sana turns to close the door on her sister standing there in the dark looking at her miserably.

"You're not real," she says as she shuts the door on her.

Thirteen

Pinky sits in the kitchen grumbling as she tries to untie a packet of yams. Murky light filters into the kitchen from the back door. A small lizard as gray as the unwashed walls darts in from the courtyard and raises its tiny head. The cockroaches in the darkness between the cupboards shiver, their long feelers trembling as they sense the approach of the predator. The tension travels to the ceiling and makes the sleeping bats dream of small hard fruit that sticks in their throat.

They move their wings uneasily.

Unaware of the restlessness around her, Pinky fiddles with the knot on the packet and swears in Tamil.

"Pinky," Sana, at the kitchen table where she is doing homework, berates her.

"What? What? You don't know what Pinky is saying!"

"I know," says Sana, glaring at her.

"You don't know nothing! You don't even know what they are saying in the films. All you know is English-English-English."

"I know a little Urdu," says Sana a bit sulkily.

"Ha! You know nothing. One English girl you are."

Sana has taken to watching Bollywood films with Pinky in the pantry in the evenings. The pair sit on her mattress beneath a bare bulb and watch films from the eighties and nineties when Bollywood, cocky and confident, turned a brash corner; blood turned more red, fights became more ferocious, and heroines grew more buxom. Pinky guffaws when women slap villainous men in triple-scene-shots and she jabs in the air and ducks during battles, bobbing her thin arms as her stained apron swishes around her.

Once, while waiting for Pinky to open a can of beans in the main kitchen, Sana discovers a corner of paper sticking out from under the mattress. The first line reads *Dear Mr. Shah Rukh Khan Sir*. Sana pulls the letter out and scans it. It is a letter to the Bollywood superstar and in it Pinky explains in painstaking detail why she thinks Mr. Khan is such a successful actor and why she admires him. She tells him that many people may admire him for his good looks or his muscles or the dimples in his cheeks, but she, Pinky, admires him for something far more important: his ability to make you *believe* in something. The other fans don't understand how hard it is to make unbelievable things believable but she *knows*, she writes, she knows how difficult it must be to make an audience believe in robots and aliens and even more difficult things like love and joy. But he, Mr. Shah Rukh Khan Sir, makes her believe in all sorts of things like perhaps men will run after trains, that maybe women can burst out in song from happiness, and maybe, just maybe, there *are* happy endings.

In the end in her scrawling handwriting, she puts:

> *The world is a hard place, Mr. Shah Rukh Sir. For a lot of people.*
> *But you make it a little easier.*

Pinky pokes at the starchy roots with a knife and mutters to herself, "Not ready."

"Pinky?" Sana says as she puts away her notebook.

"Ām?"

"Do you hear anything . . . at night?"

"Like what?" says Pinky, still prodding the vegetables.

"I don't know. Like, noises?"

"If you don't know, how Pinky must know?" says Pinky exasperatedly. "Pinky is watching her film and Pinky is going to sleep. She doesn't have time to listen for 'noises.' If you listen for 'noises' you will hear how many things! This is not a place for wild imaginations. You must be like Pinky. She is a sensible person," she says, nodding her head in agreement with herself and stirring the pot. "Even when she goes to the outhouse toilet at night and hears noises in the bushes, you think she worries about it? No, she does not," she says, wagging her spoon at Sana. "She only thinks she must brush her teeth before she goes to sleep." She peers in the pot. "Now help Pinky—this is almost ready. Let's move it off the stove before it gets too soft. Ayah, Pinky needs the strainer quickly," she says, looking around frantically.

As Sana takes over from her, Pinky complains as she throws opens cupboards. "Where is it? Oh ma, where is it?!" She mutters and moans as she pulls open drawers and rifles through the mess; dirty dishes emerge, an eggbeater, some wooden spoons, a rusting ring of keys, and an ornate baby rattle are all unceremoniously yanked out. Finally, with a yelp of triumph, Pinky locates the cracked plastic colander and rushes to pour the steaming water into it. "Must do this fast-fast, otherwise they too soft." She smacks her puckered lips together in distaste. "It must be Miss Razia Bibi. I know she must be hid it from Pinky on purpose. Like one *sour* lemon, always complaining-complaining," she says. She shakes out the yams and peels off the scratchy brown skins onto an open newspaper. Then she slices them and sprinkles them with salt and pepper. She makes two mugs of coffee and they carry their cups and plates into the garden.

They eat in a patch of sun on the grass next to the aviary. Afterward Pinky wipes her hands on her apron, leans back, and closes her eyes.

"Let Pinky catch a wink for two minutes," she says.

As Pinky naps, Sana walks through the garden.

In a sunken plot filled with muddy leaves, she spots something with a metallic sheen poking out of the debris. She sifts through the branches and finds a rusting blue bicycle. She pulls it out carefully and clears the twigs and dried leaves caught in the tarnished spokes and wheels it out of the plot. It squeaks loudly as she rolls it over a line of uneven pebbles on the path. Something about the shape of the stones makes her pause. She stops pushing. She bends down to inspect the white row of stones protruding from the ground in a distinct formation.

As she studies them a pattern begins to emerge, and she realizes she is looking down at ridges of white bone. She squats to the ground and traces them with her fingers, following the long, curved shape farther down the path until she stops suddenly.

She is looking down at a giant skeleton.

Fourteen

"Crocodile," Pinky states when Sana tells her later that afternoon. "They come from the Umgeni River nearby."

"But that big?" asks Sana impatiently.

"What you thought? You found dinosaur bones?" cackles Pinky as she throws out the water from her pot and puts away the colander.

"Why would a crocodile come all the way up a hill?" asks Sana.

"How must Pinky know? Why does a father and daughter come here all the way from Jo'burg?" asks Pinky. "Not everything has to have a reason. Why you *always* have questions?" she asks as she pushes her dirty plate into a cupboard. "This is not a place for questions."

But for Sana, Akbar Manzil is *exactly* the place for questions. It's like a big puzzle with scattered pieces of history that just need to fit into the correct spaces. She feels if she asks enough questions, if she explores the right places, she might discover something amazing, or terrible; something beyond her tragedies that will make her life feel less alone. She refuses to become like the other residents who she sees have succumbed to a kind of apathy. She asks questions, opens boxes, makes records, and writes notes.

The house watches this with a morbid fascination; no one who has lived at Akbar Manzil has remained eager for knowledge of the past for long. The desire for discovery is something the house snuffs out early by making things feel impenetrable: deepening shadows, hiding doors, accumulating objects, and cloaking itself with a sense of despair and gloom. It is not a difficult thing to do when so many who arrive at its doors are already so forgotten, their existence so battered that it is merely like blowing out a candle that is already sputtering.

But the girl has something the others do not: a questionable amount of soul.

And a questionable amount of soul is a dangerous thing. It makes people unpredictable; it can send them out in the darkness to seek things that others would never dare. It can keep a flame burning, long after it was supposed to go out.

And so without realizing it, Sana refuses to let the house lull her into submissiveness. She goes through her memories carefully, confirming that she indeed did have a pair of pink shorts with daisies at the pocket, that the cows did low at night, and that once she did see Tant Elsie who lived next door peeing outside in her yard, her gown hitched around her waist. She goes through her memories, calculating dates and summoning details.

And so, that evening, she waits until Pinky withdraws to the pantry. She steals back into the kitchen and opens a drawer near the back door. She pulls out the rusting ring of keys she saw earlier that afternoon and tucks them in her pocket.

Then she creeps to the top floor to the passage in the east wing and makes her way to the corridor where the brooms and mops are piled.

THE ELEVENTH KEY WORKS.

It fits into the lock with a creak before clicking and giving way. The door swings open and Sana finds herself in a bedroom filtered in dusty light.

The walls are covered in a rich maroon wallpaper of vines and small flowers that curl and open across the walls. Underfoot the carpet is thick and soft. Across the entrance sits a Victorian dressing table, and at its cabriole legs lies a long mirror, covered in a spiderweb of cracks. In the back of the room is a four-poster bed covered in crewelwork and draped with damask curtains. Beside the bed stands a cradle; an ornate bassinet covered in frilly lace long gone to waste.

It sits there like a mouth scraped open with gums exposed.

IT HAS BEEN eighty-two years since the room was locked.

Eighty-two years since the jasmines bloomed at the window.

The room is stuck in the incident of 1932. It has frozen there, caught in a grimace with locked limbs. Sana steps in cautiously and the entire room prickles. She steps over the threshold and feels the shape of her break into the dust; a girl-shaped hole hovers at the entrance before falling apart.

She coughs.

WHEN THE DOOR OPENS, everything inside huddles together like long-forgotten creatures. The room begins to unlodge its limbs slowly, the spine of it cracking in a rhythmic stutter as it unravels itself and wakes up, adjusts to a time new and unfamiliar.

Inside a wardrobe, disturbed by the movement outside, a djinn stirs from its nap. It stiffly crawls out and peers from behind the door. Dragging its leg, it pulls itself forward to stand behind the brocade curtains, watches from between the drapes. Then it steals along the carpet toward Sana.

Its vision has dimmed over the years, and for one wondrous moment it wonders if the dead woman has returned. But when it reaches for Sana and sees her face clearly, it hisses and pulls back its hand in disappointment.

The djinn has had this room to itself for many years and it resents this disturbance. Now it climbs onto its haunches on a wooden chair in the corner of the room and studies Sana, biting its fingers. It hisses and spits and watches her warily.

Sana moves to the dressing table and studies the assortment of objects: a mirror-backed brush, a glass flacon, lipstick, and face powder in a tin. There are pieces of paper too; they have slipped off from the mirror where they were tacked. Sana picks them up and blows off a layer of dust.

She reads faint words:

> *And beauty is not a need but an ecstasy.*
> *It is not a mouth thirsting nor an empty hand stretched forth,*
> *But rather a heart enflamed and a soul enchanted.*

On the table is a crumpled shape. Sana picks it up and finds that it is an origami flower; she runs her fingers over the complicated bends and turns before setting it down carefully. Next she picks up a heavy crystal bottle and rubs the faintly wet wand against her wrist. Instantly an overwhelming smell of roses, almost rotten in intensity, fills the room. She dabs her face with the powder, her nose, her cheeks, but the caked talcum sits on her face in clumps before slipping off. The lipstick, too wet and sticky, melts at the touch of her skin. She brushes her cheeks with crumbling rouge and draws lines below her eyes with mud-like kohl.

In the dim scarred surface of the vanity mirror Sana sees her reflection and feels like someone else.

The djinn, roused from its corner by the sudden scent, comes to sit next to her. It inhales the smell of the perfume. It feels overwhelmed. It covers its face and rocks forward and backward. It remembers the way the dead woman prepared herself before this mirror. It remembers the way the brush moved through her hair. The djinn would lean in close and inhale.

The djinn remembers it all.

Sana pulls her cheeks, sticks out her tongue as if she suspects there is another person on the other side of the mirror and she needs to confirm that it is indeed herself. She waits for the reflection to slip up, move a hand too slow, pull the tongue in too quick, give away the pretender behind the mirror.

The djinn next to her watches, then it too turns to the mirror, raises its fingers to its nose, and copies her, makes faces in the mirror.

Sana, finally convinced that the reflection is her own, stands up and walks around the room, picking up dusty objects and examining them. In a gilded frame on a cabinet sits a photo of a man and woman; the man with a fez has a dark beard; he is tall with wide shoulders and the woman next to him is small but fierce with large eyes and hair that escapes the confines of the plait slung over her shoulder. Sana picks up the frame and wipes the dust off the glass with her sleeve. The man is smiling as he turns to look at the woman, a playful expression on his face, and Sana recognizes it immediately—two shapes that have fallen into one.

In the background stands the fountain in the courtyard and sitting on its rim is a little boy scowling at the camera. Sana puts the photograph down and looks around the room, turning slowly.

This is now her secret. This is a place in the world that has been forgotten and she has found it. She has found a shape in the world that only she can fit into; a room that has been waiting for *her*.

WHEN SHE FINALLY LEAVES, closing the door behind her gently, the djinn comes out of the shadows and goes to the empty cradle. It looks down into the basket before beginning to rock it slowly.

It hums the song the dead woman would sing to the baby at night.

Part Two

One

In the summer of 1919, Akbar Ali Khan braces himself at the handrail of the SS *Karagola* as it pulls away from the Port of Bombay. As the ship swings out to open sea, he pulls his pipe from his vest pocket and carefully packs the bowl down with tobacco. Then he lights it with a match, coaxes an ember, and takes a deep puff as he watches the South Asian continent slip out from under him.

"Bismillah," he whispers as they head to open waters.

Standing next to him, his young wife steps back so that the spray does not catch her blue silk dress. With one gloved hand she holds on to her cloche, specifically ordered for this journey: brown felt with blue ribbon. Despite the sweltering heat she is wearing a tweed traveling coat because she has heard it is what the Europeans consider proper.

Although Jahanara Begum is Indian, she feels quite English and she often thinks she was born into the wrong skin. She waits in earnest for the fashion catalogs from London and she practices her English accent often, berating herself when she mixes the Queen's English with Cockney. She can even sing some English songs, and eventually word of her musical talent goes around the ship and in the evenings they have her sing Marion Harris's "After You've Gone," her sweet voice rising through the night as they clap around her and call her an Indian nightingale. She points out her husband to the other ladies and tells them that that strapping young man is her husband and they are on their honeymoon. They are going to Africa, "For a holiday, darlings, to see the lions, because he is ever so terribly adventurous," she gushes.

She says that they are madly in love. Madly. It's simply outrageous, she giggles.

The mostly English passengers agree the pair make a striking couple: the young woman with her light eyes and fashionable dress sense and the tall man with his dark hair and steady gaze. It is rare to see an Indian couple in first class, but the man comes from a fair bit of money, they hear, old farming business in a village in North India, and the woman is rumored to have royal lineage. Quite different from the usual coolies, they comment over breakfast, but best to maintain some distance, they add, as they smear jam on their scones. They are a little wary of the man; he isn't very sociable. The wife is a real looker, and friendly enough, but the man barely speaks to them and they hardly see him on the deck. He never plays cards with them or joins them for tea, and they often wonder where he could be. Still, he is, they have to admit, a dandy-looking chap. A bit darker than the wife but certainly light enough to get away.

Akbar, oblivious to the musings of his fellow passengers is often belowdecks in steerage. Unaware of time and place, he sits and talks to the Indian laborers who are traveling to Africa for a New Life. He is a tall man, taller than most, and the first thing that strikes you about him is the ease with which he carries this fact. He does not crumple himself, nor bring attention to it, but holds himself as one who is contented however he may be. He can sit huddled with the men on their crates in steerage as easily as he can sit upright at the dining table in the ballroom above. He has elegant hands that seem odd for a man of such build, and he uses them to stroke a dark neat beard when he is thinking. He is often mistaken for a seaman, and he doesn't hesitate to strip off his jacket and pull up his sleeves when he is ordered to help with the ship. He has a sea-feel about him, loose limbs and far-off eyes. The ship workers invite him to play dice with them belowdecks, where they clap his back and call him jehajibhai.

He has a persistent curiosity and a great love for adventure; by twenty-one he had already traveled to the British Isles, the Far East, and parts of the Middle East. He revels in the journey over rough seas. He longs for foreign accents, narrow streets, and strange skies. He returns to his village in Gujarat bearing skins of strange animals, ornate daggers, woven carpets, and intricate jewelry. When he comes home, he is always restless—going hunting, horse riding, or studying new places on the map. He dreams of the seas and of new lands parting through the waters. He takes his dreams seriously and sees them as Signs.

As the years pass and he announces his plans to explore Africa next, his distraught mother says bas, enough is enough; he will only be allowed to leave once he is married. He is getting older, she says, and his good looks won't last him forever (though secretly she thinks they will). His mother locates a suitable girl from their village with noble lineage, who is more than adequately fair-skinned (almost like a gora, some say), with an adequately distinguished nose, whose parents are only too keen to marry her to the eligible bachelor.

The couple travel south down the east coast of Africa, stopping in the ports of Dar es Salaam, Mombasa, and Lourenço Marques. At each stop Akbar excitedly disembarks and begins talking to the locals at the docks. He stands at the harbor among crates of vegetables and nets of fish and tries his best to communicate and learn about each new place. There are animals he has never seen before; some long and graceful and some fierce and proud. He asks people their names, tries the local fruit, and inspects the plants. He takes walks through the markets and returns with an array of medicines, roots, fabric, and a smattering of Swahili on his tongue. His wife grows increasingly aghast at the collection of seeds, plants, and fruits collecting in her designer luggage.

"Akbar, my dear," she says, as she fingers a bright roll of batik print. "Do we really need all this . . . material?"

"Yes," Akbar nods enthusiastically. "Haven't you seen how the locals use this for everything? They call it kitenge. It's beautiful. We should get something sewn for you. Perhaps a nice dress?"

Jahanara Begum is taken aback. *A nice dress*? Couldn't the man see that she had the best dresses already? Why, her double-tiered pleated skirt was all the rage in London. Why would she want a dress in that hideous print? What was her husband thinking? As it is, this journey was nothing like she had been expecting.

She dislikes the continent with its heat, large skies, and open land. She sits beneath her lace-trimmed parasol and fans herself while trying to appear unperturbed. She abhors the locals with their dark skin, strong teeth, and strange words. She does not like the food. She hates the peculiar-smelling herbs, bones, and skins. But most of all she hates the way her husband is so intrigued by it all. She throws much of his collection overboard when he goes exploring. She doesn't like the way he talks about the Africans and the way he talks about the Europeans. He doesn't like spending time with her friends on the ship and always makes excuses to leave.

Meanwhile Akbar seems to grow more and more enchanted with the continent. There is something about East Africa he says. The land is not ashamed to be itself. The green is more vivid, does she not see it too? he asks. The shadows are deeper, the lights burn more brightly, and the sea is in everything, the air, the walls, the way people speak.

Jahanara Begum does not understand. What green is in the air? What sea is in the walls that he talks about? How can the ocean be in everything? While she still tells the others their honeymoon is "Fantastic, just fantastic, darlings," she secretly cannot wait to return home and be done with this "African adventure."

Unfortunately for her, fate has other plans.

As they travel south and make their way toward southern Africa, they stop at their final destination in Natal, at the port of Durban. When Akbar sets eyes on the lush, warm tropics with its rolling sugarcane valleys, old mango trees, and sparkling ocean, he is instantly smitten. He decides this is where he wants to live. He sets foot on the land and feels the ground shudder beneath his boot and he knows it is a Sign.

He knows his travels are over.

He simply says, "This is where we will start our new life." He begins to unpack and tells his wife to settle down; they are home.

His wife begs him to reconsider, but Akbar is a man who never looks back once his mind is made up.

He wastes no time and begins business with the local Indians, a mix of previously indentured laborers and businessmen who come to seek fortune in the continent. He goes out to farms and fields to see where best he can invest. He starts business with a sugarcane farmer, and in 1920 he opens his own sugar mill in Natal.

Soon after, construction for his house on a hill near the sea begins. Akbar is a man of big ideas and he announces that he wants a palace. He wants a mansion that merges Western sensibilities with Eastern elegance. He brings an architect from India, a descendent of the great Ustad Ahmad Lahori; he asks for glass domes, guldastas, brass finials, ornately cut passages, Spanish balconies, stilted arches, stone towers, Palladian windows, and marbled floors. He orders lapis lazuli from Afghanistan, has cedarwood brought in from the Atlas Mountains and Carrara marble from Italy. He has Lebanese stained-glass windows imported from Sidon. Arabic calligraphy is etched into cornices and ivory arabesque worked into column capitals. Moroccan craftsmen build Zellij mosaic floors and walls in the courtyard.

Outside he wants a garden that will remind anyone of the promise of God's gardens in heaven. Up on the cliff, he has columns, fountains, and rectangular pools put in. Between pine trees he has pathways designed that lead to plots of roses. Bougainvillea climb up the walls and spread themselves languorously in fuchsia heaps over the eaves.

The house becomes an obsession for him, a dream where he can capture his passion for every part of the world.

When the Georgian manor with whispers of domes, Gothic towers, Islamic arches, and European balconies rises on the hill, the townspeople below shake their heads in disbelief. And when animals in carts and cages begin to arrive, they are truly convinced a madman has moved to the hill. Akbar announces that he has dreamed that his garden should be a mighty paradise bursting with God's animals. He fills the garden with peacocks, African grays, canaries, doves, and cranes. He builds a giant aviary and constructs cages for sloths, marmosets, and an array of African monkeys.

Unsatisfied with this, he introduces more animals: two zebras, several local bucks, and a giraffe that wanders the garden peering into the upstairs windows, startling the maids cleaning the rooms. At the back of the garden, he keeps a stable of horses.

He calls it his palace and "Akbar Manzil" is etched into stone on the iwan above the entrance.

Soon after his house is constructed, Akbar's father passes away in India and his mother arrives to live with him in South Africa. That same year, his wife, Jahanara Begum, gives birth to their first child.

And it seems to everyone that Akbar Ali Khan has finally begun to settle a legacy.

Two

With a place in the world that is her own, Sana begins to visit the secret room regularly.

She airs it, forcing open the timber casement window. Then she starts to clean, hauling buckets and dishcloths surreptitiously from the main kitchen into the bedroom. She creeps downstairs early in the morning with sheets and pillows and washes them in the trough in the garden. If Pinky notices, she says nothing. The work is slow and arduous; Sana sweeps the carpet, dusts cobwebs, wipes windows, and polishes surfaces, rinsing the grime from her rag every few minutes.

In the mahogany wardrobes she finds simple cotton dresses, cholis, and swaths of dusty sari fabric with zari embroidery. She goes through the drawers, finding satin slips, glass bangles, hair clips, and volumes of poetry, but she cannot find anything more about the couple in the frame. She searches the room for more photographs, until finally one afternoon, in the back of a drawer of cotton shirts, she discovers a small wooden box. Inside are a number of grainy black-and-white pictures taken inside Akbar Manzil. She lays them out on the bed carefully.

The first is of a short lady with a dupatta draped around her face as she stands before a pot in the kitchen glaring at the camera. The next photo is the man in the fez with a pipe between his fingers standing on a rolling hill with a factory spouting smoke behind him. On the back of the photo is scrawled "Akbar, 1931." In another photograph—a self-portrait in a mirror—a young woman, her face partly obscured by a camera, half smiles, with the man standing behind her. His face is hidden in the nape of her neck so they both remain faceless in the photo. Sana turns around and finds the very same vanity mirror at the dressing table across the room. She holds the photograph up to the mirror but it reflects blindly, remembering nothing.

The djinn peers over Sana's shoulder and looks at the photo.

It remembers when the photo was taken. It had been living in the roof then. The man had just gifted her the camera; he was always giving her gifts, purchasing her affection, buying her love, the djinn thinks bitterly. She had been happy when she had taken this photo, the djinn remembers. It heard her laughing inside the rafters and it had crept down to be closer to the sound. She had tried to take a photo of the man on the bed, but he had jumped up and grabbed her from behind, and her silvery voice had run through the room like light. The djinn had tried to open its hands to catch the sound. The man held her waist close. She turned to face the camera to the mirror and then clicked the shutter.

The djinn, standing next to them, looking at her, had not been captured in the moment.

The man had whispered something in her ear that the djinn did not hear. The man pushed his mouth to the woman's neck urgently and she stopped laughing and closed her eyes. The man held her hand and pulled her toward the bed, the camera already forgotten on the floor.

The djinn had climbed back into the roof sullenly.

IT IS THE LAST PHOTOGRAPH that surprises Sana. The photo is taken on the stairway landing, and through the stained-glass window she can see a large shadow behind the glass. She brings the photo close and frowns.

Something big is standing in the courtyard behind the window.

Sana tilts the photo and stops suddenly.

It's a giraffe.

That night, after supper, Sana takes out the box of photos in her room; she holds each photo up to the candlelight and studies it carefully. She wonders about the scowling boy, the man with the pipe, the old woman at the pot, but mostly she wonders about the couple that looks like one person. She tries to put the pieces together. The only thing she knows for sure is that the bones in the garden belong to a giraffe from more than eighty years ago.

Her candle sputters and she looks up.

Her sister is sitting along the window ledge looking through the quarrels.

"There's a ship coming into the harbor," her sister says.

"Why do you keep coming back?" Sana asks tiredly.

Her sister, still looking out the window, says, "You don't really want me to leave. We both know that."

"Keep telling yourself that." Sana gathers the photos and puts them back in the box.

"You shouldn't go back there."

"Back where?"

"It was locked for a reason."

"The room?"

Her sister swings her legs down and turns to face her.

"Something happened there. Something *bad*."

"What?" Sana shifts uneasily.

"You're stirring up too many things. It doesn't like it."

"What doesn't?"

A dark look draws upon her sister's face. "There's *something* in that room."

"Something like what?"

"Something old. Older than anything I've ever seen. It's different from the others. The room changed it. Made it into something else."

"I don't know what you're trying to say," Sana says impatiently. "I didn't see anything."

"You can't see it," her sister says, fixing her with a stare. "But it can see you."

Sana looks at her uncertainly, then turns back to the box in her lap. "You're just trying to scare me. Like always."

"I wish I was," her sister says flatly.

"I can't trust what you say," Sana continues. "You're just a part of my imagination."

"If only it were that simple." Her sister looks at her sadly.

"Go away," Sana says.

"Fine. But don't you worry, I'll be back later to kiss you good night," her sister chirps.

When Sana looks to the window, she is already gone.

SANA BLOWS OUT the candle and gets into bed. As she lies down and closes her eyes, she hears a heavy thump outside her door.

She pauses and listens.

It feels to her like the house is listening too. It feels like something has changed since she opened the room; as if something, a spark perhaps, has been kindled and everything feels on edge. She waits, but the silence grows heavy, and just when she decides it is nothing, a small noise starts that gradually grows, a kind of scraping at the door. She wonders if it is the mice that Razia Bibi talks about, but the scratching suddenly grows louder, more insistent, and alarmed, Sana sits up.

"This isn't funny!" she says loudly. "Stop it! I told you to go away."

The noise abruptly stops. Then it seems to Sana as if she can sense someone behind the door. As if someone is pressed against it and waiting. She gets up and goes to the door. She stands there for a moment and listens, and when she hears nothing, she puts out a hand to the doorknob and, it seems to her, something shifts on the other side.

She turns the brass knob slowly, then swings the door open.

Nothing is there.

She sighs, then closes the door and gets back into bed. She curses her sister for messing with her head.

Then she shuts her eyes and falls into a fitful sleep.

THE DJINN COMES OUT from the shadows.

It drags its mangled leg behind it as it walks toward the girl. It comes close to her sleeping face and studies her. It turns away in disgust and begins to poke through her suitcase; then it opens her wardrobe and climbs inside. It looks in her pockets and inside the hems of her pants and under the tongues of her shoes. It wanders out of the room into the main house and moves through the corridors unsteadily. In the east wing it begins to open trunks and dig inside; it tosses aside boxes and dishes, but its hands come away empty. It throws back its head and wails.

Then it sees a crimson stain spreading in the corner of the rafters. It shakes its head as if in disbelief and backs away. It begins to whimper. The rafters begin to drip like a leak and the red splatters the walls. It runs down the wallpaper and pools in the cups and saucers and spills over into the cracked bathtub.

The leak turns into a river gushing like a faucet, flooding the passage.

The djinn howls as the house begins to fill with blood.

Three

Sana paces the foot of the spiral staircase in agitation. It is raining outside; water gushes down the roof tiles and pours into the old drainpipes that creak and overflow. Inside the house it sounds like dishes clashing together and the din only adds to Sana's distress.

She pauses midstep when she notices the music coming down from upstairs has stopped. Suddenly the door at the top bursts opens and two schoolgirls run down, their backpacks bumping in the air. They pass Sana unnoticed, and laugh among themselves. One girl asks the other, "Did you *see* what she was wearing today? Oh my God—was it her *pajamas?*" The girls laugh hysterically as they disappear around the corner.

Sana climbs the stone stairs and stands outside the door, which is slightly ajar. The piano has stopped now and all she can hear is the rain falling steadily against the roof tiles. She lifts her hand to knock and then decides against it and turns quickly back to the stairs. As she descends, she hears the door swing open and a voice calls, "For God's sake, what do you want?"

Sana turns back.

At the top Zuleikha stands in the doorway. She is barefoot and wearing a bright green silk robe painted with exotic birds. Her hair is piled untidily on top of her head and a cigarette sits in her fingers. She looks impatiently at Sana. "Well, girl, what is it?"

Sana hesitates. She has been trying to meet Zuleikha properly for weeks now. Besides that one time at dinner, Sana has never seen her. She lives in the tower at the top of the house and rarely ever comes down. Pinky says she teaches piano to schoolchildren and if it wasn't for the sound of the piano no one would even know if she was dead or alive.

"Well," says Sana, twisting her hands. "I just . . . I mean . . ."

"Oh, for goodness sake. Spit it out. Lord knows you've been hanging around my door long enough."

"I have some questions," says Sana quickly. "About, l-love. Pinky downstairs said you had a lot of things to say," Sana gulps, "about it."

"Love?" Zuleikha asks incredulously.

Sana nods.

Zuleikha studies Sana up and down, then asks, "Why would you want to know about it? Are you in love?"

"No!" Sana says quickly. "No, I just, well . . . I'm sorry. I'll go now," says Sana as she turns to leave.

Zuleikha watches her retreat, then groans exasperatedly and calls out, "Fine! Come in." She turns into her room and leaves the door open behind her.

Sana follows and enters a circular and dark bedroom that is thick with cigarette smoke. A maroon flock wallpaper peels off to reveal strips of stone behind. Next to a bed with drapes stands a small humming fridge. A threadbare wing chair faces the window, but the curtains are drawn. Opposite the bed is a black grand piano.

Sana stifles a cough.

Zuleikha turns the chair around to face the room and gestures for Sana to sit down.

"Well, go on. What sort of questions do you have?" she asks as she puts out her cigarette butt in an ashtray.

Sana squirms awkwardly. "Well, Pinky and I were watching a film together. And there was this love story and Pinky was telling me that in real life that couldn't happen. She said love wasn't like that—"

"Ha! And what does that mad little woman know about love?" Zuleikha interrupts.

Sana hesitates, then opens the notebook in her lap, turns to a page, and reads:

> *Pinky says that love in real life is an unpractical thing. It slows people down and makes their brains wonky; it makes completely sensible people do all sorts of ridiculous and unreasonable things like get married or share food. She says there is no such thing as love because love is supposed to last forever and nothing lasts forever. She says love is just for the movies.*

Sana shuts the book and looks at Zuleikha.

Zuleikha considers this. "Well, she knows more than I give her credit for."

"She said that you once said that 'love is the worst thing of all.'"

"And let me guess," Zuleikha arches an eyebrow. "You want to know why?"

Sana nods.

"Because love *is* the worst thing of all."

"How?" says Sana.

"From the day a girl is born she's told she needs a love story to survive. It's everywhere: in poetry, in music, in films and books. She's told life is worthless without love. She's told *she* is worthless without love." She lowers her voice. "But what no one tells her, what no one talks about, is that it can *kill* her. That the very thing they say can save her can destroy her. Love is a trap, darling. It lures you in then digs its bony fingers into your chest, breaks open your ribs, and yanks out your bloody, beating heart, and *still* leaves you alive."

Sana looks at her aghast.

"Don't sit there goggling at me. Write it down," says Zuleikha, waving her fingers at Sana's notebook. When Sana opens it, Zuleikha continues. "Have you ever been in an accident?"

Sana shakes her head.

"Love is like that." She pauses to look at the shut curtains as if she can see the view beyond them. "You're driving along the highway, twiddling with the dials, until you finally find some good music on the radio—you're humming along, making plans for what you're going to cook that evening, thinking whether you need to defrost chicken, when suddenly a car comes out of nowhere to blindside you. And then you're skidding and sliding and screaming and everything goes black. When you wake up you find yourself in some sort of steaming wreck and you have to pull yourself out and there is blood running down your face and you're dazed and you don't know who you are or what you're doing."

Sana swallows.

Zuleikha picks up a small box by her bedside and pulls out a cigarette. She holds it close to her face as she lights the end with a match. She shakes out the flame and says, "Tell me, how old are you?"

"Fifteen."

"Fifteen," Zuleikha repeats as she sits down on the bed and leans back on the pillow and considers this information. "Such a simple age. When the world is clear and the future is mapped out. Fifteen is when you think you have an idea of the life you'd like to have, the person you'd like to marry, the house you'd like to live in. I'm sure even your dreams have clarity."

"I'll be sixteen this year."

"Oh, what a pity. At sixteen all that confidence flees. One mistake, one wrong word, and it falls apart." Zuleikha takes a puff and exhales slowly. "Love is the worst thing of all because it is a great lie. It promises you everything but gives you nothing. Love leaves, *it always leaves*."

"But what about people who still love each other?" asks Sana softly.

Zuleikha snorts. "Everyone pretends. It's the only way they can survive." She closes her eyes. "These are the things young girls who go asking about love should know," she says.

The rain comes down heavily.

Sana waits.

She wonders if Zuleikha has fallen asleep.

"It's like losing the edge," Zuleikha says softly.

"W-what?" asks Sana.

"I teach the piano," Zuleikha says. "Mostly to children with no talent. Their parents don't understand you either have it or you don't; there's this place in the music where you choose to fall or step back, this place where you can see the edge and you are not afraid to go forward. These children don't have it." She pauses. "My mother saw it in me; she recognized the edge, and instead of pulling me back she pushed me toward it and when I fell over, when I went in, I could see *everything*." Zuleikha's eyes shine. "I was *special*. I was in international newspapers and I was invited to play at concerts around the world. The next Maria João Pires, they said." Zuleikha pauses and continues in a dull voice. "I don't see the edge anymore. Not the way I used to."

With her eyes closed and the cigarette smoking between her fingers, she reaches out her hand in the air searching for something. "It used to be right there. Right there . . ." She opens her eyes and looks at Sana. She puts down her cigarette. "That's enough now. I've said all I want for today. Leave. I need to rest."

And with that she leans back against her pillow and closes her eyes.

SANA CLOSES THE DOOR quietly behind her. Inside the room Zuleikha begins to cough; it echoes off the stone. Sana takes a deep breath as she makes her way down the stairs and considers Zuleikha's words.

Surely love was not a thing that always left. She thinks of the old couple that lived next door on the farm. The old woman, Tant Elsie, was suffering from dementia and her husband, Oom Piet, always held her hand, even as he laid the table in the evenings and made soup for her. When Sana visited he would tell stories about Tant Elsie's childhood as if they were his, talk about *her* father and *her* mother and the way *she* ran around *her* kitchen barefoot as a child racing after *her* sisters until *her* mother took a broom and knocked *her* feet. The fact that he could make her memories his own made Sana believe that love was not a thing that always left.

Love, to her, was the thing that stayed.

Four

Downstairs, Razia Bibi is in a jaath.

She scowls more than usual and mutters to herself; she bangs pots in her kitchen, shouts at Pinky for no reason, complains repeatedly about the grandfather clock, and keeps entering the main house, slamming her apartment door behind her. She walks into the big kitchen determinedly and walks out just as fast.

When she sees Sana coming downstairs, Razia Bibi pounces.

"What's happening upstairs? Were they talking to you?"

Sana looks at her in confusion.

As if suddenly aware of herself, Razia Bibi adjusts her scarf around her neck and continues, "Why you always wandering around, huh? Don't you have anything better to do? My mother also died when I was small but you don't see me feeling sorry for myself. Do you see me feeling sorry for myself?" she demands.

And with that she storms back to her apartment and slams the door, leaving Sana standing there in surprise. Just then Fancy and a young woman appear at the top of the stairs; they talk softly and walk down quickly. As they reach the bottom, Razia Bibi's door flings open again.

She is hunched as if holding herself together; a wooden spoon that she has been cooking with drips in her hand. When her door opens, the two women walk faster toward the main entrance.

"How. Don't run away. So long I never see you, Preeti beti," Razia Bibi says, following them. "You didn't even come say hello-hello? I also live here you know. Maybe you forgot." Razia Bibi is smiling garishly. She continues walking toward them with the spoon in her hand, talking in a low sweet voice. "Just going away like that? Fancy, she comes *all* the way and you don't even bring her for tea?" she calls after their retreating backs. "We were like *family*. Now you don't have time for me anymore?"

The young woman finally stops and turns around to face Razia Bibi. She starts, "Sorry, Razia Bibi, I—was in a hurry. I came to visit Mum quickly and had no time to see anyone else. You know how it can be—with work and everything. Next time . . ."

"No time, huh?" interrupts Razia Bibi. "You've been upstairs since the morning. Parked your car down the driveway but I know. I know everything." She taps her nose.

"Razia Bibi, just leave it. Don't do this every time," Fancy implores.

"Leave it? *Leave it?*" Razia Bibi's voice starts rising slowly. "You think it's so easy to 'leave it.' *Pretend like it never happened.* But I remember what she did. And she can come here and act like nothing happened, but I won't forget."

"Enough, Razia! Why you must always do like this? She hardly even comes to visit me because of you," cries Fancy.

"You? *You.* And who has stopped coming to see me. *Me!*" yells Razia Bibi, almost hysterical.

At this point of the commotion, Doctor's door opens and he comes out of his room. He tries to cut in as the women bicker. Finally, he turns to the young woman and says kindly, "Preeti, I think it would be better if you leave now, beti."

"Well, I was trying to!" she says. With an exasperated look, the young woman turns around and walks briskly toward the door, shaking her head. Razia Bibi follows.

"Yes. Go. Jau! I don't want to see your ugly face here again." When the other woman is gone, she turns on her heel and marches back to her own apartment and shuts the door with a bang.

Fancy wails. "She won't even let her visit me anymore!"

"Come now," says Doctor. "You know how she is. Next time, you tell me when Preeti is coming and I'll distract her. I'll tell her I heard a mouse in my room and she'll get very excited about it. Now, let's go have a nice cup of tea."

They walk away together as Fancy continues to complain.

That night Sana sits in the gloom of the east wing.

She is pulling open boxes and going through the objects inside; she is trying to find clues to the story of the family that lived here. She pulls out a chipped porcelain tea set with a rosebud design.

"That's all junk, you know."

Sana looks up and finds Zuleikha standing there with a candle.

"What are you doing here?" she asks, surprised.

"You spoiled my nap with all your dratted questions. And then there was that big ruckus downstairs. Not the usual clock-and-bird shouting. Razia Bibi seeing burglars in the day now?"

Sana looks down at the teacup in her hand and frowns. "I'm not exactly sure. Razia Bibi was angry. I think it had something to do with Fancy's visitor."

"Fancy had a visitor? Oh—*oh*. No wonder Razia Bibi was shouting. I should have guessed."

"Why?"

Zuleikha slides her back against the wall and sits down. She pulls out a cigarette, which she lights by holding it to the flame of the candle. She takes a deep pull. "You've never wondered why those old women hate each other?" She exhales slowly. "Those two were best friends when I came. Always in each other's apartments. You see, Razia Bibi's husband left her for another woman a long time ago—although she'll give you some story about how he died from a heart attack—and Fancy's husband had just passed away. When Fancy moved in, they became fast friends. They shared all their problems and even ate their meals together, if you can believe it. Anyway, Razia Bibi had a son, her life and joy—I heard he was the only good thing that came out of that marriage of hers.

"One day, Fancy's daughter, Preeti, returned from working in Jo'burg, and she met Razia Bibi's son, Ziyaad, and they fell in love instantly. Of course, initially it was a drama—her being Hindu and he being Muslim *and* she was divorced—it went against *everything* Razia Bibi believed in. But I'll give the old woman credit—eventually she came around—it was her best friend's daughter after all. They got married quickly and of course Razia Bibi and Fancy were over the moon." Zuleikha pauses to puff. "But it didn't last. Of course it didn't; I've told you this. They say—I don't know if it's true or not and frankly I don't care—that Preeti met someone at work and she left him. The boy was devastated. They say he didn't take it well at all. After that the old women started to fight like crazy. Obviously Razia Bibi blamed Preeti for what happened, but Fancy wouldn't hear a word against her daughter; she said some things about Ziyaad that Razia Bibi didn't like, blah, blah, blah. And then a year later when the divorce was finalized, Ziyaad just left. Packed his bags and moved to Canada. He said it was the job offer but we all know he just couldn't bear living in the same city as his ex. The thing is, he also left his mother. I mean he phones and all that, but he's never been back since. He keeps saying he'll come every December but then he doesn't. It's been nearly . . . five years, I think. And the more time passes, the more she blames Fancy for everything."

"Razia Bibi hasn't seen her son for five years?" asks Sana.

"Hey, I don't blame him. Some things are unbearable. And that's how life is." She takes a deep pull so that the tip of her cigarette burns red. "Your kids abandon you, your husband leaves you, your best friend hates you, and eventually everyone dies. Trust me on this: at the end of the day, all you have is yourself."

"That sounds horrible," says Sana.

"Well life is horrible; get used to it." Zuleikha taps ash from her cigarette into a saucer and looks around at everything collected around Sana. "What *are* you doing here?"

"Looking," says Sana.

"Why? It's things people *threw away*—what the old tenants didn't want."

Sana places one saucer over another carefully. "Do you know anything about whoever lived here? Before the tenants. Like, right at the beginning?"

Zuleikha rests a pallid arm on one upturned knee. "No."

"Aren't you curious?" Sana says, pulling a rusted trunk toward her.

"The past is the past. Why should I care?" Zuleikha puts out her cigarette against the saucer.

Sana opens the trunk and finds it filled with musty-smelling blankets and books.

"See, junk," says Zuleikha, peering in.

Something in the trunk glints in the light of the flame and Sana reaches into the folds of the blanket and pulls out a narrow metal box. The box is covered in tan leather and the front has a two-tone enamel geometric design. She picks it up and studies the front panel, which is fixed with a glass disc in the center. "Beau Brownie, double lens," she reads out loud. She turns it in her hands and says, "I wonder what it is."

"Let me see," Zuleikha says as she leans over and takes it from her to study. Then she laughs. "It's a camera! A camera from the Stone Age." She tosses it back to Sana. "You should take it to a pawnshop and see how much you can get for it."

"Oh!" Sana touches it delicately. "I wonder if it's the same camera from the photo," she says, before she can stop herself.

"What photo?" asks Zuleikha.

Sana drops her head and fidgets with the camera. "Oh, it's nothing." She doesn't want anyone else to know about the photos or the room. Especially not Zuleikha, who might say something that will cause the fragile world she is stringing around herself to collapse. She cannot risk it.

"These things, they're just junk," says Zuleikha, gesturing to the passage. "No one wants anything here. People don't come to this house to remember, they come to forget. Leave the past alone," she says as she stands and picks up her candle.

Sana looks around the passage. She draws the teacup to her and studies it. "Does it stop becoming junk if someone wants it again?" she asks.

But Zuleikha is already down the passage, her light disappearing around the corner.

Sana looks inside the teacup and finds a small rust-colored stain at the bottom. She pulls her sleeve to her fingers and rubs at it but the mark doesn't budge. Eventually she gives up. She picks up the box camera, tucks it under her arm, and leaves.

AT THE END of the passage, the djinn watches from the shadows. Its eyes flicker to the rafters but they remain still. Quiet. Everything is sturdy and is as it should be. Outside the window, the rain slows. The djinn goes to the tea set and lifts up the saucers and looks under them. It picks up the teapot and tips it over but nothing falls out. It opens the sugar bowl and peers inside but it is empty.

It remembers how there had been so much sugar once, how horse-drawn carts brought tons of it up the hill, how the cellars were packed with bags, how the servants filled bowls in the kitchen until they were overflowing.

Five

The sugar business in Natal is a good one.

The rainfall is reliable, the soil is fertile and the fibrous cane thrives in the hilly tropical landscape. The demand for sugar increases in Europe and America, and Natal's point of access on the Cape Route makes it attractive for export. Business booms, the sugar mill has to be expanded, and Akbar, the businessman, is pleased. As trade increases, he acquires new machinery, hires more laborers, and begins to manufacture sweets: an array of funfair wares from loops of candy canes, lollipops, and toffee apples, to more traditional Indian fare like gulab jamuns, hot sticky jalebi, and mounds of pistachio and cardamom burfee.

Akbar's mother, Grand Ammi, oversees the production of the sweetmeats, shouting orders and perspiring over boiling vats of jalebi and cauldrons of halwa. She throws her dupatta over her shoulder, pulls up her sleeves, and inspects mixtures with her wooden spoon.

Grand Ammi had arrived from India when she heard news that she was going to be a grandmother; she quickly became the matriarch of the house. She is a little woman who wears silver shalwar kameezes and a dupatta with a heavy embroidered edge that she throws aggressively over her shoulder when she is annoyed. She has bushy eyebrows and a deep voice that makes her seem bigger than she is and she projects it so that she seems to always be ahead of where she is. This is how she keeps workers on their toes. She moves as if she always has an objective in mind, quickly, with a determinedness to her gait. She wears thick silver bangles up to her elbows despite objections that her husband is dead.

"If the people have a problem with it, they must tell me themselves," she replies when she hears the complaints. "Just because my husband is dead, doesn't mean *I'm* dead. My heart is still beating." And she thumps her chest with a clang of her bangles.

She carries herself with the confidence of a woman who knows her Role in the world. The entire household is thrown into frenzy when she arrives; she marches through rooms, rearranging furniture, ordering new carpets and wallpapers, firing servants and interviewing new ones. She is horrified with the quaint English interior her daughter-in-law has introduced to her son's house and replaces watercolor landscapes with heavy oils of maharajas and Indian forts. She discards the Victorian sofas and lamps and imports Mughal furniture made of ebony, brings in julas, damchiyas, and jalis carved in detailed teak, and puts down finely woven Persian carpets.

While the outside attempts to gracefully blend Eastern and Western sensibilities, the inside rages a war against each other. Mother-in-law and daughter-in-law are locked in an ancient battle of the civilizations.

Grand Ammi tells her daughter-in-law that it is shameful that she runs such a poor household. There is no control; nothing is in order, the house is not properly cleaned, the servants have no schedules nor do they follow instructions, and the food is just pitiful. A real lady of the house, she says, will know how to handle the servants, placate her husband, cook pilau, and still have every hair in place at the end of the day. She did not choose her as her son's wife for her to make a mockery of the position. She fires the meek Bengali cook and interviews a number of new cooks before deciding on a South Indian from Kerala who impresses her with his polite manners and dhal chawal (almost as good as hers, she admits to her son once). She rises before the sun every morning and after her morning prayers she lines the servants up and inspects their hair and nails. After inspection, she bathes, dabs sandalwood attar on her wrists, and prays for a grandson to bless her family. Then she burns a stick of incense and wafts the heady scent all over the house to ward off bad spirits.

When the baby is born and it turns out to be a girl, Grand Ammi does not mince words. She tells her daughter-in-law she is disappointed; it would have been more suitable to have the heir first, but the damage is done and they can do nothing but wait for the next one. She advises her daughter-in-law to eat more fish and drink less milk in order to produce a male.

Jahanara Begum doesn't dare speak against her mother-in-law, considering her a formidable foe, but privately in her chambers, she gnashes her teeth. When no one is around she replaces the Indian paintings with the English ones.

But come morning they are always changed back.

JAHANARA BEGUM COMPLAINS TO AKBAR. "Your mother is interfering too much in the house. Do you know she fired my cook? Without even consulting me!"

Akbar tries to placate her. "She wants to feel like she is still in control of something in her life." He tries to put an arm around her but she shakes it off and paces the room.

"No, no, Akbar. I know what your mother is trying to do. She's trying to show me my place. I won't have it, you hear? My family didn't send me away to be treated like this. I gave up *everything* to come here with you. And now? Now I can't even run my own household?"

Akbar runs a hand through his hair and says slowly, "But, Jahanara, I thought you didn't like house duties anyway. You said you would rather be out picnicking or dancing. You took months to even find that cook. I thought it would be a relief for you when Ammi came to stay. One less thing to worry about."

Jahanara Begum stops pacing and her eyes narrow. "What are you trying to say, Akbar? Are you trying to say I'm a bad wife? *Are you siding with your mother?*"

"No," says Akbar sighing. "Don't be impossible."

"Impossible? How dare you. *You're* impossible. Thinking we can just come to this strange country and pretend like we've always lived here. Like these are our people. These are not our people!"

"And I assume the European friends you spend all day playing bridge with are?" he says evenly.

She grits her teeth. "Don't twist what I'm saying, Akbar."

He pinches the bridge of his nose. "I'll speak to Ammi."

"Yes, I would expect you to," says Jahanara Begum.

BUT LITTLE CHANGES in the house. Grand Ammi still continues to run the household with an iron fist, and when Jahanara Begum gives birth to a baby boy four years later, Grand Ammi says it is only because of her early morning prayers. She pushes aside the surprised imam who has come to place the softened date in the newborn's mouth and read the azaan in his ear.

If anyone is going to feed her grandson and introduce him to the world it should be her, she says as she picks him up and begins the takbeer, preparing him for a life she has already mapped out. A life in which everyone must follow the path they have been given.

It is difficult to pinpoint the exact moment when fate veers off that designated path. Some blame a specific person, a certain action, or the consequence of a particular sin.

For Jahanara Begum it's quite simple: it's the sweet factory. The addition of the sweet factory is where it all falls apart.

This is how Grand Ammi finds out.

Shanthi Singh, who works at the reception desk, who deals with the admin and the books, who watches everything there is to be watched, reports to Grand Ammi that her son is spending an awful lot of time around the girl who sweeps the sev-and-nut floor. The next day Grand Ammi takes off her apron, leaves her boiling vats of jalebi, and watches the girl in question. She studies the young barefoot Tamil girl with her dark skin, wild hair, and coarse manners. The girl could barely string a sentence together in English. Grand Ammi scoffs; how could Shanthi even warrant this katchra as a threat? Why was she being sent on nonsensical wild-goose chases when she was such a busy woman?

Her son would never be interested in someone like that. She fastens her apron back on and drops the matter from her mind.

So you can imagine her shock when Akbar Ali Khan sweeps into the house one morning to announce he is taking a second wife, "a good woman" from the factory who has finally agreed to marry him, and that she will be moving into the house that week.

Well, Grand Ammi put her silver chappaled foot down: A second wife? A common worker? A non-Muslim?

But worse, someone who has *finally agreed* to marry him?

What has gotten into her son's head? Here is that indomitable streak of madness from his father's side that she worries about. First, coming to this wild country and building this outrageous house and now marrying the sev-and-nut floor sweeper? Yes, no one can deny that Jahanara Begum is a difficult woman, but she is still of proper caste, still noble, still *suitable*, dammit. There is a proper way to do things, appearances to keep, and rules to follow. You can't just go around doing what you like.

This had not been part of her plans for him. How can he shame the family like this? What is she going to tell people back home? Oh, she won't bear the shame. She rages and rants and beats her silver chappals against the wall. She bangs her head and pulls her hair out of its bun and wails at God for giving her such a pagla, ungrateful son. How long, *how long*, had she carried him in her womb?! What *pain* had she endured to give birth to him? How much had she given up to come all the way to Africa to look after him?

Anyone, *anyone*, except this sev-and-nut floor sweeper, she pleads. If he really wants to take a second wife, at least let it be from a respectable family from their village. She would *help* him choose. They could go to India *now* and choose the best of the best! When her words seem to have no impact, she pretends to have a heart attack and gasps, dropping to the floor, holding her chest and wheezing.

But Akbar will not listen.

He asks her to stop the theatrics. He says this woman is going to be his wife, whether Grand Ammi likes it or not.

IN CONTRAST TO HER MOTHER-IN-LAW, Jahanara Begum restrains herself when she hears the news. Akbar tells her in their bedroom as she sits on her side of the bed, slipping on her gold bangles, preparing to start the day.

"Another wife?" she says as she stops struggling with her bangle and holds still. She wonders if she has misheard.

"Haan," says Akbar, nodding as he buttons up his shirt and pulls out the collar. "Meena. She works at the factory."

Jahanara Begum begins to force the bangle tightly over her hand, wringing it until it burns her skin. "A worker at the factory?"

"Yes," says Akbar, running a brush through his wavy hair. "You might even like her; maybe she will be good company."

Jahanara Begum's flesh turns red as the gold bites deeper. "Good company?" she says through teeth so gritted she wonders if they will crack.

"You're always saying it's so boring here, all alone," says Akbar with a shrug as he buttons his cuffs.

"I have friends, Akbar. Don't do anything on my account," she says with a small mirthless laugh, but clutches the bangle tightly.

"I'm not," he says as he puts on his fez and leaves the room.

Jahanara Begum purses her lips and holds her fists tight. When he shuts the door behind him, she waits until she knows he is far enough not to hear. Then she stands up and smashes her fine crystal perfume bottles and throws her pots of powder against the wall in rage. She cannot understand it. To treat her like this, to *demean* her so explicitly, to insult her lineage, her very forefathers, by marrying not just another woman, but a woman so *common*—and then to suggest companionship! It is too much for Jahanara Begum to bear. She, who has provided two children, one of them being a male. She, who is not only beautiful but also keeps herself in the best manner. Does she not ensure she has the most fashionable frocks from London? The most stylish negligées from France? Does she not bathe in rosewater and milk at the end of the day? Does she not turn the head of every man in the street when they walk the town? She cannot fathom what this common worker can offer him. She cries and shreds her fine dresses with her teeth in frustration. How can he play her the fool like this? How can she show her face to anyone? It is humiliating. She sits at her dressing table crying until eventually she begins to quiet into small hiccupping blubs. She looks at her wretched reflection in the mirror and recoils. This will not do. She tries to organize her table, steady her shaking hands.

She sits down and paints her lips red carefully as an idea begins to form.

She will take revenge. She is from a family of noblemen, a dynasty that traces itself back to the Mughals. She is beautiful, white-skinned, *and* sophisticated. Her English is impeccable. Nothing like that filthy servant who probably can't even speak a word of it.

She dabs away the black kohl that has run down her cheeks and reapplies it carefully to the inside of her eyes. She rearranges her hair into a stylish set of curls. When she finally emerges from her chambers, she is calm and polite. She says little to him, just nods primly at the news.

She will bide her time and soon she will have her pound of flesh.

Six

Early in the morning, Akbar Manzil is filled with the sound of screaming: Razia Bibi had stepped off her bed and found her feet immersed in ankle-deep water. Her bathroom has been leaking for years but now it's finally flooded and she curses her miserable existence. Her wails fill the house as she blames everyone: Sana for having short hair, Fancy's bird for taking God's name, Doctor for being too modern, Zuleikha for never marrying, and Bilal for trying to cook like a woman. "When God's punishment falls, it falls on everyone, even the innocent!" she yells.

Bilal offers to take a look at the pipes and Razia Bibi says it's the least he can do since he was the reason it happened in the first place. He sets about mending the cracked pipe in the courtyard while Sana tries to help her clean up. Every now and then Razia Bibi comes outside to empty her mop and bucket in the garden and each time she does, she has something to say. "This bloody house will be the death of us. One day we will wake up and we will all be dead!"

"How will we wake up if we are dead?" asks Bilal cheerfully as he mixes a bucket of cement.

"You shush," mutters Razia Bibi. "It's an expression. You won't understand," she says, squeezing her mop violently into a pot of palms and sending two wandering peacocks into a frenzy as she shakes out the leftover water in their direction.

"I don't think there's much to understand about it," says Zuleikha, who is sitting on a tattered deck chair nearby wearing oversized sunglasses and sipping a glass of water.

"What are *you* doing here?" spits Razia Bibi.

"I'm here for the show," says Zuleikha, lowering her sunglasses and gesturing at the mess as if it were obvious. "The moment I heard what happened, I ran down, grabbed a chair from the junk passage, and came right over."

"If you're not here to help, you can just leave. We don't need useless people getting in the way!" shouts Razia Bibi.

"You better calm down, Razia Bibi. Don't excite yourself too much. Otherwise we might have to call an ambulance again," says Zuleikha, pushing her sunglasses back up with a finger.

"Chupkar! I told you I saw a burglar. Stop going on and on about it! Like a broken record you are," says Razia Bibi. She grabs her bucket and marches back into the house.

But it isn't the truth.

Razia Bibi *didn't* see a burglar last winter. She saw something else entirely. Something she won't admit to herself, least of all anyone else.

It happened during an unusually cold night in June. The night had been wretched, full of twists and turns and aching joints, and Razia Bibi had woken to fill her hot-water bottle. As she waited for the kettle to boil, through the hiss of the whistle, she heard a noise outside her apartment, a dull repetitive knock like someone dragging something. She switched off the kettle and cocked her head to the front door. When she heard nothing, she went to the door, bent down, and put her eye to the keyhole. Through the gap she saw the entrance hall with all its usual shapes sitting in the dim light. Then it seemed to her that something passed by quickly, just a fleeting moment of darkness that blocked her view. She jerked back from the door in surprise. The thought came to her that it might be Pinky, that perhaps the maid was wandering the house at night, looking for things to steal, or perhaps even trying their doors and coming into their rooms. Razia Bibi had always known it was a risk to take in an outsider as a servant; she wondered how long this had been going on for. She pulled out her apartment key from her gown and unlocked her front door quietly. She stepped into the hall and squinted into the gloom. Something moved in the shadowy depths of the stairway landing and she strained to make sense of the shape. At the same time the clouds outside cleared, revealing the moon, and its brightness pierced the stained-glass window, filling the hall with ethereal splendor. Razia Bibi looked to the landing and saw in the light a figure with its back to her. She almost called Pinky's name, but then the figure began to turn and Razia Bibi stopped.

In horrid fascination she watched as the figure moved stiffly around and revealed itself to be a woman with long matted hair. Her face was wan, almost without features, except for sunken eyes that seemed to pull Razia Bibi in. She wore a dress marked with dark stains and clutched a bundle in her arms; whatever was inside seemed to gurgle and move. As the woman limped forward, Razi Bibi realized the stains were blood. She gasped, stepping backward, making the woman look up sharply. Their eyes met, and the moon fled for cover. In the ensuring darkness it seemed to Razia Bibi that the woman, like smoke, simply disappeared.

That's when she began to scream.

SUCH THINGS, OF COURSE, she tells herself later, are nonsense. There are no such things as ghosts. It must have been the moonlight playing tricks on her eyes. She tries to forget it, but no one seems to want her to forget, especially the bird on the stairs that committed to memory the words she screamed that night.

IN THE GARDEN, Sana hangs Razia Bibi's wet clothes on the washing line. As she pins up scarves and dressing gowns, Doctor lays out soaked prayer mats and rugs in the sun on the grass next to her.

"Razia Bibi is never going forgive me for this," says Doctor, wiping his brow as he sets down a rolled-up rug. "She's been telling me to get that leak checked for ages."

"No one could have known *this* would happen," says Sana. "My father even says the leak doesn't make sense; the pipes are old but they're not that damaged," she says as she strings up a shawl.

Doctor leans back on the trunk of a palm tree and lets out a breath. He looks to the house through the tree and says, "Sometimes I feel like it's giving up. Like it's on its last legs."

Sana glances in the direction he is looking at. "The house?"

"It's like an old car, you know? First it starts to trouble, some noises here and there, and you get it fixed and then it starts to slow down and get stuck and then it keeps troubling and then one morning you try to start it, and you know this car is not going to move again."

They both look at the house, which sits sullen, as if listening.

"Look at you two, daydreaming here. No one knows how to get anything done in this house!" Razia Bibi yells as she passes by carrying a washing basket of objects.

Sana and Doctor quickly start working again. Sana hauls up a waterlogged rug.

"Just taking a quick break, Razia dear," says Doctor.

"Don't you 'dear' me. You know this is all your fault," calls back Razia Bibi.

Doctor mouths, "See, I told you," to Sana.

Sana smiles to herself as she carries the rug to the back of the garden. She locates a sunny patch near the rickety gate that leads down steep stairs to the beach below.

"What are you grinning about?"

Sana looks up to find her sister perched on the crumbling stone wall.

"Nothing."

Her sister pouts. "Old people give me the heebie-jeebies. I don't know how you hang out with them."

Sana rolls open the carpet on the grass.

"They smell so bad and move so slowly," her sister continues as she shudders.

Sana shakes her head as she pulls at the edges of the carpet so that it sits straight.

"Don't act so sanctimonious. We used to laugh at Tant Elsie, don't you remember? When she pulled off her gown and ran out in the fields? That was *hilarious*." Her sister cackles and slaps her knee. When Sana doesn't respond, she stands up and dusts her dress, then walks along the wall one step in front of the other, arms out for balance.

"How come you don't tell people about me?"

Sana is startled by the question. She looks up. "Tell people about you?"

"Yes." Her sister looks at her pointedly. "Are you ashamed of me?"

"No . . ."

"Then why don't you ever talk about me? Why don't you tell people you had a sister. Aren't you sad that I died?"

Sana is silent. She steps over the carpet, then says, "I am."

"Liar," her sister stops walking. "You're happy I'm dead."

Sana shakes her head.

"If that's true, then why do you want me to leave you? Don't you want us to be together?"

"Not like this," says Sana under her breath.

Her sister looks over the edge at the rocks below. "I'll show you how then. Come here. Don't be scared. All you have to do is climb up and take one step. It'll be over in a moment. Everything will be over—all your pain and worries. *Just one small step.*" Her sister bends down and offers a hand to her. "If you really feel bad about me, you'll do it."

Sana looks at her sister's small, pale hand outstretched toward her. She imagines taking it in her own, feeling the cool flesh against hers, stepping up onto the crumbling wall and standing on the ledge looking out to the bright blue ocean. She can feel the wind on her face. The glittering expanse before her. She can feel how it would be to just close her eyes, shut it all out, and take that simple step forward, off the edge into the tumbling darkness where the world would tip over and end forever. There would be a flash of pain and then nothing.

No fear. No anger. No sadness.

Nothing.

She looks up at her sister and her sister has never looked lovelier. Her skin blushes with color. She looks warm, inviting, kind even. Her eyes are full of softness and she smiles beguilingly. She looks like what a sister should look like, a dear friend, a companion for life. Would it be so bad to join her?

She finds herself lifting her hand.

And yet, there is something. An unease. A flash in the eaves. A rattle in a box.

Nothing is ever so simple.

With great difficulty she lowers her arm and shakes her head at her sister.

Her sister drops her hand. Her face turns cold and lifeless once again. She whispers hoarsely. "*You always choose yourself.*"

"That's not true," Sana mutters.

"It's always been like this," her sister says bitterly and turns to face the sea. "You're the one who got to live. I'm the one who got to die. I'm stuck here and you don't care. If you cared, you would come with me." She looks over her shoulder and smiles. "But don't worry, you're going to pay, little sister."

Then she steps forward and falls off the edge.

Sana rushes to look over but all she sees is foam crashing into the rocks below.

Seven

"As it is, it's so confusing when Big Madam came from India and took over from Small Madam. Now there's another one—what do we call her? And do we have to answer to her?" complains Daisy, one of the maids, as she sorts through a pile of laundry in the servant's quarters.

"I thought it was just a rumor," says another maid, fanning herself at the table.

"No, Big Madam herself told me to get a room ready in the east wing," says Daisy, flapping out a pillowcase.

Iqbal Babu, the animal caretaker, sneers from across the table. "Ha! Don't you worry your little head about what you have to call her, Daisy. No matter who comes here, it will always be Big Madam who has the say! She's the lady in charge 'til the day she dies. Yes sir!" He dunks a hunk of bread sloppily into in his tea adding, "And if you have any doubts about the matter, ask our man, Pappu, the dear fellow will confirm it."

There is laughter from the other servants in the room that stops abruptly when Jahanara Begum opens the door and bursts in. Iqbal

Babu swallows and flattens his oily hair down on either side with his palms.

"Daisy! Where is Daisy?" She turns to the maid. "Where have you been? I've been ringing the bell for ages. Are you deaf?" Without waiting for an answer, she continues, "Have you seen my red shawl?" she snaps. "It was in my armoire."

"Your what, Madam?" Daisy asks nervously.

"My cupboard, my cupboard!"

"No, Madam. I haven't," answers Daisy.

"It was there." Jahanara Begum narrows her eyes. "I put it there yesterday. I'm very sure."

"I'll look for it as soon as I'm done with the ironing for Big Madam."

"Oh forget it. You're useless," she hisses, offended at the reminder of her inferior position in the household hierarchy. She sweeps out of the servant's quarters and slams the door behind her.

"Different as night and day those two, master and mistress. It's a bit early in the morning for her tantrums, isn't it?" observes the gardener, Nkosi, as he sips his tea in the corner of the room.

"I like her like that," says Iqbal Babu, his eyes bright. "Feisty. I bet she wakes up that way in the morning—all turned on, looking for a fight." He grins and spits onto his hands before flattening his hair down once more.

"Poor thing," ventures one of the newer maids. "I think it must be the stress. It must be *so* difficult knowing the master is getting married again. Really, it's too sad," she says as she folds sheets. "I wouldn't stand for it if I were her. She already has the two young'uns. She should have put her foot down and told him. It's 1930. Times are changing."

"Hey wena, what do you know?" asks Nkosi. "You haven't been here long enough. If I had a wife like that . . . hawu! I'd also find a new one. Such a sour face with nothing good to say to anyone. She doesn't deserve our master. He's a good man."

"Good man? Bah," spits Iqbal Babu. "A good man who doesn't know how to treat a fine woman. If *I* had a woman like that, I'd treat her like she was something special. Oh yes, I would," he says with a gleam in his eye.

"She *is* special! They say she's related to them big kings and queens before in India. All fancy-like. Those what you call it . . . Mongols . . . Mughals. Yes, that's it! Don't you know?" says the young maid excitedly. "Come from royalty, she is. That's why Big Madam chose her in the first place. We ought to show her some respect at least; she's basically a princess."

"Ha! Princess, my foot! Wouldn't she like to hear that," says Daisy. "Big Madam only chose her because she knows that she can control her. She wants a daughter-in-law that will listen. When Big Madam says jump, Small Madam must hold on to her skirts and ask, how high? Same like all of us."

Just then Pappu the cook comes in wiping his hands on a dishcloth. "Eh, what you talking about, Daisy?" he asks, smelling trouble.

"Your mother," replies Iqbal Babu.

Pappu ignores him. "I hope you all not talking about Madam-ji again. I keep saying she's an honorable woman who deserves our respect. We'll have none of that dirty talk here. Remember the hand that feeds you—"

"Not another lecture, Pappu. We've had enough bayaans," groans Iqbal Babu.

Pappu continues. "She's under a lot of pressure, our Madam-ji; you all know what she has to put up with. That mad son of hers who can't sit still and that rude daughter-in-law, and now, can you believe it? A new daughter-in-law—a non-Muslim even!" He throws up his hands in the air. "They can say what they want about her converting but we know that she's not a *real* Muslim. Arreh baap. Who can blame our poor Madam-ji for being so tired and shouting all the time? She works the hardest in the house. The *hardest*! It's a wonder she hasn't collapsed from exhaustion. And don't forget how she nearly had a heart attack when she found out he wanted to get married again. I thought she was going to die! But our Madam-ji is a tough one. You can't break her. Oh no, you can't!" He throws his dishcloth over his shoulder and nods to himself.

"Yes, I don't disagree with you on that. She's the toughest of the lot, gives everyone a run for their money; even the little girl can't compete!" laughs Iqbal Babu.

"I almost forgot! You know what she did the other day?" asks Daisy with an exasperated sigh. "She purposely wiped chocolate on the newly washed sheets on the line. She actually *looked* at me as she did it," says Daisy as she shivers. "And then she went away smiling, twirling her plait behind her as if she hadn't done a thing in the world. Oh, if there was a child I wanted to smack it would be her!"

"Well, look who's the mother," says Pappu as he begins to wash his hands in the communal sink. "Small Madam is *always* irritating Madam-ji. Remember how she kept changing all Madam-ji's *lovely* paintings upstairs. How nice Madam-ji made the house! So welcoming! And when our Madam-ji has her important dinners, Small Madam *never* helps. Not one finger she will raise. So what you expect from her daughter?"

"I wonder how the new madam will fare here," says Daisy as she begins to heat the electric iron. "I hope she's nicer than Small Madam. The poor master needs someone who will treat him better."

"I hear she's no better than us. In fact, *worse*. She used to sweep the factory floors," whispers the young maid conspiratorially.

"No!" says Daisy, her eyes widening in shock. "Say it isn't true."

"Yes!" says the other maid excitedly. "My cousin in Tongaat told me. She came from the settlement, same as all of us."

"Well, if I knew I had a chance I should be wearing my red lipstick every day!" says another maid, guffawing as she slaps a hand to her knee.

"I think it's wonderful," says Nkosi. "Finally, someone from outside making it into their world. Good for the master, I say."

"Oh please," Iqbal Babu scoffs. "The master is just thinking with his—" and he makes a crude motion to his crotch so that the ladies gasp. "That's all there is to it, he's a man, same like us."

"For once, I must agree with Iqbal Babu," says Pappu. "There's nothing noble about what he's doing. She's a cheap woman. You can find someone like her on any street corner. She doesn't belong in an important house like this. This is a decent family. You can't just throw katchra in it. Oh, our poor Madam-ji," says Pappu, shaking his head.

"I bet she won't last one month," says Daisy.

"Ha! Now there's a joke. Forget a month, I'll wager she'll be out before the week is over. Our Madam-ji will eat her alive," says Pappu in glee.

Everyone bursts out laughing.

Akbar never planned to take a second wife.

It is not something he ever imagined. His passions are engrossing and it is doubtful that if his mother had not intervened he would have married at all. He had hoped in marriage he and Jahanara Begum would find common interest, perhaps even love. Unfortunately, he discovered quickly they are very different people. His wife is not interested in activities like horse riding, archery, or listening to poetry, and he finds himself restless or annoyed in the company of her friends. She has a short temper and complains often—if not about his mother, then the weather or the servants or the food. He protests when she insists he wear suits instead of kurtas or tries to take him to dances and tea parties. The more demanding she grows, the more frustrated he becomes. After eleven years he accepts that their marriage is not ideal and throws himself into his house and business. He retreats to his library and reads more poetry than ever. He devours Yunus Emre, Hatef Esfahani, Rumi, Hafez, and other Sufi poets. He tries to recite verses to Jahanara Begum but she grows fidgety and tells him to stop, that he is giving her a headache. So he reads the poems to his children, bending low over their beds, whispering the words of al-Ghazali in their ears.

After a long time he feels the old urge; he wants to be at sea again. He takes to riding his horse along the beach and only returns late at night when the house is dark. He feels stuck and searches for Signs in the night skies, but for once he feels at a loss at what to do.

It is during this period in his life that he returns home one afternoon honking his horn with a large container attached to his Tin Lizzie. In it, he introduces his shocked family to a large male lion that he has purchased from the circus in the town below. Have you ever seen anything so magnificent? he demands. He saw the animal and immediately knew it was meant for him, he says. He has large steel cages built into the walls of the garden and hires a lion tamer. The wild cat is allowed to roam the gardens freely on Sundays when all other animals are bolted up and the giraffe is pushed to the front of the house. The servants huddle on the landing and watch through the stained-glass window as the lion paces proudly up and down the courtyard and tries to attack a stray peahen that someone has forgotten to put away.

IQBAL BABU, the "King of the Ring," arrives with the lion, and he is as vain as he is proud. He had once been a famous lion tamer, well known in Bombay's circus scene for his death-defying acts involving fire and wild cats. At the height of his career, he boasted that he could get any woman he wanted—why, he just had to wink at them in the crowd, and married or not, they would be waiting for him at the back of the tent after the show.

Then came the incident in the ring and everything changed.

Unlike other trainers who had affection for their animals, Iqbal Babu hated his charges and often went into a mad rage just looking at them. He was merciless, often beating them savagely on their paws so that the scars could not be seen on their pelts. One fateful afternoon a lioness suddenly tackled and killed his assistant during a performance, and in the ensuing chaos tore off Iqbal's own ear. The traumatized crowd vowed never to return to his shows.

His missing ear was a gory reminder of the mess in the ring that stood out in Indian circus history. It wasn't good for business, this reminder that the shows were just shows; the infallibility of the circus was at risk. It interfered too much with the fantasy that circus folk took decades to cultivate.

And so Iqbal Babu was forced to leave India, defeated and deaf in one ear. He joined a small circus in Egypt that toured parts of Africa, moving among small circuses around the continent because he could never keep a job long enough with his bad temper and attitude. He was in South Africa when Akbar made him the offer. He did not want the job, but he was forced to accept it when the only lion was removed from the circus. The fact that he had been reduced to menial animal caretaker in a rich man's home filled him with great bitterness.

AT THE HOUSE, he takes bets with the servants to prove how strong he is; he lifts the heaviest rocks and breaks bare wooden boards with his fists. He flexes his muscles and tells them how he was a famous lion tamer in India and how for the love of travel he gave it all up to see new parts of the world. His ear mishap occurred when a particularly enthusiastic lover had bit it off in lust. He had even been to America, he says, where the roads are so wide you can't see the other side. He won't be here for long, he will be off soon and this is just to pass the time. He twirls his fingers around his mustache and looks up to the bedroom windows to see if Jahanara Begum is watching. If she is, he asks if anyone wants to challenge him to a fistfight.

He stands at the end of the garden with only a leather waistcoat over his hairy barrel chest, flexing his muscles and yielding a whip as he oversees the lion.

"Hut! Hut!" He beats his whip on the ground. "Salla kuta!" he shouts at the beast, knowing it makes for a powerful display for the huddled servants inside the house.

He can take on anyone, he says, even the lion.

One Sunday when he feels he has a particularly large audience in the surrounding windows, Iqbal Babu begins to beat the pacing lion with his bullwhip until blood streaks the pelt of the animal. He smiles and looks up at Jahanara Begum's window, but a moment later, he feels a strong hand on his arm as Akbar tackles him, grabbing the whip and shouting, "What the hell are you doing? Are you crazy?" As Akbar wrestles him to the floor he shouts, "Don't *ever* touch this animal again. Your job is to make sure it doesn't hurt anyone. Not to hurt it! Do you understand?"

When Iqbal Babu refuses to answer, Akbar raises his voice, *"Do you understand?"*

Iqbal Babu nods meekly, burning with embarrassment and rage.

"This is a creature of God. The most beautiful creature in the world. Don't forget it," says Akbar, as he throws the whip to the floor and walks away.

THIS IS TRULY what Akbar believes.

Until he meets Meena.

When Akbar sees Meena for the first time he finally understands what they mean about *falling* in love. It is as if you are standing at the edge of something for a long time, not knowing you are at the edge of anything at all until suddenly you feel yourself going over.

She is a twenty-year-old woman who has arrived fresh from Madras. Her family arrived to work as laborers in the sugarcane fields in Natal. She is small built and her abundant hair is pinned in loose curls above her head. Her brown skin shines across the rise of her cheekbones and a tiny ring glints in her sculpted nose in the light from the factory windows. She has deep dimples when she smiles, although this is rare and happens in small, quick bursts when she thinks no one is watching. Her large eyes seem to reflect her feelings and it seems she knows this, for she keeps her gaze down, her head lowered as if to protect herself from their betrayal. In the shadows she looks like she is carved out of teak and in the shafts of light she looks like she is on fire.

The first Sign is that he begins to dream of her. In his dreams she comes to offer him handfuls of lotus flowers, but whenever he reaches for them, to taste their thick leaves and hollow stems, she disappears into a river, dropping beneath the water like a serpent.

Akbar takes his Signs seriously. Every morning he rises early and looks to the sea for Signs; if the sea is dark, he takes it as a Sign that the day will be difficult, but if it is calm, it means that the day will be good. His journey to Africa had been spurred by a dream in which he had been swimming for many years in the Indian Ocean until, exhausted, he climbed onto shore, where he found a herd of zebra grazing in a vast land with grass so green it made his eyes burn.

His dreams of Meena trouble him because it is not a Sign he can interpret. He becomes feverish and quiet. His mother makes him mixtures of turmeric and ginger to break his fevers and calm him down. After that his dreams takes on a new twist. Now Meena bows before him offering him baskets of ginger and turmeric roots.

The second Sign is that he begins to see her when she is not there. As he sits in his office, he sees her pass the window, but when he steps out he finds that she has been downstairs all the time. He sees her in his study perusing the bookshelves, or walking outside in the garden. He rubs his eyes wearily. He finds himself writing poetry to her, long poems about lotus leaves that float like open palms in the river Jhelum. He begins to watch her work, the way her hands move over the floor in confident, wide strokes.

It seems to him as if she is dancing. As if she is a flame flickering in a darkened room.

The Signs go on for months until finally an exhausted Akbar decides that it is clear: he will have to propose. He calls her to his office and asks her if she will take him as her husband. He is, he explains, already married, but Islam allows him to wed another.

MEENA FOR HER PART is not surprised by the request from the factory owner, who has not said a word to her in his life. She has heard many stories of the eccentric landowner, ranging from rumors that he requests shark meat every night to stories that his strange mansion is filled with underground passages that run all the way to Zanzibar. Meena regards him as an impulsive narcissist. She assumes this request is just another of his fanciful whims that will dissipate, and she does not take it seriously.

No, she tells Akbar, she does not think it a good idea that they marry as soon as possible.

Perhaps, she adds politely, Sir-ji just needs another horse in his stable.

When she returns to her small home in Tongaat and tells her parents what happened, they are aghast. She must, absolutely *must* marry him, they insist. She is still too young, too headstrong and hopeful to understand that life is unbearable most times. They will be paying debts off for their journey to South Africa for years to come; suffering would be their lot in life if they continued this way. She wasn't going to get a better offer than this: a rich landowner offering to take care of her future. She would be a fool, a *fool* to turn this offer down. So the man is a bit crazy—they should take *advantage* of his craziness. What if he came to his senses? It was unlikely, but they shouldn't take any chances. It would change everything for them, *everything*, her parents announce joyously in their tin shanty. When Meena remains stubbornly irresolute, her parents try a claim of conscience: Doesn't she see how noble he is? "He's not trying to sleep with you, like the other factory owners, Meena. He wants to *marry* you! This is different!" Meena retorts that it's not, that he wants her like any other man—he's simply packaging it in a presentable way for himself. When Meena brings up the question of religion, they say that God is the same for everyone, all she has to do is say there is only one God and cover her legs.

When she still refuses, they threaten her; if she doesn't take this opportunity, they will make her leave the house, put her out on the street. Meena, aghast, refuses to speak to them again. It is all to no avail. The next day, Meena's father wears his best white shirt, combs what little hair he has left on his head, and goes to the factory to tell Akbar that he would be honored to give his daughter to him.

So Meena marries Akbar, unwillingly and resentfully. She says little to anyone before the wedding and wanders away from her singing relatives, who try to pinch her cheeks and apply wet turmeric to her face. At the nikah ceremony, Meena rejects the Arabic first name they offer her and insists on keeping her own.

So they call her Meena Begum.

THE DAY THE NEW BRIDE enters the house, a hush falls over Akbar Manzil. The servants hover in the corridors, whispering among themselves, standing on their toes trying to catch sight of the new lady in the house. Grand Ammi stands at the entrance in her silver shalwar kameez looking grim.

As Meena Begum enters with Akbar, Grand Ammi goes forward. She pulls her new daughter-in-law close as if to embrace, and when her face is near the other woman's, she whispers in her ear, "Listen to my words carefully, you filthy coolie. You might have fooled my son, but you will never fool me." As Akbar watches, she pulls her tightly into the embrace and adds, "You will *never* be welcome in this house."

Then the old woman turns away and walks up the stairs, throwing her heavy dupatta behind her as the servants hurry to follow.

Eight

Meena Begum is not the kind of woman to easily accept a fate so miserable.

She refuses to believe that her life will play out as a second wife to a vain and arrogant master. She briefly considers running away, but in the end it is an unexpected contempt for her new mother-in-law that persuades her to stay; she decides to remain long enough to agitate the proud old woman who threatened her the day she entered the house. Of course, she also expects Akbar to eventually weary of her and toss her out like a toy he has grown tired of. Her family will have to take her back and she will get a new job at another factory.

In the meantime, she explores the house from her new bedroom in the east wing. She has never been in such a house before. She walks through the deeply carpeted passages running with French boiserie, studies the heavy oil paintings, inspects the delicately painted japanned cabinets and numerous sitting rooms that no one sits in. She finds a room filled with portraits of Victorian kings and queens and fussy gilt-wood chaises. She wanders the gardens behind the house, feeding pieces of fruit to the monkeys and studying the bright parrots that climb crookedly up the nets and stare at her from sideward eyes.

Outwardly she seems calm but inside she is full of boiling rage. She has been thrust into the mouth of the very thing she detests.

The very thing she had tried to escape.

IN HER VILLAGE in south India her parents had worked on a cotton farm for a British landowner, and as a small girl she had roamed the giant manicured gardens of the main house in awe while her parents were working. One afternoon she accidentally entered the large house through the wide veranda doors, and she had wandered the passages seeking an exit until she reached a door at the end, where she found the most fabulous room in the world, with deep carpets and a great white bed piled high with pillows. She had never seen anything like it; at home they slept on grass mats on the floor that they rolled up during the day. Unable to help herself she kicked off her sandals and climbed onto the bed, just to feel the *softness* of it for a moment, but before she knew it, she had fallen asleep. She was awoken by the Memsaab, who shook her violently and kept screaming at her, "Disgusting! Disgusting!" and other English words she didn't understand. The Memsaab threw her out of the house, and all Meena Begum remembered was the ringing in her ears as she walked back home without shoes.

As she grew older, she became aware of the differences between the white people in their big homes and the brown people who worked for them. And even at a young age the differences made her angry. Something rippled over her skin when she thought about it. *The injustice.* When she was a teenager, she would creep to the window of secret village meetings at the schoolhouse and listen to members of the Justice Party and the Indian National Congress Party discuss the changes needed in the land, that the British Raj could not continue their tyranny if action was taken swiftly. She heard the stories about the bravery of Tipu Sultan against British forces, the mutiny at Vellore, Bal Gangadhar Tilak's advocacy of the Swadeshi movement for Indian nationalism, and Vanchinathan's sacrifice in the armed struggle. She stole copies of *The Hindu* and had friends translate the English into Tamil. She squatted in the dust and listened to how a radicalization of the system was the only way out of the colonizer's hands. Once, her father found the newspaper in her room; he tore it to shreds, telling her not to cause problems for them. They ought to be grateful for the opportunities they had, he said. Other people were not so lucky. She asked him if he thought they were lucky, if he thought his wife going nearly blind from working long hours weaving for the British was "lucky." He said she shouldn't say such things. He said someone might hear. When they left for South Africa to work on a farm, she thought they were escaping. She thought, as many of them did, that it was a way out. The new land showed promise: Indian indentured labor had been abolished, opportunities were arising in the growing Indian settlements in Natal and Transvaal, neighbors and friends were all leaving. They said it was better in Africa for them. But her family realized too late, the British were the same whether they were in South Africa or India; their brown skin would always hold the same currency. Her family still lived in poverty, they were punished for their skin color, and they were still answerable to the white man for everything they did.

It was still slavery, just in different packaging.

So MEENA BEGUM is particularly repulsed to be living in the home of such people. The fact that they are Indian makes it worse to her because they should lend to the struggle, or at the very least, share out their wealth and not make a display of it. All the English paintings and furniture she finds upstairs convince her that these people are as bad as the colonizers. Their skin may be brown but their wealth turned them white, she thinks.

So Meena Begum scorns everything lavish; she turns away the meals of saffron chicken and rice, opts for tinned fish and pap, which she takes from the pantry and cooks on the stove as her mother-in-law watches. She makes her bed herself, shooing away the maids who come to clean the room. And as for the man she has been sacrificed to, she ignores him. Refuses her part in what she sees as an ancient play of the poor performing for the caprices of the wealthy. When Akbar speaks to her, she looks away, and if he stays in her room too long she disappears into the bathroom and does not return until she hears him leave. She eats her meals, takes walks in the garden, and continues her job at the factory, where she has refused to stop working; she is quickly promoted to a higher position so she does not have to sweep. On the weekends she removes her sandals and sits in a low garden of rose bushes and reads books from the study, practicing her English to herself.

"How'd you do? How do you do?" she asks the pink flowers. She knows that language can be a weapon, that if you can harness it properly, you can use it against a people.

In the house she uses every opportunity to provoke Grand Ammi. She walks around barefoot and leaves her hair open. She speaks in Tamil, eats food with her hands, and refuses to answer to the Arabic name Grand Ammi tries to force on her. She has not yet spoken to the other wife and her children behave cautiously around Meena Begum, as if torn between being inquisitive and remaining aloof. They stop short when they see her in the passages upstairs, seemingly wanting to speak and then, as if suddenly recalling something, scoff and run off, bumping into her as they pass. The servants, too afraid of the retribution of their matriarch, leave her alone and say little. It seems that everyone moves around her and avoids her, even lowering their voices in her presence. She drifts through the house as she pleases and everyone seems to avert their eyes as she passes. As if she is not real, a mere inconvenience that they must endure for a while.

But one day in the upstairs passages she takes a corner too quickly and almost bumps into Jahanara Begum.

"Watch it!" the other woman says before she can help herself.

FOR ALMOST TWO MONTHS now Jahanara Begum has successfully ignored the presence of Meena Begum. She simply pretends that the other woman does not exist. If she sees her in the room or at the table, she ignores her, lowering her eyes and stiffening her spine. Once, in the kitchen, she accidentally dropped an orange that rolled away and hit Meena Begum's foot and the younger woman bent down and picked it up to offer to her, but she simply walked away from her outstretched hand.

Now, flustered, she turns away from Meena Begum, and then as if reconsidering, she pauses and turns back and says, "You know it's not real, right?"

Meena Begum looks back at her watchfully.

"The marriage. Akbar's so-called love. All of it. It's not real."

Meena Begum says nothing.

Jahanara Begum continues. "Akbar gets these strange fancies. He thinks the world is a big, wonderful place where you can do what you like. If he has a feeling he follows it, without any thought." She laughs bitterly. "You're just here for a moment because he's a man and he's bored. It's fun for him. I would hate for you to believe that any of this *means* anything."

Meena Begum says nothing.

Jahanara Begum shakes her head. "I shouldn't have expected you to understand." She makes to go, then adds, "If I were you, I would leave this place before I embarrassed myself any further." As she walks down the passage, Meena Begum calls out to her.

"I will leave. Soon."

Jahanara Begum stops, then turns. "You will?" she says arching an eyebrow.

Meena Begum nods.

"Good," says Jahanara Begum and gathers her skirts as she walks away.

Nine

The cold season come downs harder on the house than usual.
Winter is not particularly cruel in Durban, but this time the house on the hill seems to freeze over; pipes turn to ice, fireplaces fizzle out, and the windows fill with frost. Razia Bibi walks around wrapped in knitted scarves, clutching a hot-water bottle and complaining while Fancy seems to disappear, completely buried under a pile of blankets in her room.

The cold alters the secret room; damp spreads across the walls, bubbling under wallpaper and pushing out plaster like erupted wounds. A cold wind starts up; it rattles the wardrobe doors and shudders at the windows. Sana checks the panes for cracks and feels under the doors, but she cannot explain where it is coming from. Each time she enters the room it seems to grow colder and darker until eventually she retreats from it back into the passage, spending more time looking through the collection of objects, trying to find clues.

She is no closer to understanding who the room belonged to than when she first unlocked it. She sits with the photographs and the camera next to her trying to piece the parts together. She wants to know more about the man and the woman and how they have merged so seamlessly that she can't even see where one begins and the other ends.

She has to know who they are.

She visits the municipal library in town. She asks for information on the history of the old house along the cliff, but the staff are underpaid, overworked, and uninterested. They say they cannot find anything, that not every building and its history is recorded by the city. One librarian asks Sana if she knows the surname of the family that lived there but Sana shakes her head. She knows nothing about the family, she says, except that they are one shape not two. The librarian does not understand.

Later, after trawling newspaper archives, Sana finds a single article in the *Daily News* from 1969.

It announces the Durban Municipality's implementation of a "Rejuvenation Development Program" for the city. One of the projects includes an abandoned property on the cliffs above the CBD. The article states the unusual residential property was abandoned in the 1930s and had begun to deteriorate. After attracting vagrants and thieves, the esteemed city council took the decision in the interest of public safety to refurbish the existing house into community flats. They planned to utilize the structure to house some of the dozens of Indian-classified families relocated out of the Casbah with the 1950 Group Areas Act. This was a generosity provided by the apartheid government to the Indian people, and the project was expected to be a successful example of rehousing under the act.

Sana prints the article and keeps it with the box of photos in the secret room. She collects her clues like an investigator trying to draw a map. After she puts away the box, she wraps her arms around herself and looks at the cold dark room wondering what happened.

She puts her mouth to the wall and whispers, "*What happened to the family who lived here?*"

She presses an ear against the wall and listens.

The house is quiet.

Ten

Meena Begum continues her simple life: cleaning her room, learning English, overseeing the floors at the sugar mill, and waiting to be kicked out of the house.

But eventually the problem becomes clear: Akbar shows no signs of relenting.

Months pass and still she refuses to talk to him or share his bed but he neither becomes angry nor does he evict her.

ONE AFTERNOON, Meena Begum sits on the jula in the sitting room, swinging herself back and forth on the balls of her feet, listlessly staring out the window as storm clouds begin to gather outside. The intricately carved teak swing creaks every time she rocks back on her heels. She senses a shadow at the door.

Her mother-in-law has taken to standing in doorways and glaring at her if she finds her anywhere in the house, but Meena Begum has learned to ignore her, stoically remaining where she is, unwilling to let her disapproval affect her.

Grand Ammi enters the sitting room.

"Don't push so hard. It's antique," she says as she begins rearranging a crystal vase of pink roses on the credenza. *"An-tique.* It means it's valuable. It was passed down for generations in my family. Nothing like the stuff your family has, I'm sure."

Meena Begum continues to swing.

"I hear you still won't let the maids in your room to clean. You must enjoy living in your own filth. No wonder my son never sleeps in your chambers."

Meena Begum stops.

"Oh yes, I know everything. He is my son, after all. He only married you because he took pity on you. He was always too softhearted for his own good. Even as a child he gave beggars his money, though they were all drunks," she adds as she reinserts roses. "But he's coming to his senses. He told me he didn't know *what* he was thinking when he married you, that he's going to tell you to leave, so you better prepare your things. If I were you, I'd leave quietly; there's no need for a fuss. Akbar doesn't take kindly to women who make scenes. Just accept it when it happens." She stops arranging the flowers and turns to Meena Begum.

"Because it *will* happen."

THE TRUTH IS GRAND AMMI doesn't know what will happen. Akbar married this impudent girl with her wild hair and vulgar ways and brought her into their home, but it doesn't seem like the two even speak to each other. She would throw the girl out herself, but something about Akbar makes her hesitate, some look in his eyes that makes her think she may not win this one if she takes it into her own hands. She tries to find other ways to express her anger; she follows the girl around the house, flinging insults and threats, hoping that if she harasses her enough, she will leave on her own. When Grand Ammi does her agarbatti rounds with her incense in the morning she deliberately leaves out the east wing, permitting any lurking evil to wander into that area if it pleases.

But the girl just seems to grow more and more insolent. In fact, it seems to Grand Ammi the more she goes after her, the more stubborn the girl gets. Recently she's started turning up at the dinners Grand Ammi throws for important company. While the esteemed guests are tucking into their tandoori chicken and sipping their rose sharbats, Meena Begum will suddenly appear at the table in a messy state with unruly hair and rumpled sari. She seats herself at the table and helps herself to dhal with her hands, smacking her fingers while the astonished guests try not to stare. And Akbar, that foolish boy, just continues his meal with an expression that looks like amusement.

Grand Ammi grinds her teeth at the memory as she turns back to the roses and gives them one last adjustment. Then she throws her dupatta over her shoulder in a huff and leaves the room.

MEENA BEGUM SMILES to herself as Grand Ammi leaves and then sighs when she remembers her predicament. It is the fourth month of marriage and still Akbar has not shown any sign of wearing. She tries her best to annoy everyone, walking around in messy clothing, singing childhood Tamil songs, and irritating visiting guests. She wonders if she should just sleep with Akbar, that the anticipation of the act is bolstering him and that once he has his way with her, he will finally abandon her. It is certainly what some of the women at the factory say happens with other men.

He himself says little and nothing has happened between them—except for one afternoon when she returns from a bath and does not know he is sitting in the room. She shuts the door and drops her towel, gathering the clothes that lie on her bed until she senses that there is someone behind her. She tries to quickly pick up the discarded towel, but she is too slow, and then he is right behind her, his hands resting lightly on her wet shoulders. She is frozen, unsure of what happens next, unsure of what is expected, and he stands there for a minute, his breath close to her neck. She can feel the drops of water from her hair running all the way down her back like fingers. It seems like the whole world slows down—the sound of the birds outside has disappeared and the usual commotion of doors opening and shutting below has stopped, and for one small moment she allows herself to close her eyes, to feel his breath at her neck, the bristles of his beard almost brushing her skin.

And then he is gone.

That is the closest they have come to any intimacy.

After that, he has returned only to sit in her room after dinner and read the newspaper. When it becomes late, he taps out the ash from his pipe, folds his paper, and bids her good night as he leaves the room.

As she contemplates this moment, the storm that has been gathering outside suddenly breaks. The rain pours and a gust of wind slams the cliff, smashing the rain into the bay window she is sitting at. While she watches the downpour morosely, she notices the washing lady hurrying outside with her basket to collect the clothes hanging on the line. She stands up quickly with the intention of helping her when she sees Akbar rush out to the clothesline. He begins to unpin garments quickly with the washerwoman. When they fill the basket, he opens his jacket and spreads it over them both as they hurry toward the kitchen entrance.

Later that evening as is his custom, Akbar knocks, enters the room, and sits in an armchair in the corner. He loosens his collar and settles into the chair, then stuffs his pipe with tobacco and lights it with a match, blowing at the embers. He pulls out the daily newspaper to read as he puffs away. Meena Begum is now used to this; usually she sits undisturbed on her bed, reading a book.

This time, however, she watches him agitatedly over her book. She returns to her page and tries to read and then looks up again.

Finally she starts in broken English, "Why you help her?"

Akbar continues his sentence to the end then closes the paper and folds it over, turning to face her.

"Why did I help who?" he asks.

"The maid. Today—it rain and he—she—take washing, you also go. So, why?"

He contemplates her for a moment and then says simply, "It was raining, she needed help, and I was there."

Meena Begum shakes her head. "No. No. Uṅkaḷ vakai appaṭi illai. People like you—not helping. Not . . . for people like us." She seems genuinely perplexed.

"People like me?" He is smiling now.

"Yes, yes, like you," she nods her head vigorously. "You know—what I meaning." She gestures at her big room.

He puts his paper down. "I'm afraid you don't know me, dear Meena. How can you? And let me be clear," he says, leaning forward slightly. "I don't blame you. Anyone in your situation *should* be angry. I am very sorry that I am keeping you here where I know you don't want to be. But I can't see any other way to solve this."

She stares back at him, unable to reply.

He taps his pipe into an ashtray, bids her good night, and leaves the room.

That night outside the window, a small red bud begins to emerge on a twist of jasmine vine.

For the first time in their marriage Meena Begum begins to actually *notice* Akbar.

She thinks she understands everything about this aristocratic family—its domineering matriarch, who has made it clear she thinks her inferior; the arrogant first wife, who holds the reserved air of one who wishes not to be contaminated. Oh yes, Meena Begum understands—their bourgeois distaste for the destitute, which, to their horror, has been brought right into the bowels of their home by the misguided, indulged man of the house, leaving them with nowhere to hide their pretensions.

But now, she considers she may perhaps have been wrong about the man.

It is true that he is impulsive and rash and occasionally hotheaded, but she sees that he is also kind, and that he bears through trials with a faith that seems unshakable. He talks about angels and devils as if he can see them in front of him, and he believes in the consequences of actions. She overhears the servants talk about him with respect, sees that he treats the workers at the factory with genuine concern. She hears about his distaste for British law, his involvement with the Natal Indian Congress, and how, when he can, he helps his workers with their debts. She discovers that he pays higher wages than other sugarcane farmers in Natal and that immigrant workers fight to work at his factory. She watches as he hears out his overbearing mother and attends to the requirements of his cold wife and notices in him an unexpected tenderness when he handles his children.

Much to her own surprise, Meena Begum finds herself unable to continue to ignore Akbar.

She looks out for his voice in the house when he returns home. She makes excuses to go downstairs to catch a glimpse of him in the dining room. She wills him to enter her room when he passes by upstairs and begins to comb her hair and check her reflection in a mirror. When he visits her room, she peers over her English books and watches him read his paper. She studies his dark eyelashes and thick beard and finds herself lingering over the upper parts of his arms. She wonders how tall he is. She wonders what she would look like next to him. Or even, beneath him. She begins to occasionally respond to his conversation and to eventually accept the tiny trinkets of flowers and poems he leaves at her pillow, instead of tossing them out immediately.

And just like that, quietly and reluctantly, Meena Begum finds herself falling in love with her husband.

ONE EVENING, Akbar does not arrive at her room at his usual time. Meena Begum seats herself on the bed and waits. Then she walks around the room wondering what could have happened to make him late. She peers out the window into the darkness and then goes to the top of the stairs and tries to hear if anything is being said about his whereabouts. She finds herself annoyed and then overcome with an unexpected concern; perhaps he has tired of her rejection. Perhaps he has finally moved on.

She paces the room in agitation.

More than an hour later there is the usual knock on her door and Meena Begum hurries to the bed to sit casually in her spot. Akbar seats himself on the armchair opposite her. He lights his pipe, opens his newspaper, and makes himself comfortable. This time, Meena Begum is too wound up to even pretend she is reading. She keeps glancing up at him and then down at her book until finally Akbar puts his newspaper down and asks her if something is the matter.

"Where is you?" she asks.

"What do you mean?"

She stumbles. "You late."

He pulls out the watch from his pocket and glances at it. "Ah, yes. It was work," he says as he snaps the face shut and puts it back. He rubs his eyes tiredly. "There was a problem with the boiler—I had to stay late today," he says as he pulls open his newspaper again.

Meena Begum does not know what makes her do it; it is a mixture of frustration and relief. While Akbar is speaking, she stands up and goes toward him. As he looks up at her she bends down and kisses him softly on his mouth, feeling the sharp bristles against her lips.

He is still for a moment, surprised.

Then he puts the paper down and kisses her back.

Outside the window that night, white petals begin to emerge like tissue paper from inside their buds.

Soon the air fills with the scent of jasmines in bloom.

Eleven

Sana battles to open the window against the old knotted jasmine plant outside. The crank in the casement window creaks as it struggles to extend and she gives up and leaves it a quarter way open, hoping this will be enough to air the damp room.

She goes to the bed and lifts the crewelwork bedspread and flaps the sheet to shake off the dust. Every now and then she comes in to clean the room, and each time she does, she is perplexed to find it more dusty, as if it is shedding something in her absence. She goes to the dressing table and begins to wipe it with a soft cloth.

The djinn sits morosely in the corner of the room and watches the girl. It gnaws at its fingers. The girl is interfering too much; she is upsetting the house; it can no longer hold on to its secrets the way it used to. More and more of the past is slipping through its fingers, and the house begins to break down further; pipes start to leak, cracks open in the walls, mold spreads, and the cold becomes unbearable. History is beginning to emerge, and the more the house fails to hide it, the more the djinn's own terror grows. Its eyes flicker to the ceiling, then away.

Sana runs her cloth over the back edges of the dressing table and her fingers come across something wedged behind it. She pulls out a piece of paper that she missed. She unfolds it and reads the faint words:

M,

Think not you can direct the course of love, for love, if it finds you worthy, directs your course.

Love has no other desire but to fulfill itself.

She takes out her notebook and sits at the table. She copies the words from the paper into her book.

The djinn watches this with a peculiar feeling. The dead woman had been this way too; bent low, writing in her diary. Putting down words it could not understand. The djinn creeps slowly to the girl and watches her scribble the words down. She finishes writing and holds the piece of paper in her hand as she studies it.

Under her breath she says, "Who is M?"

The djinn knows. It will never forget. Its head begins to throb. It closes its eyes. It is tired of aching. It is tired of everything hurting. It holds its head and rocks back and forth.

It had not always been this way.

Once the djinn walked in the world of mankind. A bit quieter than most, a bit more lonesome, but a djinn that walked nonetheless.

It walked to many places in the world and swam through many seas. It moved among men and watched how they lived and how they fought. Men were the same everywhere—power-hungry creatures always engaged in wars. They smelled bad and were selfish and told lies, especially to themselves. The djinn grew to hate men and tried to stay as far away from them as possible. It moved from its forest in the steamy south of India to the capital in Delhi, where there were many other djinns, but the smog made it choke; it hacked out globs of phlegm and rasped out coughs that left it clutching its throat.

It escaped north toward the Himalayas. There it discovered Kashmir, and in the green valley, among the lilies of Dal Lake, it bathed away the smoke and dust. But winter came and the valley filled with snow and the djinn had to creep out to the houseboats of men to warm its hands on the kitchen fires. Even so, it was too cold. Winter deepened, the lake froze, and the djinn fled west. In Eastern Europe it wandered through ruined buildings and tightly cobbled streets. It lived for a few days in a bombed-out house. It sat beneath a sink and watched the frozen sky through a missing roof. It passed through different countries, briefly resting in destroyed castles and abandoned homes.

The scent of war hovered in the air wherever it went.

It finally reached Scotland, where it lived in a small cave along the North Sea in the high-walled cliffs. It lived there for years undisturbed, until too many young people from the growing cities with too much free time began visiting the cliffs. They laughed and smoked things that filled the air and made the djinn choke. It hissed and threw small stones when they came too close but they refused to leave. It tried to draw the smokeless smoke, the ash inside, forcing itself to appear, but it had tried for too long to disappear from the world of men and it could no longer willingly show itself. It could barely muster an outline, and those who saw it thought it was a hallucination. More people began to visit when rumors spread that the cliffs were haunted.

The djinn left.

Everywhere it went, it was the same. The world was becoming more full; there were too many people and noises and smells. The djinn held its hands over its ears and longed for quietness. It swam until it reached Egypt, where it liked the warmth of the land.

It walked along the coast for many miles, making its way to the end of Africa, to the point where two coasts joined to become one.

One day as it walked on the sand, it saw a young woman on the beach.

She was standing along the shore in the moonlight, singing something so sweet and so delicate it could not help but creep closer to hear her better.

Her voice sounded like the stars. Like a language it knew from another world and another time. It spread through the sky like scattered glass. She sang of her village far away in another land. Of her longing for home. The djinn watched the words linger in the air.

She is different, thought the djinn. She is a different human.

She sat at the sea and watched the sun rise over the water. The djinn sat next to her. It watched a tendril of her hair flutter in the wind and tried to reach out and touch it. When she left for home, it followed her. It watched her make a fire and cook rice in a pot for her mother and father and family. It watched her roll away the mats they slept on. Darn clothes. Sweep the courtyard. At night it watched her sleep, one arm slung over the other, her fine eyelids quivering in dreams. It wanted her to sing again. It went close to her mouth and tried to pry her lips open, but nothing happened. It stayed with her for months, walking with her beside the sea and as she worked in the factory.

When she got married, it followed her up the hill, up the stairs to the big house. It watched her walk the gardens and feed the animals. As she learned English, as she wrote in her diary, as she slept in a new bed, one with fine silks and drapes. It sat beside her on the jula and wondered how it had never known how very lovely human beings could be.

It watched as she fell in love and then it climbed out the window through the jasmines to cry at the sea. It wished it could leave. It wished it could walk in the world again.

But all that mattered in the world was here.

THE DJINN HOLDS its aching body tight. It goes to the long mirror lying broken on the floor. It looks into the shattered surface, at its blank reflection, and then looks at the girl at the dressing table. And it does not know why, perhaps because it is so very tired or because it knows what it is like to want something that may never come, it decides to answer the girl's question.

The djinn closes it eyes.

The house shivers, turning in horror to the djinn as it realizes what is happening.

A feeling of heat begins inside the djinn, slowly at first and then like a flame it spreads red hot and burning. It ignores the pain and draws on an essence of itself it has not in a long time. The house howls. It begs the djinn to stop, to reconsider. To keep the last of their secrets. A big breath of something like air surges through the djinn's body; it pushes up its rib cage and fills it until its skin is stretched thin. Then it bends down and carefully blows on the dressing table, at the pot of powder, which shifts and shudders and then topples off the edge of the table onto the glass below.

S<small>ANA TURNS SUDDENLY</small> at the sound.

She walks to the mirror and looks around curiously. She cannot see anyone. She bends down to pick up the fallen container, and through the scattered powder on the glass surface she sees something.

Something amiss in the ceiling reflected above.

She turns and looks at the spot that has caught her eye; in the corner of the room a square panel in the high ceiling sits at an odd angle. She puts the pot down and goes over. She stands below; there is a tiny opening where the square does not sit flush with the ceiling.

It is an opening into the garret.

She drags out a tall wooden ladder she remembers seeing among the objects in the east wing and pushes it into the gap.

The panel shifts and gives.

She climbs up.

The house watches all this with a peculiar kind of horror. It knows that things cannot remain the same forever. It has watched from its high perch how the town below changed over the years. It has seen roads cut through the landscape, buildings erupt, and people multiply.

It knows that nothing can escape change. That the djinn just opened the way for what was always going to happen.

Still, it cannot bear to witness this.

The reopening of history like fingers digging into a wound.

Twelve

In love, aside from sipping the wine of timelessness, nothing else exists.
There is no reason for living except for giving one's life.
I say, "First I know you, then I die."
He says, "For the one who knows Me, there is no dying."

It is raining outside and Akbar sits at the desk in the library, reading to Meena Begum, who is lying on a rug looking up at the glass dome.

"So, jaan, love is to forget yourself," he says as he shuts the volume.

Meena Begum props herself up on her shoulder and turns to him. "Tell me, have you forgot yourself?" she asks.

"Entirely," he says.

"Why?"

"Because we were made for each other before we even met. Our souls found each other on the plains of heaven. I knew it when I saw you."

"Did you not say you fell ill and tried to forget me?"

Akbar smiles. "A foolish effort to fight fate."

Meena Begum's eyes laugh up at him. "You know I do not believe in such things as fate, sir."

"Perhaps you are in need of more poetry," says Akbar.

She laughs then, her dimples flashing. "You are a madman."

"So I have been told," he says. "Shall I read more?"

THEIR COURTSHIP sprung over words; he reads to her from the works of al-Ghazali, Hafiz, Rumi, and from more contemporary pieces in his collection, like Gibran and Marrash. He tapes poems to her wardrobes, her mirrors, and leaves them on her pillows at night. She practices her English with him and he helps her with her reading. In return she teaches him Tamil, laughing at the way he pronounces the words.

"Not eppatti irukkirka! You're mumbling it. It's eppatti irukkirirka!"

MEENA BEGUM HAS GROWN different in the last few weeks. She is fuller, firmer, a fish in a river with silver salty skin.

Her body feels alert; everything seems brighter and louder, her flesh constantly burns. She can hear the blood running through her. She smiles more often, her dimples flashing like pebbles in a pond. Her nipples ache. She looks up more often, no longer hiding beneath her lashes.

Love is the last thing she expects from life and she certainly does not expect it in this way. It is strange to her that she is capable of such joy, that she responds with such delight to another, as if she were a wick just waiting to catch alight.

She cooks him small dishes of uthappams and sambars and rubs warm coconut oil into his hair while they sit outside in the garden. In return for his poems, she fashions him small paper flowers, a craft she learned while sitting in the dust below the school windows. While she listened to the secret village meetings she would fold and crease paper, her fingers automatically twisting and turning as she listened to talks about communism and revolution. The repetitive movements and small intricate steps calmed her down, blunted the anger when it bloomed to the surface.

She is fascinated by him, the calluses on his hands, the hair on his arms, the girth of his thighs, the small cleft in his chin that she finds when she digs her fingers into his beard. She loves his poetry and the way he urgently whispers it in Urdu to her even though she does not understand all of it. She wonders how he loves her so deeply, withholding nothing.

"Tell me everything," she says. "Tell me everything you have ever known," understanding then what it is like to be in love, to want to know another person as much as yourself, to know their secrets and desires, their histories and hurts. She wants to envelop him, swallow him entirely until she and him are one.

She runs her hands over him, always wanting to touch him; even while reading she stretches out absentmindedly until she can hold on to something of his (a finger, an ear, a tuft of hair).

They talk and talk as if there are not enough words. Low and quiet they whisper everything they have kept within their selves. They are two lonely boats floating in a pitch-black sea and when they find each other they hold on. In the dark she tells him about her village and the way she would fish in the river with a simple fishing stick she made herself. She tells him about the fat bodies of the fish and the way she shrieked as they thrashed and how over time she learned to bash their heads on the rocks to keep them from sliding out of her small hands. How she gutted them with a penknife and how she brought the little silver bodies back to her mother to cook.

She tells him of hunger, how it gnawed at her belly some days when all they had to eat was a fistful of rice or a boiled fish head.

She tells him about how one afternoon the youngest son of their landowner discovered her fishing while wandering with his friends. Adjusting to adolescent power, sensing their growing authority as men of the land, the boys surrounded her, mocked her bare feet, her simple dress, laughed at her stick of a rod. When she steadily ignored him (even then, the defiance, the glint in her eyes emerging like frost at the frame) the landowner's son grabbed her by the back of her head and pulled her down to the ground, forcing her to apologize for her insolence.

When she kept silent, he called her brown filth, tore open her blouse to reveal her unformed breasts, sneered, and then shoved her against the rocks until everything went black. She awoke long after sunset in the same spot on the bank, with a wound on her head that came back sticky when she put her fingers to it. She made her way home in the dark, through the jungle filled with creatures that rustled as they moved around her. Her parents comforted her but refused to say anything, too afraid for their jobs and their lives—it was best to keep quiet, forget it, they whispered. God would ensure those terrible boys were punished, her mother said.

But Meena Begum could not wait for God.

And so at eleven years old, with a keen determination for justice, she marched to the grand house and knocked on the door. She waited in a fine sitting room while the butler called the Memsaab. She stared at her grubby, small self in numerous gilded mirrors and looked out at the fine patio that held deck chairs and orchids in glass vases. The Indian maid who brought her a glass of water urged her to go home before she caused trouble for her family.

When the Memsaab arrived, tall, drenched in pearls, with lips as red as ripe cherries, the young girl remembered the way the woman had grabbed her years ago, screaming and slapping at her, horrified to find a brown child in her white bed. The Memsaab did not recognize her. She had come because she found it amusing when the butler told her there was a village child there demanding to see her about an important matter. She listened as the child told her what her son had done. She furrowed her brow, clicked her fingers for something sweet, hmm, perhaps some jalebi? Something to calm the little girl. Then she called her son, who was outside in the garden practicing his archery.

Was this true? she asked him, did he really attack this *poor* girl?

It was the way she asked, so calmly, so perfunctorily, that made Meena Begum realize that the Memsaab did not believe her. The boy without blinking said he had never seen her before and walked away with bow and arrow in hand. And the woman in her pearls and red lipstick had tutted and shooed her out, expressing disappointment at village girls who told lies. The Memsaab said that little girls shouldn't find such vile ways to get the attention of boys they liked. Such girls were wicked and deserved to be punished, she said as she shut the heavy door on her.

Meena Begum tells Akbar she took her revenge two years later. She stole a traveling snake charmer's cobra basket and tipped its contents into the boy's room through his open window at night. Later in the village they heard about a commotion at the big house: the young master had discovered a snake in his bed one night and screamed with such terror that the snake felt obliged to bite him. His hysterical mother had rushed him to the nearest doctor only to discover that the boy was fine because the snake's venom had been removed.

Still, the whole incident jangled the Memsaab's nerves so badly that she convinced her husband to pack up and take her back to England.

HE, TOO, TALKS, bursting with words as if he himself does not know that he has been waiting for a companion to share them with. He tells her why he thinks Iqbal's ideas for a new Islamic Republic cut off from India is problematic, how the fall of the British is nearing, and how he fears for the fate of his children in this New World. How he worries that his children will not understand that life is a gift, that they will become simpletons, soft and pliable under the incessant fingers of his overindulgent mother. How his dreams have troubled him at night from the time he was young, and how he always looks for Signs from God to guide him. He says the most important thing you can do with your life is search for the Signs. He says the Signs can be in ordinary things like the dew at dawn or the way a tree grows, but it is how you *recognize* it that makes the difference.

Some evenings they ride together on the beach on his white Arabian stallion. Later they dismount and walk along the ocean with the horse trailing behind them. Then Meena Begum runs ahead and shyly removes her sari, the smooth skin of her shoulders and breasts suddenly emerging from the folds, defiant and glistening in the moonlight, before she beckons him with her luminous eyes and then disappears into the water, slipping in like the fish from his dreams of afore.

IN THE LIBRARY Akbar continues. "As much as I laud the great Persian and Urdu poets—because let's be honest, they are the only ones who can capture the ecstasy of love—the Western ones can sometimes surprise you. Yes, their language will never be adequate and the English constantly reduce metaphors to simplicity about nature, but occasionally they capture the essence of some feeling. Take for instance this American fellow, he's quite good," and here he flips through a volume next to him and says, "Ralph Waldo Emerson. An essayist more than anything but a decent poet. Listen to this one, just the end:

> *Though thou loved her as thyself,*
> *As a self of purer clay,*
> *Though her parting dims the day,*
> *Stealing grace from all alive;*
> *Heartily know,*
> *When half-gods go,*
> *The gods arrive.*

He shuts the book. "Kya baat hai," he says, unable to help himself. He kneels to lie next to her on the carpet and gently takes her hand in his. He looks up at the rain, hurtling toward them through the heavens. Her dark hair spreads open underneath her and she smells of jasmine. He lays his head on the hair that is fanned out. He brings his mouth to her neck and breathes her in.

"So I can go? It will be okay?" she asks mischievously, drawing her own conclusion from the poem.

"Forget those damn Western poets. What do they know?"

"You said they were decent enough!"

"Not if they are giving you wrong ideas."

She laughs. "That's not how poetry works, Mr. Akbar Ali Khan. You can't control how people understand it."

"Arreh, the student surpasses the master," says Akbar in mock surprise.

In fact, he is shocked at how quickly she learns. She picks up English easily and uncovers metaphors and meanings, sometimes even before him.

"I can think of some who may be happy if I leave," she says, circling a finger over the carpet carelessly.

"Don't talk like this. They cannot separate us," he replies solemnly. "Now only God can do that."

She turns to look at him as she tightens her hand in his. Her body moves up against his without her even knowing. Twisting, turning, adjusting her shape into his until from the sky above, the heavens see them as one.

One human being with four legs and four arms, wrapped in unspoken understanding.

Thirteen

There are things that never see light again.
 They scream and bang at their fate, hoping they will be discovered. A forgotten letter beneath a file, an ivory button in a couch, a handprint against a window. These things tremble in rage at their apparent insignificance. Eventually they calm down; they take deep breaths. They resign themselves to their fate and watch time pass.

But they hold on to hope.

They hope one day they will be discovered, find small ways to be found: a glint in the grass, a rattle in the drawer, a flutter in the wind.

A misplaced panel in the roof.

So when the ceiling floor cracks open and a young girl's head pops through, the attic stirs sleepily, almost in disbelief.

Its hope had become frail like the bones of birds.

THE ROOM IS THICK with cobwebs and the smell of timber. There are two dormer windows whose filthy panes filter in murky light. Beneath them sits a mahogany writing desk and a wooden chair. In the dim background are boxes and trunks covered in dust.

Sana pushes open one of the dormers; the silence revolts as a deep creak cuts the air.

The djinn follows Sana up; it has not been here since the incident of 1932. It has not even glanced into the mouth of the monster since then. It runs its finger over the thick dust on the dead woman's table; it peers at her papers and books and crawls onto her chair and lays back, overwhelmed suddenly. It remembers the last time it was here.

A few cockroaches scuttle about. On the writing desk are pens and loose papers, but right in the middle of the table sit two leatherbound notebooks. Sana picks one up, dusts it off, and opens it.

On the yellowing pages in small, neat writing it reads:

9 November 1931

> *It's windy at night. I'm not sure if I should bring the baby upstairs because of the draft but I feel I can't leave him alone for a moment. I don't trust them after what happened.*
> *They watch me. Especially the children.*
> *I only feel safe when I'm up here.*

Fourteen

As Rome and Berlin can attest, a great and common purpose can cause the most unlikely of unions.

The marriage of Akbar Ali Khan to Meena Begum threw Grand Ammi and Jahanara Begum together in a sudden and fierce allegiance. They had watched with horrified fascination as the love story of Akbar and Meena Begum began to unfold in the house, as vines on the east wall filled with an abundance of jasmine.

The two women sit together for hours in the parlor discussing the intruder upstairs in hushed voices. Grand Ammi assures Jahanara Begum that it is only a matter of time before Akbar's fascination with Meena Begum wears. Men have phases, she says, and he will soon grow weary of the novelty of dark flesh in his bed. She says history is full of such women who try to ensnare great men, women with no morals or faith to keep them in check.

Time is the enemy of these women, she says. Time reveals the fallacy of their plots.

Jahanara Begum listens intently. It echoes what some of the ladies at her bridge club have said too. Men, no matter what their color, are all the same, they agree as they survey their cards and bring drinks to their lips. While they cannot relate to her particular issue of a second wife, they know well enough about mistresses, and it can't be much different—short-term thrills, they say, and those kind come and go. You are the one who gave him children and that counts for something, they declare as they pick up and put down cards and nod to one another.

Laddoo, as he is affectionately nicknamed by his grandmother, gets back on his blue Colson's Fairy and starts riding through the garden again. He had paused beneath the parlor window to overhear what Ammi and Dadi Ammi were talking about, but when he realized it was not, as he hoped, plans for the dessert menu but yet again talk of the new lady in the east wing, he went back to play. Laddoo is a small boy with thin arms and dark eyes. He was born a silent baby and did not utter a sound even when the doctor shook him upside down. As a child he spoke little and hid away, listening to conversations that he ought not to be listening to and knowing things that he ought not to be knowing. For instance, he knows that Ammi and Dadi Ammi have vowed never to tell any of the family in India about the second wife. And he knows Ammi calls the other woman a "harlot" although he is not quite sure of its meaning. He stores this information with all the other secrets he keeps, packs it between the knowledge of a mouse living in the third drawer in his bedroom and the time he overheard Dadi Ammi say Ammi is a "matlabi."

The bicycle he is riding was a gift for his fifth birthday, and it took him some time to learn how to ride it. He still remembers the moment, the morning when he *knows* he can master the machine; his knees are raw from falling but his father insists he get back on, and then suddenly he is pedaling and nothing is crashing—the world is straight up and he is laughing and his father is shouting that he is doing it, *he is doing it.*

Now he zips through the garden feeling fearless as he shoots down the path with the wind in his hair, moving like a bullet, avoiding startled bucks, veering away from screaming maids, and chasing peahens that scatter helter-skelter into the trees.

He is cycling fast when he brakes suddenly, the loose pebbles grinding against his tires as he comes to an abrupt stop. He has ended up on the side of the garden where the cages are kept. He jumps off his bicycle and wheels it over as he peers between the leaves of a hedge; up ahead of him Iqbal Babu is sitting on a stool outside a cage. Every now and then he draws something up in his chest and spits toward the darkness behind him.

There is a faint snarl from the dark. Laddoo turns around, hops back onto his bicycle, and pedals as fast as he can, his brow wet with perspiration.

On Sundays he climbs into his cupboard and waits there for hours. His sister calls him a scaredy-cat; she shouts for him to watch with her from the stairway landing, but he refuses to join. If he hears roaring at night, he pulls up his covers and pushes his fingers into his ears.

Once, he tried to be brave and crept to the top of the stairs to peer through the balustrade, but then he heard a low growl outside and turned to flee, running straight into his mother. She grabbed his arms and stopped him, asking him why he was running. When he reluctantly explained, she said that he should be ashamed of himself. That this was not how Khan men behaved, crying and running away like little girls. She expected more of him, she said disappointedly as she shook her head. After that, she forced him to stand at the window to watch the lion with everyone else, keeping a strong grip on his shoulders so that he could not turn away.

When he reaches the courtyard, Laddoo slows down and drops his bike against the fountain. He hikes himself onto the flat stone rim, looking down into the water at the silver-orange koi. His heart is beating fast and he tries to calm down by imagining what they are going to eat that evening. He hopes with all his might that Pappu will make his famous custard and jelly boats. He catches his reflection in the water and notices his nose is smudged with dirt. He pulls his sleeve over his fist and wipes; he tries to attract as little attention as possible from his grandmother. She is always making a fuss over him, and even if he enters a room as quietly as possible, she knows and calls for him. If she sees his face like this, she will exclaim in distress, grab him to her bosom, and attempt to wipe his face with spit on her thumb.

Laddoo is a very fussed-over child. Every morning his grandmother will rub amla oil into his hair, dress him herself, and slip him small pieces of her famous laddoo while pinching his soft cheeks. "My little rajah, these are just for you. Don't tell your sister, okay?" she coos in his ear as she pushes sweetmeats into his mouth. And so, if he is a little spoiled, it is not really his fault. He mainly concerns himself with finding unique hiding places in the house and chasing peacocks in the garden on his bicycle. Mostly, he just wants to be left alone to play.

It is the older sister who is the problem, really.

THERE ARE SOME CHILDREN that wait to be born. When God gives their souls a body in heaven, they shiver in anticipation, waiting to be let loose on earth. Soraya Bibi Khan is such a child.

She was born four years before her brother, and unlike him, she came out screaming and it was a scream that only ended when she was put to the breast, where she suckled greedily. She is a demanding child who grows into a tall and sturdy young girl with the promise of her mother's beauty. She wears two oiled plaits held together by white ribbon and has an unusual darkness about her that worries even her grandmother. From a young age she would pull koi from the fountain and watch as they flapped fatly against the paving, gasping for breath. She pinches small children on their legs and steals hairpins and vials of perfume from the servant's quarters only to throw them away. She flings flour onto the carpets after the servants have cleaned and she makes mischief by spreading stories, pitting her grandmother against her mother and servant against servant.

When her mother notices anything—if at all—she chooses to believe her daughter acts this way because she is special. Jahanara Begum says her daughter is a little firecracker, a cheeky princess who knows how to get what she wants. It's clear she comes from a line of formidable women, she says. She buys her daughter the finest ribbons and lace and dresses. She teaches her to rub turmeric on her face every night, to sleep with her hair wrapped in silk cloth—advises her to avoid meals after six p.m. if she wants to maintain a slim figure. When tutors or servants complain about her, Jahanara Begum replaces them, so they learn to be quiet and let the child have her way. She ignores Akbar's warning that their daughter needs to be kept in check.

And so it is Soraya Bibi, who months after Meena Begum arrives, suggests to her younger brother that they ought to do something about the witch in the house.

"The witch?" Laddoo asks wide-eyed.

"The witch. That's what Dadi Ammi says. I heard her tell Ammi that that is the only way she could have caught Abba. She did jadoo. Do you know what jadoo is? Of course you don't know. You're just a little twerp." She leans in close to her brother's face with her two plaits hovering between them and hisses, "Black magic. She did black magic on Abba and that's why he *thinks* he's in love with her. Dadi Ammi says no normal man can love someone like that. She must have gone to a witch doctor and he must have given her the muti to put in his food. Who knows what kind of black magic these kalyas do in Africa," she says. "She stole our father from our mother . . . and now, now she's going to steal him away from us. Ammi says so. He won't love us as much with the baby on its way. And he's so bewakoof he won't even suspect the child might not be his. God knows if we will even get the inheritance now that there's a bastard on the way," she says, echoing her grandmother.

The children had seen their mother turn white when she heard news of the baby; they had seen her clutch the banister and fall into a fever that lasted for weeks. They had heard from their hiding places that their mother wished the baby dead, let everyone hear it—she didn't care anymore, she didn't care about the bloody servants, she would never accept that thing in this house, she would leave, God ki kassam she would leave, she wasn't afraid to, she would take the children and go, she would show that man what she thought of him and his katchra mistress.

Soraya Bibi tells her brother that they must make the witch pay. They have to teach her a lesson.

They have to teach her that she and her bastard don't belong in this house.

THE BABY BOY IS BORN one morning without much fuss. The nurses quietly make their way upstairs and Grand Ammi pretends to go to bed as Meena Begum's moans fill the house. Meanwhile Jahanara Begum in her room in the opposite wing begins to pray fervently. In her life she has barely ever sat on a prayer mat, but now she prostrates herself on the intricately woven carpet and clutches her prayer beads tightly in her hand. She prays that mother and child die in birth. She knows once there is a baby, Meena Begum's place in Akbar Manzil is established and she is truly linked to Akbar. It isn't a joke anymore, a phase like her mother-in-law promised. It would no longer be a charade she could ignore; the new woman would be a part of Akbar's life forever.

She lies on her prayer mat and cries out. God knows, God *knows* the humiliation she is going through. He knows how that wicked girl tricked her! Made her think that she didn't even want to be in this house in the first place. Feeding her lies about leaving so that she would drop her guard and think everything would soon return to normal. Her mother-in-law had been right—this was all part of that treacherous girl's plans. She had been biding her time, worming her way into Akbar's heart, and now had cast her final move to set her place in stone.

Jahanara Begum sits the whole night whispering earnestly in the dark. She no longer knows who she is pleading to, the light or the darkness; it is all the same to her. Whatever power will let this be. She holds on to her elbows, pacing her room, muttering to herself while biting her lips until they bleed.

Early in the morning the sound of a baby crying breaks through the house and Jahanara Begum weeps bitter tears. When Akbar comes into the kitchen with the soft-bundled baby to show her her new grandchild, even Grand Ammi cannot deny the child is his, with his dimpled chin and deep eyes. But Grand Ammi turns away from the babe, refusing to bless the newcomer. She calls him an abomination, a sin against the family. The child changes nothing, she says.

They name him Hassan Ali Khan.

He is the living manifestation of Akbar and Meena Begum's love for each other. Together they go through his tiny fingers and toes and admire his catlike eyes that open and close slowly as he blinks at his new world. They look for signs of him and of her and inhale in surprise when his face changes into hers and then suddenly into his like a revolving door that can't decide where to stop.

One afternoon as she puts the baby to sleep, Akbar enters the room with a long wooden ladder. He smiles.

"A small gift for you, my jaan," he says, carrying it in carefully.

She cocks an eyebrow quizzically, then breaks into a grin and says, "Why, my love, it's what I always wanted."

He winks. "No. *This* is the gift." He carries the ladder to the end of the room and pushes one end against the roof until a panel in the ceiling dislodges. Then he motions for her to follow him as he climbs up. Inside the sloped roof beneath the attic trusses, Akbar has had a room prepared. It is cleaned, carpeted, and lit with lamps, and under the dormer windows sits a writing desk with fresh flowers.

"You always say you don't feel welcome in this house. So I had this room prepared—it's your own secret room, *your* space in this house that no one needs to know about. I thought you might like to practice your writing here. I know it is a small thing but perhaps it will help you feel like this house is your home too."

Meena Begum looks around the clean and cozy space; the desk has reams of fresh paper, new pens, and an English dictionary. A crystal vase holds fresh jasmines and next to it is a red diary, bound in leather. On the wall below the horizontal timber beam sits a painting of a river beside a lush green bank.

Akbar clears his throat self-consciously. "Forgive me, it is foolish." He places a hand to the small of her back to lead her down again.

She turns and puts a hand to his chest to stop him.

"This is more than I could have wished for," Meena Begum says, her eyes shining.

He pulls a sprig of jasmine from the vase and tucks it into her hair, drawing her close to kiss her forehead.

LADDOO LIES IN THE DARKNESS, under the bed as still as a cockroach, and watches the night-frill-edged world of the witch's room. She isn't what he expects of a witch; she doesn't have hands like claws and a mouth full of sharp teeth. She has a soft voice and she speaks kindly to him. But his sister says it's all an act, that she just *pretends* to be nice, that she wears a mask made of the skin of children to cover her true face, a face that is more gruesome than he can imagine. His sister says that she is just waiting for the right moment to attack them and eat them like succulent pieces of chicken. She will chew on our bones and spit them out at the first opportunity, Soraya Bibi says. Keep your eyes open, she warns, the witch can attack at any time, especially if you make eye contact. So Laddoo is careful to avoid her gaze; if he hears her nearby, he ducks into passages or behind chairs. He keeps his eyes downcast if she speaks to him; he walks away quickly if he sees her close.

Now he lies under the witch's bed, shivering a little as he sees her come down the ladder with his father. He is under strict instructions from his sister to collect as much information as possible and return quickly to her. Soraya Bibi wants all the details—what the witch eats, what she reads, what she does, and where she goes. Laddoo watches the witch with his big eyes and tries to remember everything. Later when he returns to his sister's room, he tells her that the witch sings songs to the baby that sound nice, he tells her that Abba speaks to her in a special way, he tells her that the witch always says thank you and please to the maids. She even cleans her own room. She doesn't seem witchlike, he adds.

Soraya Bibi says that she is a *very* good actress. The nicer she seems, the worse she actually is.

It is Laddoo who informs her that Meena Begum goes to bathe every morning after she makes the baby sleep.

One such morning, the pair steal into her room. They push apart the lace curtains of the crib and Soraya Bibi lifts her four-month-old sleeping brother. She is not exactly sure what she is going to do. Everything in the house has changed since the new woman has arrived. Her mother, who normally spends her time doting on her, is now too distracted, too consumed by something to see to her needs. Her father too, who has always been a little cool with her, is different; he seems lighter, full of life, and she, knowing it has nothing to do with her, resents it. She has the idea that if she can just get rid of the child somehow then everything will be okay again. That somehow, order will be restored in the house.

While she carries the baby, she tells Laddoo to place one of her china dolls in the crib. It will buy them a little time, she says. Buy them a little time for what? asks Laddoo, but she shushes him. When they leave the room and go into the passage with the baby, Laddoo, his eyes wide with fear, asks, "What are we going to do now?"

"Give me a second," she scowls. She looks around furtively and then motions for him to follow.

She walks around the upstairs passages, and spying the door to her father's library, she quickly enters and shuts the door behind them. She searches around and then on seeing a window ajar, she walks over and looks out to the grounds far below. She glances at the baby in her arms and then at the window. When she picks the bundle up to the ledge and holds it out, Laddoo looks at her in shock. But she hesitates, drawing the blanket back toward her, and walks further into the library, looking around frantically. She has not thought this through.

They dig among boxes and shelves until they reach some trunks that are packed away at the back of the room. They empty a heavy trunk of old volumes and carefully place the sleeping baby inside. They look at the tiny bundle wrapped in his blanket and watch as he breathes.

"He looks so small," says Laddoo.

"Well, he'll grow up soon enough. And then we'll be in for it," replies Soraya Bibi.

"Where are his horns?"

"What?"

"You said he has horns. Because he's a devil-baby," whispers Laddoo. "You said witches have devil-babies."

"Oh, yes. They're there, under his skin. They'll come out soon enough."

"What will happen to him here?"

"I don't know, okay. I don't have all the answers," replies Soraya Bibi testily.

She shuts the lid of the trunk and turns away. When she reaches the entrance of the library, she turns around to find Laddoo looking down at the box.

"What are you still doing there?" she hisses as she goes back to him and pulls at his arm. "C'mon, before someone comes."

"But where's the tail?" he asks as she drags him away. "You told me it had a tail."

"The witch must have cut it off!" she says as she shuts the library door.

Fifteen

Sana returns home from school to find Razia Bibi in the foyer waving an envelope in her hand.

"Over-the-seas!" announces Razia Bibi. "Who *she* knows from over-the-seas?" She turns the letter over. "England! Hmm. My Ziyaad went to England, you know? He went to the Buckingham Palace where the queen lives. He even saw the Big Ben. He says the goras there *only* eat Indian food. Imagine! They got bored with the fish and the chips." Razia Bibi studies the letter again. "I wonder who she knows there. She's always going on and on about traveling here, traveling there, but I thought she made that up." She studies the letter for a moment again, then reluctantly hands it to Sana. "Well, give it to her anyways; must be advert or something." As Sana goes upstairs, Razia Bibi calls after her. "Good luck trying to wake the rani at this hour."

Sana climbs the spiral stone stairs and knocks loudly, but no one answers.

She bends down to slip the envelope under the entrance, but just then there are muffled footsteps and the door opens a crack. Zuleikha stands there with a blanket wrapped around her shoulders, her eyes half closed.

She squints through the slit in the doorway and, on seeing Sana, throws the door open and shuffles back into the room. Sana follows as Zuleikha stumbles into the bed, where she pulls the covers over her head. The curtains are drawn and the room is cold.

Zuleikha mumbles from within, "Why the hell are you here so early?"

"It's two o' clock."

"It's even earlier than I thought. Go away," she groans.

"A letter came for you."

There is a small pause, then Zuleikha emerges from under the covers.

"A letter?"

Sana hands her the envelope and Zuleikha squints at it in the dark before jumping off the bed and pulling open a curtain. Bright light pierces the room and Sana is blinded for a moment. Zuleikha stares at the envelope.

She looks horror-struck.

After a minute she looks up at Sana, almost fearfully, and says, "I don't want it. Take it back. Do what you want with it." She sticks her hand out with the envelope, then snatches it back just as quickly and looks at it. She turns it over and over in her hands. Then she falls back suddenly into an armchair.

"It can't be," she says to herself. "Not after all this time." She draws one knee up to her chest and places an elbow on the chair arm, resting her forehead in her hand. After a moment she looks up and says, "My cigarettes and matches—" and points in the direction of the kitchen table and makes an urgent beckoning motion with her hand.

Sana passes her the boxes and Zuleikha opens the matchbox unsteadily before lighting a cigarette. She takes a deep breath in and blows out slowly. She glances at the envelope she has put down next to her and takes another pull.

"What do you think it is?" she asks.

"It's from England . . . do you know anyone there?" asks Sana uncertainly.

"I know it's from England. I can see that; I'm not an idiot." She swallows and glances at the envelope again. Then finally she looks up at Sana and says, "You can go now. I need to be alone."

As Sana closes the door, Zuleikha puts her face into her hands, the cigarette smoke rising against the window from her extended fingers.

Later at night Sana sits in the attic with the diaries. She has found six altogether.

They are old and dusty and the pages almost crumble beneath her fingers. The words in them are sometimes so faint they are barely visible. The earliest entries are in Tamil, although the text begins to switch into English later and the scribbled sentences begin to make more sense to Sana. After studying the pages, Sana slowly begins to glean a story.

The writer, a young woman named Meena, starts the diaries to practice her English soon after her marriage to a man named Akbar Ali Khan in 1930. She lived in the house he built, as his second wife.

Her writings are filled with definitions, poetry, and excerpts of conversations.

7 *December* 1930

Akbar told me that there are 99 names of God. His favorite is Ya Fatah—the Opener. The Opener of all ways and all things. The one who opened our paths to each other.

The djinn sits with her while she reads. It does not like the dead woman's things being touched, but it also finds an odd relief that her books are being opened, that her words are in the world again. As if she has been unlocked somehow.

It listens as Sana pauses to read aloud a line of poetry from a page. It is not as soft in the girl's mouth as it once was in the dead woman's, but at least it is something that was once hers as a sound in the air. The djinn scrambles, trying to reach for it, to grasp it, but its hands come away empty. It turns morose, slips under the bed, and whines.

As it nears midnight a loud creak in the main house cuts through the steady quietness and Sana looks up from the diary suddenly. She hears a door shut somewhere and then after a moment she thinks she hears a sound on the stairs. She pauses then closes the book. When she hears noises at night sometimes, she usually ignores them, thinking her sister is trying to provoke her. But this time the noise is different; it feels more real, solid. She climbs down the ladder and mutters, "You had better not be playing tricks again. I'm warning you." She exits the room, and on the main stairs she spies a fleeting figure shutting the front door as it steps out. She hurries down and opens the front door to sees a shadow heading with a lamp out to the stairs that lead to the alcove below the house. She follows, and at the bottom she finds a woman in the shallow cove beneath the rocks, looking out to sea.

In the stinging wind, she recognizes Zuleikha.

"Why are you following me?" Zuleikha asks, still facing the sea.

Sana startled, stops.

"I asked you a question." Zuleikha turns to look over her shoulder.

Sana steps forward tentatively. "I heard a noise. I came to see . . . what it was. And then I found you here," she starts uncertainly.

"Well, I'm sorry to disappoint you. It's just me." She turns back to the ocean.

Sana scrabbles down next to Zuleikha and sits down. The rock is cold beneath her fingers.

"What are you doing here?"

"Always with the bloody questions." Zuleikha pulls a lit cigarette to her lips and sucks, cupping it in her hands to shield it from the wind. She is quiet, then says, "I needed to think."

"Here? Why?" Sana peers down where the waves crash into the rocks below.

Zuleikha shrugs.

Sana wraps her arms around her knees as the wind cuts across her face.

"I didn't open it," Zuleikha says softly as she looks into the distance. "Why should I? I don't want to know what it says. I know every version of what it can hold and I'm not interested in any of it." She takes another puff of the cigarette. "Shall I tell you a story?"

Sana tightens her arms around herself and nods.

Zuleikha closes her eyes, takes a breath, and begins:

"Once upon a time there was a girl. She liked music. She liked how sound could erupt out of nothing. How it filled the air like a physical thing. Her mother encouraged it. Her mother used all her savings so that her daughter could do what she loved. The girl grew up ambitious and fearless." Zuleikha suddenly laughs. "And she was *beloved*; she was loved instantly by everyone.

"But she? She loved no one. No person evoked emotion in her, not even a flutter in her chest. She was proud and selfish. And she deserved to be, she'd worked hard. Then one day she met a man who came to listen to her play. He was handsome and charming and she fell in love with him." Zuleikha pauses then lowers her voice. "She was a *fool*. She loved him like it was the end of the world. Like everything was falling apart and he was all she could hold on to."

A SHIP APPEARS on the horizon. They watch as the cargo ship filled with construction material heads steadily toward the harbor. Two tugs head out from the berth to guide the large vessel in.

The ship's lights twinkle in the sea.

"So what happened?" Sana asks through slightly blue lips.

"What always happens," Zuleikha replies. "They fell in love. They loved each other like crazy, like those people you see in the bus staring at each other as if the rest of the world doesn't exist. He was funny and gallant and she was happy . . . happier than she'd ever known. But his love was like a flame; it came intensely and went out just as fast. They started to fight, often, and then he started to disappear for months, leaving her to wait in agony. Every time he left, she wrote him music, scores and scores trying to express her feelings. Finally, after a magnificent fight in which they threw things at each other, they wept and embraced and agreed to marry."

Zuleikha takes a deep puff of her cigarette and holds it in before exhaling slowly.

Sana looks at Zuleikha. "That's not the end of the story, is it?"

"No," Zuleikha says. She looks down at her cigarette and twists her lips, lifting the slim white cylinder that has gone dead in the wind. She sighs, then continues, "On the day of the wedding, they waited for hours at the mosque before they realized he was not coming. The girl pulled down the flowers from her hair and threw them away.

"The boy disappeared. He never came back nor did he ever phone. The girl went into a kind of shock; she waited at the telephone; she became delirious with fever and would only drink jugs of iced water.

"She slept for one week, and when she awoke she gave up her music and left. There was so little music left in her by then anyway. She traveled to the East and to the West, and she learned to choose her destinations by simply pointing a finger on a map and making her way there as best she could.

"She ended up in many strange places with many strange people. She met people like her; people running, people searching for something.

These people always find one another, you know, drawn by some invisible thread. They would all stand together on the side of roads and in small bars and under the night sky rubbing their hands together and stomping their feet in the cold. They would take long drives on dark roads, smoke strange things, talk nonsense, laugh for no reason, sleep beside rivers in tents, and put out their fires in the mornings. They would talk about their childhood memories. About their dog that died, the girl they once loved, the sickness that took their parent, how the stars made them ache, how they ached all over.

"All the time."

Zuleikha is quiet then. Sana shifts closer on the rocks, then asks, "Did the girl ever go home?"

Zuleikha nods faintly. "She did. She went back to bury her mother, and she decided to stay because there was nothing left then. When there's nothing left, you can only go home."

THE SHIP ON THE WATER moves steadily now; the light at the end of the harbor flickers. A group of hadadas call mournfully to one another in the sky.

Sana rubs her hands together and blows them. She waits for Zuleikha to continue.

"THE THING IS, IT'S HAPPENED, and nothing will change anything. It's too far in the past to bring it back and too much has happened to hold it to the light again. There was a time when an explanation, an apology, anything really, would have made sense. But the time for that has passed. Seasons have come and gone. People have died. The world is another world now.

"The girl, she is another girl now. There's nothing to be said."

SANA RESTS HER HEAD on her knees and turns to Zuleikha as if considering her. Finally she asks, "Do you think the girl will ever read that letter?"

Zuleikha flicks the butt of her cigarette into the water. "What letter?"

The sea crashes against the rocks below them. The moon shines brightly as the ship enters the harbor.

Somewhere far off a horn sounds.

Sixteen

Meena Begum is sitting at her desk in the garret writing when she feels her breasts swell with milk and realizes that Hassan has not woken for his feed. She climbs down the ladder, goes to his crib near the window, and bends down. She pulls apart the net curtains and turns back the covers on the small figure.

A porcelain doll dressed in white lace is nestled inside, its dark eyes wide open. Meena Begum gasps in horror as she picks up the doll, flinging it to the floor, where it cracks across the face. She frantically searches the cot. When her hands come away with nothing, she looks around the room, searching under the bed and in the bathroom, before finally yanking her door open and rushing through the house into the west wing, where she bursts into Jahanara Begum's chambers and demands to know where she is hiding her son.

Jahanara Begum, seated at her dressing table, is startled at first, then returns to her dressing mirror and continues to pat her face with powder.

"Leave my room immediately," she says evenly, without turning back.

"Tell me where he is *now*," demands Meena Begum.

Jahanara Begum looks up at her in the mirror's reflection and pauses with the velvet puff in her hand. "I have *no* idea what you are talking about. Leave."

"Liar!" Meena Begum screams. "You know where he is!"

Jahanara Begum puts down her powder pot gently, stands up, and turns to her. "I will not have you in my room making a scene. If you were any bit of a lady you would know this is outrageous behavior. I have endured enough for my husband. I have given up everything and moved to this godforsaken place. I have put up with his strange whims and peculiar fancies. But I will not have his harlot barging into my bedroom screaming accusations at me! He may think this is his world and we are all here to please him, but even I have my limits!"

"Enough, I don't have time for this! We both know you and Akbar were not happy!" shouts Meena Begum. "The trouble was already there, with or without me. Now, *where is my child?*"

Jahanara Begum's eyes flash violently and she grips the back of her dressing chair to steady herself. "*How dare you?* I don't know where your bastard is, but I hope to God you never find him," she spits.

Meena Begum screams and is almost upon her when Daisy, who has rushed to call Grand Ammi, returns with the old woman.

Grand Ammi places herself firmly between the two women and shouts, "Bas! Enough. This is not a brothel. *What* is going on?"

"My son is gone! Someone took him!" Meena Begum screams as Daisy tries to calm her. By then the servants have gathered at the stairs to listen to the commotion and even Pappu, who is trying to clear them away, stops to listen. Grand Ammi asks Meena Begum if she has checked her room properly, and when she says she has, Grand Ammi pauses for a moment and then she nods, telling Daisy to call for Akbar from the factory and begin a search immediately.

Meanwhile the children sit silently in their rooms. Soraya Bibi keeps brushing her hair and doesn't even look up when the adults rush in and ask if they know what happened to baby Hassan. Do they know who put the doll in the crib? Do they know anything at all? Laddoo keeps his eyes down and furiously shakes his head at the questions.

Jahanara Begum swears she has nothing to do with it. Meena Begum weeps and rails at both Grand Ammi and Jahanara Begum, saying she knows they are responsible for this somehow. While the search continues, the servants are lined up and questioned. No one is to leave the house and no one is to enter.

Akbar Manzil is on lockdown and everyone waits in their rooms in tense anticipation.

Everyone except Jahanara Begum, who rejoices quietly. She knows that fate is finally on her side. This is what God planned. This is how He punishes the wretched of the earth.

That night the house is quiet except for the sound of Meena Begum's wails.

At dawn the next morning, the police leave and a doctor sedates Meena Begum. Akbar sits at her bedside wearily, his lips moving in prayer. In the half-light of the morning, a little shadow approaches the bedroom door in the east wing and beckons Akbar.

Laddoo leads his father by the hand through the passage to the library and takes him to the trunk at the back. In the dim light he watches as his father opens the trunk and pulls out the little bundle. The baby has turned as blue as its blankets. He watches with large eyes as his father rubs his big hands over the baby's cold chest, then pinches the baby's tiny nose and blows into the blue lips of his mouth. He moves backward and crouches in a dark corner of the library with his arms around his knees and watches his father in the faint light as he gently pumps his brother's chest. He hears his father's voice break as he gathers the small body close to him and murmurs that it is not time yet, it is not time to leave. Then he sees something begin to move under the blanket and soon a frail wail fills the room.

"Allahu Akbar, God is great," Akbar whispers hoarsely, his head bent low into the baby's blankets. "Allahu Akbar."

Later that day, when things have calmed down and the doctor leaves, Grand Ammi tries to defuse the situation.

They were just children, she says. *Children.* They were playing a game. A terrible game of hide-and-seek. The boy was a baby himself. He didn't know. And no real damage had been done at the end of the day, she tells Akbar. Yes, it was a scare, but a lot worse could have happened and it didn't. The baby was okay, the doctor had said. He had to be observed for a few days, but he would be okay. The children should be given a suitable punishment and then they should put this unpleasant incident behind them.

Akbar paces the room as he listens. The relief when he found Hassan was so great that he could think of nothing else. But now he bends down to his eldest son, whose face holds the remnants of the tears he had shed earlier. Squashed, small, and wet like a bruised tomato, he cannot meet his father's eyes.

"Why did you do that? Aren't we all a family? Why would you do something like that?" he asks.

Laddoo's face melts a little as if he will cry again and he shakes his head with an I-don't-know expression.

Akbar turns to his daughter and his face hardens slightly. "And you? Aren't you old enough to know better? To put a *baby* inside a trunk and then *lie* about it. We asked you, we asked you if you knew what happened to your brother and you said no. And don't say you were playing a hide-and-seek game, I won't believe you."

"He's not my brother! He's a bastard who deserves to die!" Soraya Bibi suddenly shouts back at him, her face red.

Everyone turns quiet, and even Jahanara Begum pales.

Akbar steps forward and grabs her by her arms, shaking her. "What did you say? *What did you say?*"

Soraya Bibi glares at her father but does not answer, her eyes defiant.

"Tell me what you said," Akbar roars, shaking her harder, until her eyes roll back and Laddoo begins to cry loudly.

Grand Ammi comes forward and lays an arm on her son's shoulder. "Akbar, she's a child. Calm down. This will help nothing."

Akbar whips around to his mother. "Did you hear what she said? She *wanted* to kill him. She *wanted* to—" He stops suddenly and his expression changes as he turns to face his mother fully. "You're right, it's not *her* fault, Ammi. It's *yours*. You and"—here he turns and points to Jahanara Begum—"she are to blame. Not these children. They hear you two talking and they believe this vile rubbish you spew. Are these the kind of things you're saying? That my son is a *bastard*? That he deserves to die? No wonder they thought they had to get rid of him!" His hands are shaking. For a moment there is only the sound of his heavy breath, then he straightens suddenly and speaks clearly. "I'm telling you now, Ammi, if my child had died, *if my child had died*, I promise you I wouldn't have thought twice about throwing you both out." Akbar strides to the door and throws it open, then he turns to them. "This is not working. Meena will be moved elsewhere. In the meantime, you are all banned from entering the east wing."

And with that he slams the door behind him.

Much later, in the middle of the night, when the moon slices through his room like a white blade, Laddoo, who has been staring up at the ceiling, climbs out of his bed and tiptoes silently into the east wing, where he makes his way to the room at the end of the passage. A light is on and the door is ajar. He pushes himself through the gap and stands at the entrance of Meena Begum's room.

Meena Begum has just finished feeding the baby when she notices the little shifting shape standing in his pajamas in the doorway. Laddoo with his back to the wall shuffles in slowly in his slippers looking up at Meena Begum fearfully, his cheeks still red. The light from the lamp throws his shadow across the room.

Meena Begum watches him carefully as he stands there and says nothing. In the dimly lit room, the circles under her eyes grow deeper. Her face is pale. She picks up the baby and puts him gently over her shoulder as she pats his back. She begins to sing a Tamil song softly. Laddoo listens at first from his place at the entrance and then slowly but surely inches toward the bed. He climbs onto the foot of the bed, still watching her warily from his dark eyes. She continues to sing in a soft voice until the song's end, and then she puts the baby down and tucks him into his crib.

She sits back on the bed and looks at Laddoo in the faint light of the lamp. He looks back at her.

"He's okay," she says.

He stands up suddenly then and flees the room, his face hot.

Seventeen

"Arreh. Rounder! We not making world maps here," Razia Bibi scolds, waving a rolling pin as she shouts. Sana sits next to her on the small kitchen table covered in flour, trying to roll rotis. "It's all about concentration!" Razia Bibi states. "If your mind is here-there-everywhere, you'll never be able to roll rotis. You must think about what you're doing and then they come round."

As part of Razia Bibi's plan to turn Sana into a Good Girl she has started giving her cooking lessons. "If you learn how to cook from a man, God knows where you'll end up in life. You'd better learn from me," she says. "These men who cook, they know the surface things, in fact they're *very* good with the surface things—but when it comes down to it, when it comes down to the *facts of the matter*, these men are useless."

She is sharing now the basics of samosa making as they roll, telling Sana how to make the perfect mince filling.

"Onions, lots and lots of onions," says Razia Bibi as she bustles around the kitchen, "are the secret. If you're lazy and you don't use enough, you're asking for trouble. Some women are so shameful nowadays they buy their fried onions. Hai Rabb, can you imagine? Too lazy to fry onions? Have you heard of such a thing? Even that no-good Preeti—she didn't know how to cook when she married my Ziyaad. So big girl she was and she didn't know. She was living alone for so long, you know? Tell me, which girl lives alone? I should have known from then something wasn't right. Let me tell you, at the end of the day you can only blame the parents," she says as she pokes her rolling pin in the air to make her point. "That's why it's my duty to teach you. God put you in this house so that you can be raised right. Rule Number One is *always* fry your own onions. That way, even if it doesn't come out right, you can't be cheated by anyone else but yourself. And Rule Number Two is *homemade is the best made.*"

"Isn't that the same as Rule Number One?" interrupts Sana. "Also, don't you sell . . ."

"No. They are all different. You keep quiet and let me talk. I've been in this business for forty years! You think I don't know what I'm talking about? Everyone said I won't make it. Even my husband, he said, Razia, no way someone will pay money for your samosas. He laughed at me. But ha! Look at me now. I got customers coming all the way from Ballito! They love my samosas so much! Go down to Gora's café in town, his wife, Jameela, you think she can make like my samosas? Oh, I'm sure she tries, but she can't come close!"

"Fancy is always saying how good your samosas are," Sana says as she tries to discretely pull back an extending blob of roti with her finger.

Razia Bibi stops moving about and looks at her. "Eh? What you said?"

"Fancy always says you're a good cook," say Sana, hovering her rolling pin over the flaw.

Razia Bibi pauses and then continues to roughly break out pieces of dough. "Well . . . she must just mind her own business. I don't care what she has to say." She notices Sana's roti and shakes her head. "Your head is in the clouds, my girl. At this rate, no man will marry you." She adjusts her scarf around her neck and continues. "Don't make your face like one sour lemon. You don't marry for love—that is modern thinking. Girls today wait for love and then it's too late. You just find someone decent who will be there for you when you get old. Before you get aches and pains and cataracts, and then no one will want you." She clicks her tongue and moves around the kitchen. "Life is lonely enough as it is, and when you get old, well, it's just . . . bad."

Razia Bibi peels one of her rotis off the table and tosses them between her hands, testing the evenness of the weight. "My Ziyaad, of course, he wouldn't have left if he didn't have to. But he got *big* job offer in Canada; you don't get jobs like that in a hurry. I told him, if you have to go, you have to go. I'll be okay, I have my business to keep me busy. So he packed his bags and went. I haven't seen him for . . . a while. He says he's coming to visit in December," she says as she lights the stove and puts down the tawa to heat. "I'm going to make *all* his favorite foods. Lamb kalya, aknee, paratha, butter chicken. Poor thing hardly gets home food there. Those American Indians are very different. Not like us. They're working *so* hard there—no time to cook. Only work-work. And no maids! Can you imagine? They have to clean everything themselves. At least Ziyaad will have a break when he comes back. Maybe we'll have a small party when he comes, hai na? And I might even ask your father for the recipe for that gajar halwa. It was . . . decent—for a man. And maybe you can make the rotis."

She picks up one of Sana's oblong rotis and grimaces.

"Or maybe you just watch."

Just then Pinky wanders in through Razia Bibi's door as if unaware of exactly whose room she has entered, so unannounced. Her face is entirely pale.

Razia Bibi admonishes her. "Don't you know how to knock, eh, Pinky? What we have doors for?"

"What's wrong?" asks Sana.

Pinky sits down on a chair with a hard thump and even Razia Bibi looks up in alarm.

Wordlessly she hands the envelope in her hand to Razia Bibi, who says, "What's this?" and draws up her glasses from around her neck. She pulls out a sheet of paper and reads aloud, "Dear Pinky . . ."

Before she can continue, Pinky says in a hoarse whisper, "It's from Shah Rukh Khan."

"What?" says Razia Bibi.

"He sent Pinky a letter. She got it now in the post. She said to herself, who will send Pinky a letter? Then she opens it and it is from"—she gulps—"*Him*. He says—he says it has come to his notice that I am his biggest fan in South Africa and he . . ." Pinky is too overcome to continue.

"He says he's very happy to hear you enjoy his movies and he's glad to have a fan like you all the way in South Africa," says Razia Bibi, scanning the letter.

"It's . . . unbelievable!" says Pinky. "How can he know Pinky?"

"Well," says Sana, keeping her eyes evenly on the roti she is rolling. "These actors, they know everything nowadays. They get their information from the internet. They can even find our home addresses online."

"Our home addresses?!" says Razia Bibi horrified, clutching her hand to her chest.

"You're squashing it," yelps Pinky, grabbing the letter from Razia Bibi. She holds the letter to her heart. "This is the *best* thing that has happened in Pinky's life." She stands up, a small hazy smile on her face, and wanders to the exit mumbling happily to herself.

"Ey, at least close my door, Pinky! Don't act like you're too big for your boots now," Razia Bibi shouts after her.

Eighteen

After an hour of producing rotis that progressively grow less and less round, Razia Bibi shoos Sana out of her kitchen and tells her to return when she has learned to concentrate.

Sana leaves her apartment, relieved to be free of instructions and rotis. She dusts the flour from her hands and climbs up the stairs. At the top, she bumps into a tall somber-looking man, carrying a bag and wearing an array of beads, leaving Fancy's apartment. Fancy, at her entrance, catches sight of Sana, flushes, and shuts the door quickly.

A few second later she opens it a crack, looks around nervously, and beckons Sana with an urgent whisper.

Fancy's apartment opens into the heart of a pink kitchen that leads into a small bedroom with a wrought-iron bed covered in an array of frilly cushions and hot-water bottles. The kitchen, which serves as dining room/sitting room/laundry room, is covered in jewelry, cereal boxes, and medicine bottles. In the center, a large dressing table is littered with dishes. Kitchen drawers bulge with clothing and Mr. Patel's cage sits atop a pile of towels. Sana goes to where the bird is sitting, on a post next to his cage.

"Hello," she says.

The green parrot looks at her from a sideways eye and then shuffles along his perch until he has his back to her.

Fancy moves around her cluttered kitchen and makes tea. She pushes away perfume bottles with her arm and places the tea on the dressing table.

"Now, dear," she says, wringing the gold necklaces around her neck. "You have to promise you won't tell anyone about my visitor." Fancy looks around furtively. "Razia Bibi will never let me hear the end of it. And she's looking for *any* excuse to get me in trouble with Doctor. But you see . . . it's for Mr. Patel!" Fancy bursts out and looks as if she is about to cry. "Oh Sana, he's been so ill lately. He's losing all his feathers and he's getting night terrors. Night terrors! He screeches at night and throws himself against the wall. I just didn't know what to do! The vet couldn't explain it—he just said Mr. Patel is stressed. But stressed from what, I don't know! Oh Sana, I was at my wit's end. It just didn't seem . . . *normal*. So I called a—a witch doctor. I know I shouldn't have, but he came very well recommended. My friend Lolly said he helped her cousin walk again. And, well, I had to try *something*!"

"What did he do?" asks Sana, leaning forward.

Fancy lowers her voice. "Well, he didn't say much, just walked around and studied the room while I explained the problem. Then he threw his bones on the floor—bits of twigs and shells and animal bones. He said he was talking to the ancestors of the house."

Sana's eyes widen.

"He was whispering to himself. Then he went very quiet. He looked troubled. Eventually he said there are bad spirits here. They are giving the bird nightmares, he said."

Sana looks uncomfortable. "Bad spirits?"

Fancy nods. "Unnatural things from the spirit world. Things that try to imitate our ancestors, he said. He gave me a potion and told me to burn it in the yard."

Sana hesitates. "Do you think that will work? Do you think it can—chase away the bad spirits?"

"I hope so! Poor Mr. Patel. Just look at him," she says, turning to the parrot. "Bechara. He's so troubled. And now-now . . ." She stutters on the verge of tears. "He can't even go to the stairs to look at the courtyard anymore because of Razia Bibi. He can't help what he says. I put him outside but there the peacocks don't leave him alone. They strut their feathers, showing him how pretty and big they are." She sniffs. "As if they're anything so special."

Sana exits Fancy's apartment and finds Zuleikha lying in the carpeted passage outside. Her eyes are closed and she looks more disheveled than usual; her hair is piled wildly, the circles around her eyes have deepened, and a cigarette, dangerously close to burning out, dangles from her fingers. Without opening her eyes, she breaks into a lazy smile and says in a singsong voice, "I heard Pinky got a letter today."

Sana steps over her, bends down, and pulls the burning cigarette from her fingers, crushing it against a saucer nearby.

"Funny thing about that letter," she continues. "No one seems to notice; it was posted *in* South Africa. Strange, no?"

Sana shrugs.

Zuleikha opens her eyes and props herself on one elbow. "Don't give yourself grand ideas, darling."

"What do you mean?"

"You can't save us." Her voice takes an edge. "So stop trying."

When Sana says nothing, she leans back on the floor and clasps her hands beneath her head and continues, "So you saw, huh?" Zuleikha winks as she cocks her head toward Fancy's apartment. "Fancy's little visitor." When Sana remains quiet, Zuleikha clicks her tongue, "What, not so chatty today? Not in the mood to share anything?" She looks at Sana, waits, and then says, "For God's sake I know who was just there! Why do people think I have no bloody clue what's happening? I know, I just don't *care*." She looks up at the ceiling, then says, "Although . . . I would like to tell Razia Bibi, for fun. She would lose her head, that one, and I'll get to see some fireworks around this place—it's been *so* boring otherwise," she says as she stifles a yawn.

"Don't," says Sana quickly. "She's just worried about Mr. Patel. He's sick."

"She called a witch doctor to the house for her *bird?*" Zuleikha rolls her eyes.

"Yes."

Zuleikha roars with laughter. "Oh man. I really want to tell Razia Bibi now." She turns to Sana and makes a mournful face. "Oh benevolent savior, I beg thee, let me tell her, *please*."

Sana rolls her eyes.

"Listen," says Zuleikha, as she props herself against a wall. "These people can't fix anything. They make money from other's miseries. Do you know how many 'aalims,'" she says, motioning quotes with her fingers, "my family took me to because they thought something was wrong with me? Because they couldn't understand who I was? They thought I was broken because they couldn't believe I *chose* to be the way I was. They couldn't believe I didn't *want* to be like them. And why would I want to be like them, tell me? They sit in their cubicles in their high-rise offices in their middle-class jobs with their discounted smoothies and dysfunctional families and wait in queues at the bank but all they're really waiting for is some big change. Some big change to take them out from their misery. *The same misery they want me to endure.*" She lowers her voice and leans forward. "And they have the nerve to *pity* me. I see it in their stupid dull eyes. They think I live in this big broken house without anyone so I must be suffering. Yet they're the ones still waiting and I'm the one who's free."

Zuleikha stands up suddenly and turns to leave.

"Oh and Sana," she calls out sharply. "Stop hiding the cigarettes in my room." Her voice disappears down the passage. "I don't need any favors."

Nineteen

In the library one afternoon, Sana comes across a Tamil-English dictionary. The weathered book is worn and some of the pages are damaged by water, but she manages to use it to work slowly through the early sections of the diaries. It takes time, and she spends hours slowly deciphering the Dravidian language. The pages have sat in the sun for a long time, and some sections are too faded to read while others are written so unintelligibly she cannot make out the words. She makes notes and pencils in guesswork for certain entries.

Bit by bit she begins to learn about the family that lived at Akbar Manzil. She meets Akbar, Grand Ammi, Jahanara Begum, Laddoo, Soraya Bibi, and the servants.

As she learns the history of the house on the hill, it turns away, ashamed of its secrets and its inability to keep them hidden. It grows old, turns stiff and hoary. In the rafters the bats turn leathery with age; the smells go sour; the custard curdles; the fish rots.

In the beginning of the diary the woman, Meena Begum, reflects on her childhood in her village and the journey over the sea to work in the sugarcane fields of Natal.

She wrote about how the ship swayed at night and how sick she had been. How everyone belowdecks had been vomiting on the first day. How she thought the ship was the worst place in the world and she wanted to escape, only to discover the next morning the sun was bright, the water was still, and the whole world seemed full of wonder. How they ate the watery dhals with iron spoons and how one clear night she and some of the others left their mattresses to climb to the upper deck and watch the stars while eating apples stolen from the kitchen. They chased one another through passages, reaching out in the dark, daring the others to run faster until they finally reached a large room at the end that glowed red and hot, and she told the younger ones that it was hell because hell was a place you could carry with you.

She wrote about the fine young women on the upper decks with their parasols and lacy hats and how she envied and disliked them all at once. When they arrived on the new continent all she could see were rolling green hills, and the strangeness of it made her feel so alone. She wrote about the homesickness, how terrified she was to talk to others and how she missed her friends in the village. How her cousins, long settled in the new lands, mocked her. She wrote about her job at the factory, how she swept the floors while her parents worked in the fields. She wrote about Akbar's marriage proposal and her contempt for him.

And then she wrote how it changed, how love came in quietly and softened her edges. Even her writing seems to change then; it turns looser and languid, as if everything of her has altered. Sana's heartbeat quickens.

She gathers the diaries out of the cold garret and climbs down the ladder, clutching them to her chest, not wanting to leave them for a moment now. In the waning light through the dormers, she fails to notice the stains in the floorboards, the smears across the cabinet, the print of a trapped hand against the glass.

She leaves the room and closes the door after her.

THE DJINN WAITS A HUNDRED YEARS

T HE DJINN CLIMBS DOWN and crawls into the four-poster bed. It seizes the sheets and begins to weep. A hollow rasping sound comes from its throat. It turns to look up at the ceiling and watches dismally as blood begins to drip.

Twenty

Doctor sits on the balcony looking out at the sea.

He is lost in his memories. It is his first day at medical school and a girl with blond hair is asking him if he can move down so she and her friend can sit in his row. He is so startled by her fair hair, her blue eyes, and the chirpy way she talks that he just stares. She asks again, and when he does not respond, she and her friend giggle and wonder aloud if he speaks English. They leave to find another seat, and he, suddenly embarrassed, keeps his head bent low for the entire class.

The scene plays out on the surface of his eyes until he closes them and fast-forwards to graduation, then to the darkness after his mother's death. He had gone to the mosque then and tried to pray; he remembered the feel of the prayer mat against his forehead, the whispered recitation of the Quran around him. He had closed his eyes and tried to call out to God, but had felt like God was not listening or that he was not trying hard enough. He began to believe that God knew he was not a good man. He wavers in the memory. Then his thoughts pick up pace and run again and he is back in the war, with shrapnel through his calf, then Kenya, then the moment he sees his wife for the first time at the hospital; he pauses here, wallows in the scent of gardenias before he is pulled out and continues to flit through his life; through his marriage, his wife's death, his return to the sea, and then he is back in the present, on his chair looking out to the ocean.

He opens his eyes and looks down at the teacup shaking in his hands. The past is rising too quickly and it is taking longer to place where he is these days. He puts the cup down and looks at his table, trying to remember for a moment what he had been doing. His eyes skim unseeing over the documents, the papers, the pencils, and the envelopes on his desk. He picks up a yellow-skinned pencil and studies it carefully, wondering if he had been writing something that he has forgotten.

Someone is knocking at his door; he looks up to see Sana entering the apartment. Relieved that he has an excuse to discard a fruitless search, he puts the pencil down and welcomes her.

"Asalaamwa'alaikum. How nice to see you, my child. Come, sit," he says as he gestures toward a sofa in his sitting room. She wades through the cassettes, pushes aside some old magazines, and sinks down into a seat.

He limps to a chair and sits down. "Chai?" he offers.

Sana shakes her head. "No thanks, I just had some by Fancy Aunty." She shifts in her seat. "How are you, Doctor?"

"Alhamdulilah. Can't complain. And you? Where have you been? I hardly see you around these days."

"Well, I was busy with . . . a project. And now Razia Bibi is trying to teach me how to cook."

"I should have guessed," laughs Doctor. "Are you enjoying it?"

Sana pauses. "I'm not very good at it."

"I'll tell you a secret; neither am I. Your poor father showed me so nicely but I forgot everything."

Sana smiles. She looks at the television screen, which is paused on a black-and-white scene of two people looking at each other. She gestures to the screen. "Which one is this?"

He turns to the television and brightens. "Oh, one of the finest films ever made," he says. He leans over and puts a hand to the screen. "*Kaagaz Ke Phool.*"

Sana studies the man and the woman in the half shadows looking at each other yearningly.

"It means paper flowers," Doctor continues. "Guru Dutt was the director and actor—he was a master in his field. They called him the Orson Welles of Indian cinema." Here Doctor opens his hands to express the name in lights. "This is one of his best works. Even better than *Pyaasa*, I'd wager. His films were magic—they spoke the language of life. He died heartbroken and a drunk, but let me tell you, those people—those people who live at the edge are the ones who are really living—they know what it is to *exist*. He tried to show us how fickle and fragile this life is. You can have everything, *everything* in this world today, but tomorrow you can have nothing and no one."

He looks out to the sea once more.

"This world is full of flowers, my child, but they're all just made of paper."

Twenty-One

The darkness in Jahanara Begum is not an instantaneous thing. It begins as smoldering coals in a fireplace, but as time passes and logs of bitterness are added, it soon becomes a roaring blaze, a pyre of revenge that she prostrates herself at.

When she first heard about the baby she fell into a dark sickness. She had convinced herself that they did not sleep together, that he merely visited the other woman's room to read poetry. The child had jarred this fantasy. She spent those nights in a fevered haze, awakening with a start, covered in sweat. She took to wandering around in her room muttering to herself, listing the names in correct order of descendants that link her to Mumtaz Mahal, consort of the great Shah Jahan himself. She counted off the names on her fingers and clawed at her hair in frustration if she stumbled. Under her burning lids she thought she saw dark shapes gathered around her bed. She screamed at them to leave, to stop tormenting her, that no one had given them permission to enter her chambers. Other times she conspired with them, plotting to slit Meena Begum's throat in her sleep or poison her soup. Sometimes when Grand Ammi passed the room late at night, she heard Jahanara Begum whispering and laughing.

The lines of the world Jahanara Begum had drawn herself were blurring and she had to find a way to gain control.

Late one night as she paced her room, she caught sight of her reflection in the mirror. She paused.

"Why, look at you," she said, holding a hand to her chest. "You're as white as a sheet." She raised a hand to her cheek. "And look at your eyes. So dark. What happened to their color? They were violet, were they not? That's what they called them in the village, pure violet. Even Ammi didn't know what 'violet' meant. She thought it meant that your eyes were imperfect. But Abba told her, Abba told her that it meant you had *special* eyes. 'The girl with the magic eyes,' they said. They said your eyes meant that you were destined for great things. And *you were*. The most handsome and richest man in the village married *you*. But now look at you. Look at your dark eyes and hollow cheeks. Why, are those wrinkles around your eyes? Is this greatness? You disgust me!" She spat and turned away from the mirror. Then slowly she looked back over her shoulder, turning to face herself once more. In a softer voice, almost pleading, she said, "Why can't he see how special I am? How could he even"—she stopped to choke—"*look* at another?" She lowered her voice even more and moved closer to the mirror. She whispered, "Do you know? Do you know that there's a baby?" Then suddenly her voice changed into a high-pitched scream. "What do you mean, you want to know where babies come from? Is that any kind of question for a decent young woman to ask, Jahanara?! Get out of here and wash that filthy mouth of yours. We don't ask such questions in this house!"

Jahanara Begum pressed closer until she was nose to nose with her reflection. She smiled.

"He'll come back to you. He has to. You wait and see!"

Finally, after a month, her fevers subsided.

When she recovered from her illness, she apologized for her outbursts and returned to the household, calm and composed. She was disgusted with herself for falling apart and revealing weakness. She went back to calmly crocheting in the sitting room, reading her London fashion catalogs, playing bridge, and learning new English songs as if nothing had ever happened.

She kept the flame low, burning only enough to keep going.

But when Meena Begum burst into her bedroom that day demanding to know where her child was, the fire had crackled. How could this miserable peasant who had tried to aim for more than her lot in life barge into *her* room and make accusations? And when the trunk incident came to light and Akbar had *dared* to turn his wrath upon *her*, the flames of her bonfire burst forth, licking the sky in fury.

She had threatened to leave but she had known it was impossible; she had more pride than to return home, the disgraced and pitied first wife. She had sat for hours in front of her dressing table, crossly having a discussion with her reflection.

"Obviously you have more talent than her. So she reads a lot—but you, you can sing. Only a few people in the world can sing as well as you. Even Anna Marie, the queen of England's great-grandniece on the ship, said she hadn't heard a voice as sweet as yours. Why, she even hinted she might mention you to the queen. Just imagine! Obviously that puny beggar is no match for your fine features. No match at all. These features were passed on from the great Mumtaz Mahal. *The Chosen One of the Palace*, named for her astounding beauty by Shah Jahan himself. The nostrils of Mughal emperors. You are certainly better than her on all accounts," she whispered vehemently.

She knew if she returned home the rumors would run wild, how she had been usurped from her palace in Africa by a Madrasi factory sweeper. There were many family members who envied her, she was certain. Who would love to see her downfall. In fact, she was sure they were waiting for it, plotting and planning her ruin. Waiting to bathe in her misfortune.

She would never give them the satisfaction.

One evening Daisy prepares Jahanara Begum for bed; she brushes her silky hair carefully, then parts it into sections as she sets about braiding it. As she reaches for a ribbon to fasten the end, she remarks that Small Madam must be looking forward to bed as she looks rather tired. Jahanara Begum slaps Daisy's hands away and inspects her reflection in the mirror. She has just turned thirty-one. She studies her large eyes with their violet gleam, her soft white skin, and glossy long hair. Although she is still beautiful, she begins to notice the small signs of aging around her eyes. She moves her face closer to the mirror; she is losing the light of her youth; she can see it, the freshness is beginning to fade.

"Is it going?" she murmurs. "Is it finally going? Not this early. Surely there must be more time?" She turns suddenly to Daisy. "Am I getting old? Is that what you're saying? Do I look *old* to you?" Her voice takes on a desperate appeal. "Do I look old?" And then, almost pleading, in an uncharacteristic gesture, Jahanara Begum grabs the servant's hand. "Tell me I'm beautiful. Tell me that it's not all over."

Daisy steps back uneasily and drops her mistress's hand. "Of course, you're beautiful, madam. You're *always* beautiful."

Jahanara Begum's expression changes. Her face turns cold. "Get out! Get out! What do you know, you fool!" She grabs a glass bottle of perfume from her dresser and throws it at the back of the retreating servant; it smashes and breaks against the door. Instantly the room is filled with the scent of musk.

She returns to her dressing table and turns calmly to her reflection as if continuing a conversation.

"You've been a patient woman. I admire this. You've bided your time.

But the time is coming for you to show everyone that your legacy will not be tainted. He *will* return to you. And then you will make him pay."

Jahanara Begum has a plan. When her husband returns to her (for surely, he must), she will take revenge; she will make him suffer. She will show everyone that *she* has the power. Despite Grand Ammi's esteemed position in the community and Akbar's wealth, it is Jahanara Begum who has the *real* control. When Akbar returns to beg her to take him back, beg her on his very knees, *pleading* in front of everyone, she will sneer and laugh in his face. She will make him promise to leave this godforsaken continent before she even considers his return to her.

She plays the moment over in her mind a thousand times.

She can see her cold and glorious face looming over his sad and remorseful one as he tries to explain the stupidity, the madness that overcame him when he made the decision to marry another. She will kneel down to cup his jaw and then she will slap him across his face and the people around her will gasp and admire her strength. They will see her for the real queen that she is.

The time is coming for her husband to return, and if he will not, she will force his move.

Daisy returns to the servants' quarters, her hands shaking.

"What wrong with you?" asks Iqbal Babu, who is finishing up his supper at the dining table.

"She's gone mad," says Daisy shakily. "She just threw her perfume at me."

Iqbal Babu snorts. "Well, you must have done something."

"I absolutely did not! I was just doing her hair, getting her ready for bed, same as usual, and she went off at me," says Daisy as she begins to sniff.

"Oh hush now, you know how Small Madam is," says Pappu, coming forward to comfort Daisy. "Unpredictable as the weather in summer, she is."

"She's gotten worse since she got sick. She just screams at me all the time. I don't know if I can take it anymore," complains Daisy as she dabs her eyes with the handkerchief Pappu offers her.

"Well obviously she's gone worse. Her husband's mistress has a baby now. She has a lot to deal with," says Iqbal Babu.

"She's not his mistress, he *married* her," says Nkosi from a stool in the corner, where he is polishing his boots.

Iqbal Babu cocks his good ear to listen and scoffs, "Oh please. That's not even a real marriage. That little *coolie* is a nobody with nothing."

"Oh she's nice enough, Iqbal! I'll be quite disappointed when she leaves. I heard the master say she'll be going soon." Daisy makes a face. "It was real nice having her around."

"You know, that just wasn't right. Whatever you say. That just wasn't right what happened to the little one." Nkosi shakes his head.

"Now, now, there's no truth to that rumor," says Pappu. "The children were playing and there was an accident and that's all we'll say on the matter."

"We all know they tried to kill it," says Iqbal Babu.

"Hush!" snaps Pappu.

"And we all know that ugly tramp deserved it."

Daisy gasps. Before she can say anything, Pappu interrupts. "That's enough from you! Go finish your meal outside."

Iqbal Babu grabs his plate and saunters to the door.

"She's the same as all of us. She can go in that big fancy house and think she's somebody important but she'll get what what's coming to her soon enough," he says as he shuts the door.

One hot morning in February, nine months after the birth of Hassan Ali Khan, Jahanara Begum bursts into the factory and announces to her husband that a telegram has arrived from Gujarat with news that her father has taken ill with typhoid. He is in his last days, her mother has written, and she must return with the family to see him. Jahanara Begum commands Akbar to take her to her ailing father's bedside in India immediately.

Her father, of course, is perfectly well. The fake illness and the journey to India has been concocted after months of plotting with Grand Ammi. They write to Jahanara Begum's mother, who is more than willing to mail a letter with news of her father's ill health. They decide that all Akbar needs is some time alone with his *real* family. Away from the evil influences of Meena Begum, he will have time to get ahold of himself and see clearly the reckless error of his ways. A ship journey will remind him of his younger self and his adventurous honeymoon with Jahanara Begum. In India, among both their family members, sense will soon be restored and he will realize this situation with the factory worker is not feasible.

It is just matter of getting him away from her.

"Come with me, jaan," Akbar says to Meena Begum as she lies with her head in his lap. They are sitting on the sand in an alcove sheltered by the cliffs before the house. He strokes her hair as the water laps at their feet. At the foot of the stairs that lead up to the house stands a lantern, and next to them in a basket of blankets sleeps Hassan.

She lifts her head halfway to look at him properly and then laughs before dropping her head back. "You can't be serious."

"I am."

"What? You, me, your mother, and wife on a ship for seventeen days? It sounds delightful. It's just like you to think something like that would work," she adds softly and raises a hand to his cheek. "The world of a man is so wonderful and simple."

Akbar protests. "We can go to the south after and visit your village. I'm sure the family there will want to see you. You keep telling me about how beautiful it is. I want to see the river you talk about. The one you caught fish in when you were a girl."

Her eyes are quiet and serious now. "I want to go back." She looks up at his face, into his dark eyes. "But this is not the time. Hassan is too small for such a journey. And," she raises herself up on her elbows, "I know my relation with her is not . . . ideal, but she is your wife and you should be there for her, Akbar." She sits up and faces him. "I think you should do this for her and only her."

He is quiet then. He strokes his beard thoughtfully, then sighs and seems to nod in reluctant agreement.

She falls back against him and stares out at the sea. "You're the one who told me that you must follow the road even if it takes you far from where you want to be."

Akbar sighs. "I don't know if I can be so long without you."

"Love is best when mixed with anguish. In our town, we won't call you a lover if you escape the pain," she quotes Rumi to him in reply.

He looks at her in surprise then bellows with laugher. "How have you turned the master's poetry against me?!" He smiles, then pulls her closer and wraps his arms around her. They are quiet for a moment as they look out at the dark ocean. It opens before them like a mouth into another world.

"Time will pass quickly, Akbar. It always does," she says.

"As soon as I'm back, we'll settle you in your new home."

The water laps at the shore.

"I won't keep the servants when you're gone," she says softly. "I won't need them."

"Are you sure? Not even one or two?" he asks.

"No, I can manage on my own. I'm perfectly fine alone," she replies.

He puts a hand to his chest in mock hurt. "Won't you miss me?"

"Oh, I'm just waiting for you to go. I already have my eye on the silverware and your mother's Dutch tablecloths." She smiles impishly.

THE DJINN WAITS A HUNDRED YEARS

"I knew this was your plan all along!" he says as he grabs her waist and pinches her playfully. She bursts into a peal of laughter.

When they settle down, she says, "I'll wait for you, Akbar. As I always have, even when I did not know it. I'll come here every evening with a light and call your name until you find your way back to me."

Twenty-Two

Akbar Manzil is filled with a great frenzy as the Khan family prepare to leave for their journey across the Indian Ocean. Servants hurry about, clothes are washed and pressed, trunks are taken down and dusted out. Jahanara Begum packs all her clothing and jewelry in anticipation of never having to return.

Grand Ammi asks the servants to lock away the fine china, pack away the linen, and take down the oil paintings, for she wants nothing touched by her tainted daughter-in-law. She orders Pappu to keep an eye on things—to visit the house and make sure that little wretch is not inviting hordes of her Madrasi family for banquets in the dining room. She can just picture them, drinking sherry in her Bohemian crystal glasses, staining her Dutch tablecloths, and swinging on the antique jula, laughing as they gossip about her.

She tells Pappu she wants detailed reports.

WHEN JAHANARA BEGUM HEARS the news that Meena Begum is emptying the house of servants while they are away, a small, infected root of an idea takes hold.

If for some reason Akbar cannot see sense, *if* for some reason he wants to return, she has to eliminate the risk. She needs an insurance policy. There will be only one opportunity and she knows she has to take it. As she sits at night at her bedside pushing back her cuticles and rubbing cold cream into her hands, she knows what she has to do.

The next day at sunset, as the peacocks call to one another in the falling darkness, she paints her lips crimson, brushes out her silky hair, and enters the garden. Beneath a mango tree, she beckons Iqbal Babu to the stables. Cocky, curious, and confident that the mistress has finally succumbed to her desire for him, he approaches with swagger, twirling the ends of his mustache. At the stables in the rays of the last light, Jahanara Begum takes out a small velvet bag from within the folds of her dress and pulls out six gold bangles. She leans in close to him, so close that he can smell the musk at her throat, and he is confused, unsure of whether to look at her heaving bosom or the gold gleaming in her hands. She says she has a small favor to ask of him; she wants him to do something, then leave and never return.

It is a such a *small* request; it almost doesn't count, she says as she bats her eyelashes and moves closer. He doesn't have to do anything that he *doesn't want to*, but she knows his heart, she says, she *recognizes* it, and she knows this is something he *wants* to do. Iqbal Babu is hypnotized by her sparkling eyes, glossy hair, and the glittering gold in her hands; he moves his barrel chest closer to her and listens to her proposition. She whispers her request in his good ear and his eyes widen. Then she leans in and seals the deal with a small hard kiss for good measure.

Fate will decide everything else, she adds breathily before she leaves him, pressing the gold into his hands.

Although it is hot and humid, the sky above Akbar Manzil is filled with dark clouds on the morning they leave. Jahanara Begum waves her hand fan agitatedly around her face while Grand Ammi orders the servants about as they carry luggage to the cars.

"Be careful, my crystal is in there!" she yells to Nkosi as he throws a trunk into the car. She stops Daisy and inspects a box before nodding at her to continue. "Yes, that's fine, put that there. Ya Rabb, be careful, these things have to reach India in one piece! Oh Pappu, what are you doing standing there and gawking? Be a useful fellow and do something with yourself!" she yells at the cook, who apologizes and runs quickly inside.

IN THEIR BEDROOM Akbar promises Meena Begum that it will only be two months and that he will return as soon as he can. He tells her that he will remember her every day as he pushes a sprig of jasmine into her hair.

"So that you don't forget me," he says as he tucks it behind her ear.

"Nī eppaṭi ippaṭi collalām? Eṉṉāl uṉṉai maṟakka muṭiyātu," she replies. It is only a few weeks and time passes so quickly. She will be waiting at the rocks every evening, waiting for him to return to her, she says.

As the SS *Takliwa* sets off from the port of Durban, the sky rumbles. Akbar reads Ayatul Kursi under his breath and blows the blessed prayer of protection over his family on land and at sea.

Then he lights his pipe and leans against the stern, taking a deep puff as the African continent pulls away from under him.

BY LATE AFTERNOON the last servants, too, are leaving the house and Daisy comes to say goodbye.

"We're leaving now, miss. Is there anything you'd like before we go?"

"Please, Daisy, I always tell you, just call me Meena," says Meena Begum as she towels her hair dry in her room. "And no, I'm fine, thank you. Are you excited for your trip?"

Daisy lights up. "Yes. We leave to see my sister in Transvaal at the end of the week. Raj and the children are so excited. We've never been on a train before. Thank—thank you again for the tickets," she says shyly.

"Of course. I'm so glad to hear the children are looking forward to it."

Daisy makes to go, then pauses at the door.

"Miss—Meena."

"Yes?" Meena Begum stops drying her hair.

"I just wanted to say—it's been lovely having you here. I know I speak on behalf of everyone when I say we'll be sorry to see you go."

"Well, maybe not *everyone*," laughs Meena Begum. "But thank you, Daisy. That's kind. When I first came here, I didn't think I would stay longer than a few days, and now it feels . . . it feels like my life really only started here. How strange, hai na?"

Daisy nods.

"This life is indeed a strange thing," says Meena Begum, putting down her towel. She goes to Daisy and takes her hand in hers. "Goodbye, Daisy. I hope you have a safe journey."

"Goodbye, Meena," says Daisy squeezing her hand.

Daisy leaves the room, and soon the house is silent except for the sound of animals calling from outside. Meena Begum wanders the house in the dying light trying to switch on lamps, but Grand Ammi in an act of vengeance has ensured that the electricity in the house is cut while they are gone. Meena Begum lights candles, and as she moves through the passages, she find that her mother-in-law has locked most of the rooms. Her bedroom and Akbar's library are the only places left open to her upstairs. She goes to the library and lies on the floor with an atlas, tracing her finger gently along the Indian Ocean from South Africa to India. Under her breath she softly sings a song about lovers.

THE DJINN HANGS BEHIND HER in the shadows of the shelves, peering through the books and watching. It is feeling something new, something strange in its chest; the smokeless smoke inside is swirling, pushing against its rib cage, forcing its breath out, straining against its skin until it is unbearable. It feels something wet on its eyelashes and looks up. There is a fine mist in the air, settling on the shelves and books, causing droplets to form and cling to everything. The air feels full, heavy with possibility.

A fine rain begins to fall in the library, the scent of earth rises, and the djinn steps out of the shadows. Vines begin to climb the walls and cover the surfaces and small buds emerge on their branches as blossoms break open. The library seems to turn into a garden, and in the midst of all this lies Meena Begum on the carpet paging through the atlas, unaware.

The djinn looks around in wonder. It is beginning to understand what is happening; for the first time in its long and weary life, it is experiencing joy, and when joy erupts in the djinn, the world turns to rain; it pours into rooms and forms them into gardens.

To have her to itself had seemed impossible. Without all the others—the old woman and her maddening incense, the chatter of the servants, the noise of the children.

Without the incessant man.

The djinn holds out its hand to the rain and raises its face to the glass dome above. To be alone with her, listening to her voice fill the darkness, is all it has wanted from the moment it saw her on the beach. It turns to watch as she runs her finger over the pages in the book. As she sings, it closes its eyes.

The greenery deepens.

The rain is everywhere.

Twenty-Three

"How much brighter the stars shine in the sky when you know you are loved," reads Sana under her breath as she sits in the east wing among the objects.

"Why are you so interested in that dead woman's life?" her sister asks sulkily from a corner.

"Are you jealous?" Sana replies as she turns a page.

"Hardly," her sister scoffs. "Why would I be jealous of someone who fell in love with a man who forced her to marry him?"

"It wasn't like that," says Sana continuing to read.

"You're just a stupid romantic. You think love can fix everything. If I had been given my life on this earth, I would have made sure to break every heart I could. While you'll probably fall in love with the first person who pays you any attention and stay with them, even if they treat you badly. Bah! What a waste! I would never be as pitiful as you." Her sister picks up a jewelry box, studies it, then says, "I saw how you looked at that boy on the beach." She sets the box down. "As if he could save you."

"I know he can't," says Sana in a low voice.

Her sister smiles and turns to her happily. "Yes, he can't! No one can love you like I do. I'm glad you see it." Her sister flounces toward her and grabs her hand. "Does this mean we're friends again?"

"We've never been friends." Sana pulls away her hand.

"We were once, for a bit," her sister says sulkily. "When Mother was sick."

WHEN SANA THINKS BACK to her childhood, all she remembers is the lack of sound. Her memories run through her mind like the reel of a silent film; the sun shining in the fields as she combed her doll's hair, and the landscape moving with her as she ran toward the house; sitting in a bath of quickly cooling water waiting for her mother to appear; at the dinner table, glancing at her parents wondering why no one said anything.

Her parents had been quiet people; her mother merely murmured and her father only made any real noise when he whistled as he worked, although even that stopped eventually. Her sister too didn't say much those early days, just hovered in the shadows and sucked at her fingers, sulking.

At first she had found ways to compensate for the quietness. She would "accidentally" drop things, hammer things noisily, clang dishes in the kitchen, and scream, trying to drive some sound into the walls of their home. She would talk extra loudly to her parents and turn the volume on the radio up. When her father read the paper, she would climb into his lap and move his mouth with her fingers, making the sounds for the words she pretended he was saying.

But like dust, the silence resettled on everything, and eventually even Sana began to turn quiet, tiptoeing through the house and whispering when she needed to talk. Eventually sounds began to become so painful that her ears hurt if someone shut a door or window too loudly.

The Second Tragedy arrived quietly one Tuesday afternoon when a doctor in the hospital pulled out a chart and announced to Bilal Malek that a mass had been discovered in his wife's breast. They accepted the news as they did everything else: quietly and simply. Her mother seemed satisfied with the results, as if she had been expecting it. She refused treatment. She became sick quickly; indeed it was as if she embraced the news. She stopped walking and reading; she became still, waiting in her room for the curtain to fall.

Sana was eleven years old.

She had turned to her sister waiting in the shadows then. She sat with her in the field and braided little grass rings that they exchanged. She told her sister that she was worried. That she didn't know how to live in a world without their mother, even though she had hated her so much. Her sister said it was for the best, that their mother wasn't fit to be a mother, that if she couldn't raise her child properly then she deserved to die.

Just before the end, her mother suddenly began talking, as if she realized she had a voice. She started telling Sana stories, stories with no ends or beginnings, stories that made little sense, but always, always stories with little girls who picked grapes from other people's gardens. She spoke until she was hoarse, but still she continued long into the night. Some nights she would wail, terrifying screeches that rent the air and made the sheep shuffle in their pens. When Sana stopped listening, unable to bear the grating sound of her voice anymore, her mother would spend the night talking to Bilal. He would sit next to her and listen intently to everything she said. She told him about all the places she wanted to see and all the things she wanted to learn. It was her dearest wish to learn Mandarin, she said, so he bought her books and tapes, but she read them only for a few moments before tossing them to the floor. What she really wanted to do was taste mulberries, she said, the kind she ate from the side of the road on the way to madressah when she was a girl.

Every day she came up with new requests for her husband, who painstakingly tried to fulfill them. Why did he love her so much? she demanded to know, screaming so that Sana could hear it in her room. Why did he love like this? It was suffocating the way he tried to please her. It was pathetic, she said. He was a pathetic man. A real man would have discarded her a long time ago.

Later she cried and said she would kill herself if he ever thought of leaving. It was her fault they had lost the other baby, she said, it was her fault and she knew it. She began feverish talks that meandered into gibberish toward the end. Then, even her husband couldn't make sense of what she was saying anymore.

The last memory Sana has of her mother alive is her father lying with his head in her lap weeping and asking her to tell him what else to bring; he would bring it, he'd said. He would bring her everything if only she would stay.

And then there had been the funeral and it was just the two of them. And her sister.

"We weren't friends then," Sana says.

Her sister frowns. "Why do you always try to hurt me? All I've ever done is help you."

"*Help me?* You've never helped me," says Sana incredulously.

"Who was with you when Mother left you alone in the bath? Who was with you when she forgot to dress you, or clean you, or feed you? Who was with you when you were so sick you couldn't even get out of bed?" her sister demands. *"Who sat with you at Mother's funeral and held your hand?!"*

Sana puts down the diary. "Yes, you were *there*! You watched as I nearly froze to death in that bath. Watched as I nearly burned myself trying to cook, and yes, you watched when my fever ran so high I was delirious. But don't fool yourself, you didn't *help*. You *hoped* I would freeze, or burn my hands, or get sick and die; you were there, whispering every moment that it was my time to go. I remember! And please, you weren't there for me when Mother died. You were just pretending to be kind so I would come with you. I won't forget what you tried to do to me in the bath afterward," Sana whispers. "You're not stuck here and you're not my friend, you're just here because you can't bear that I am."

Her sister studies her for a moment, a muscle twitching in her cheek. Then she puts her hands together and begins to clap. "Bravo! Look at you. Standing up for yourself. My little sister, ladies and gentlemen!" she says, turning to the dark passage and bowing to the collected objects. "It seems living here is teaching you how to speak up." Her sister goes to her and chucks her under the chin. "Now you're making me proud." She looks at Sana's face in her hand. "Even if you are carrying that hideous chin of our mother's," she says disdainfully.

Sana shakes her head out her sister's grasp and turns away to pick up the diary from the floor. She puts it under her arm and leaves the passage.

"Wait for me, little sis," her sister calls as she hurries after her. "I'm coming too!"

Twenty-Four

Meena Begum misses the food of her village: the idli, uthappam, dosas, sambars, and especially the spicy meen kuzhambu. She begins to cook fiery, colorful curries for herself. Nothing Grand Ammi (who claims northern cuisine is superior) would have approved of. Meena Begum goes to the fresh market and buys baskets of aubergines and Indian flat beans, fistfuls of curry leaves, various dhals, blocks of sticky jaggery, shards of coconut, and packets of sharp flavors with tamarind, cardamom, peppercorns, and cumin. She grinds coconut and fries small bulbs of purple onions and beats urad dhal and cream of rice together.

She goes down to the lagoon and buys fresh fish from the fishermen. She kneels low on the rocks and inspects their baskets of freshly caught blacktails, shad, sardines, yellowfins, and rock crabs. She checks to see if their eyes are clear and their skin is firm. She bargains with the fishermen and soon they become friends. She squats along the shore with the tail of her sari trailing in the water as she watches the men thread hooks into bait. They tell her that chokka, a small squid, is the best bait for all kinds of fish, but sardines are decent enough too; rock worms are good for the big blacktails, and white mussels, although difficult to come by, are good for catching the evasive galjoens. They show her how to throw the reel out and wait for a bite, and then how to brace herself for the catch, how to lift the top of the rod out, and how to slowly lower it back as she reels the line in.

At the end of one such day, she makes her way up the hill with her pram and her basket of fish and vegetables. She cooks her dry fish dish of nethili varuval and her spicy aubergines in kathirikai podi varuval and eats them on Grand Ammi's finest china. She drinks her spicy masala mors in the Bohemian crystal goblets she finds packed away in the top cupboards.

Some mornings she visits the factory and afterward she walks around town with Hassan in his pram. She spends her afternoons in the dining room on the jula reading volumes of Akbar's favorite poetry. At night she writes in her diary in the attic and later, with Hassan sleeping in a basket, she makes her way down to the alcove with a lantern. There she strips off her clothes and wades in the sea. She sings songs from her village and throws jasmines into the water. The djinn sits nearby on the rocks listening.

The days pass into weeks and soon a month has gone.

As Meena Begum predicted, time passes quickly.

ONE AFTERNOON AS MEENA BEGUM sets Hassan down to sleep in his crib, she hears a racket in the garden. She goes outside and finds the monkeys screeching and running agitatedly around their cages. The birds too fly around, squawking as their brightly colored feathers flutter to the ground. She calls for Iqbal Babu, who had been there that day to see to the animals, but no one responds. He has always been particularly indignant toward her, sometimes even pretending not to hear when she addresses him. She wonders if he is doing that now. She searches through the gardens calling for him and then decides he must have left already.

She returns to the house and puts a record on the gramophone as she piles her loose hair up into a bun and pulls on an apron. One of Akbar's favorite songs, the ditty he would spin her to in the library, begins to play. She goes into the kitchen to cook the rock crabs she bought this morning. Soon Marion Harris's rich voice fills the house and drowns out the monkeys' chatter. Meena Begum removes the crustaceans from their dish and goes to work. First, she rinses off the excess sand under a running faucet and then begins to break open the main body, pulling out the mouth, the small stomach, and then the gills.

She hums along to the words coming in through the dining room.

> *It had to be you,*
> *It had to be you*
> *I wandered around, and finally found*
> *The somebody who*
> *Could make me be true*
> *Could make me be blue*
> *And even be glad*
> *Just to be sad*
> *Thinking of you*

She breaks off the main pincers and smaller legs and rinses them in a dish with salt. Then she grinds a piece of coconut, some garlic, and cashew nuts in a mortar. She cuts up the plump tomatoes she bought this morning from the wet market and adds them to chopped onion with curry leaves in a pot. In a separate dish she roasts chili powder, garam masala, cumin, turmeric, and fennel.

She does not notice the shadow that passes the window, entering the open courtyard.

THE DJINN WAITS A HUNDRED YEARS

She adds her ground ingredients and spices into the onion and tomato. She throws in the crab, swaying to the music. Then she lowers the heat and wipes her hands on her apron and goes upstairs to check on the baby.

She enters her room and finds him still sleeping. He has an amused expression on his face.

"You silly uruḷaikkiḻanku," she whispers affectionately. She puts a hand to his head and finds him sweating slightly. She adjusts his blankets and opens the window. The room fills with the scent of jasmine.

She pushes her door open and props it with a doorstop so that she can hear when he wakes up. She makes her way through the east wing back to the kitchen, when she pauses; it almost feels to her as if someone has brushed her cheek, said her name. She draws a hand to her face and holds it there. When she hears nothing else, she shakes her head at her foolishness and continues.

At the top of the stairs the music drifts up from below:

Some others I've seen
Might never be mean
Might never be cross, or try to be boss
But they wouldn't do

She takes the first step down but for some reason she hesitates. Something feels off. She hears a small noise, then something heavy bumping into something else. She slowly bends down to peer through the balusters.

She gasps.

For nobody else gave me a thrill
With all your faults, I love you still
It had to be you
Wonderful you
It had to be you

Part Three

One

16 *February 1932*

The house feels so empty without Akbar. I miss him so. I miss his poetry that shows me how words can make the world come alive.

But also . . . I am glad not to feel everyone's eyes on me anymore. I feel free. More like myself. It sometimes feels to me that the house seems more alive, almost as if it seems to be blooming along with me. Sometimes, I swear I can almost see the flowers move on the tapestry . . . but it must be my eyes playing tricks on me. Perhaps it just the feeling of being so free.

I hope it will be like this when I move to our new home. A place where Hassan can grow up knowing who he is and not what he is expected to be. A place where he is so free, he will feel like the house is a garden.

Sana reads the words slowly. She feels as if she knows Meena Begum now, as if they are friends just separated by time, like two people in different time zones. She feels the love that Meena Begum has for Akbar and it makes her feel whole somehow. It is not the silent fraught kind between her parents, or the kind Zuleikha tells her about that is like a car wreck. Nor is it like the love that Pinky says is only for the movies, or the fracturing sort that brought together Razia Bibi and Fancy's children only to separate them. It is perhaps something like what Doctor talks about when he tells stories of his wife or when Oom Piet remembered for Tant Elsie. Still she knows that none of these stories she collects, these scattered little fragments that shimmer and reflect, could ever show her the whole truth—the enormity of what love can be.

But here in these pages of this woman's story, love is spread open to her, laid bare, generously shared, and it is like she has finally found the shape she has been searching for. She slips into the diaries, and among the words she is no longer a broken thing.

She falls asleep at night, holding the diaries close to her, dreaming of the house blooming like a garden.

Two

Ya Fathah.
The One who opens solutions and removes obstacles.
There are 99 names of God. He is the Merciful,
 the Compassionate, the Wise but this, this one is my
 favorite, jaan. For God is the opener of everything. He
 makes any way possible for anyone who asks.
Ya Fathah.

In the darkness, these are the words she holds on to. The only sound that makes sense.

There are sirens going off somewhere in the distance. A great cacophony of bells that ring incessantly. She tries to open her eyes but they feel stuck together and the darkness remains. There is a sticky wetness beneath her legs. She continues the zikr furiously.

Ya Fathah. Ya Fathah. Ya Fathah.

Then gradually, after what seems like an eternity, her breath slows and she begins to become aware of her surroundings. She manages to crack open her eyes and the world enters in painful bits and pieces. She looks around in the semidarkness—she is in the attic, on the floor. She tries to pick herself up but the world tilts too much, so she remains low, wondering how she has ended up here.

The noise in the background begins to emerge more clearly and she finally understands what it is: the baby is crying. She lifts her head slightly and looks over her shoulder.

Hassan sits next to her on the floor. His face is red and streaked with tears as he howls and kicks.

Then she notices the blood.

She runs her palm through the dark puddle on the floor and looks back at her wet hands in disbelief. Still unsure of what is happening but consumed with the innate instinct of motherhood she shakily sits up and pulls the wailing child to her and holds him to her chest until he calms down in wild hiccupping coughs. She looks around fearfully, unable to make sense of anything.

She rocks the child.

She tries to remember what happened and eventually it comes to her in jagged pieces.

THERE WAS SOMETHING BIG and heavy moving in the hall.

She crouched on the stairs and broke into a sweat. She clutched the carved baluster and steadied herself.

It could not be.

The record in the dining room ended and the scratch of the needle in the run-out groove suddenly filled the air with an ominous drone. Meena Begum held her breath and tried to stand up as quietly as possible but the stair below her gave the smallest of creaks and the giant face swiveled in her direction.

She turned and ran.

Everything was a blur after this. She was leaping through the passages. A pounding in her chest, a *thud thud thud* that filled the air. She couldn't breathe. The awareness that there was something heavy bounding up the stairs after her. Her mind racing. Where to go? There were only two unlocked rooms. The library was nearest, but her bedroom was open and her child was in there. *Where to go?* She made up her mind and raced toward the east wing. She heard things topple behind her. A sudden turn right into the open doorway. The crib ahead. The child now in her arms. One foot was already on the ladder when she heard a crash behind her as something skidded into the room and smashed into the dressing mirror. She was climbing. She was almost away. Then a sharp hot blinding pain as something sank into her ankle and tugged her off the swaying ladder.

She held on. Held tight.

Gritted her teeth. Struggled until she was free.

She scrambled higher. Flung the child in. Pulled herself up.

The teetering ladder fell backward onto the ground as she hit the attic floor and everything turned black.

Three

If Jahanara Begum has any remorse, it does not show.

On the ship she paints her eyelids peacock blue, pins her curls into cascading spirals, dons her most luxurious silk dresses, and entertains the other passengers with her renditions of Gene Austin's "Carolina Moon" and Wayne King's "Good-Night, Sweetheart."

A crowd gathers around her each evening to hear her sweet voice lift up into the night air. In the evenings in the dance hall, she looks like a film star with her coiffed hair, feathered headbands, heavy eyelashes, and crimson lips. She laughs with the other passengers and entertains them with her stories about life in Africa. How she does it, even she doesn't know, she says. Akbar is dutiful, taking her on his arm when she asks to dance and listening politely when she begins a story for a crowd. She tells him that she worries for her father, of course, but it doesn't mean she needs to be miserable. He wouldn't want that, she says.

She entreats him to attend social events on the ship, where she encourages him to wear the Western suits she has packed. She curates conversations with guests and sets up points for Akbar to nod or interject, and he, knowing the expected role, turns morose, quiet, and then aloof. He longs for his cotton kurtas, he misses his factory and the rolling green hills of Natal. It is strange to him that even while traveling he can feel the same restlessness as before. Sometimes he leaves his cabin at night and stands at the rails, smoking his pipe as he looks out at the dark sea. He thinks of the young man who thirsted for adventure, who traveled across the oceans, playing cards beneath the decks, collecting daggers and animal skins, and he wonders how life can change so quickly. He remains there until early morning when the dew gathers on his clothes and he can see dolphins leaping in the distance against a pink sky.

Jahanara Begum remains oblivious to her husband's state of mind. She is elated that her plan has worked and is overcome with the thrill of a new setting, one where she is not relegated to inferior madam or wife. In her new company, with social activities and the attention of so many, she barely notices how quiet Akbar has become. In her delusional elation she mistakes Akbar's distance for introspection, and toward the end of the journey she decides that once he returns to her, she might *think* about showing some mercy.

And then Africa will be a horrible memory that they can put behind them.

A FEW DAYS LATER the cargo liner docks in the bustling Port of Bombay.

Grand Ammi wraps her silver dupatta around her head and gathers her grandchildren around. It is time for them to return home, she says. Jahanara Begum powders her nose and rearranges her curls as she takes Akbar's arm and they disembark.

Akbar walks down the gangplank with his family and enters the busy crowd carrying bales of cotton, sacks of rice, and crates of tea, as cargo ships are packed for their journeys to England. He is upset to find he feels a sense of trepidation as he places his foot down on the land of his forefathers.

He turns to look back at the water, shading his eyes from what feels like more than the sun.

Four

In her bed at night, Sana turns the pages of the diary. She finishes a passage and reaches for a pencil.
In the light of her lamp, she underlines it:

6 December 1930

"Did we really meet in the heavens before?" I asked Akbar today. "Of course," he said. "And that is why we recognized each other on earth." "How come I didn't recognize you at first?" I asked.

"Because you had closed your heart to the Signs," he said.

Five

Meena Begum lies in the attic in a feverish haze.

Her right leg bleeds profusely; there is a ragged gash at the bottom of her calf. She clenches her teeth and drags herself away from the garret opening to a dresser where she finds a number of rags to wrap tightly around the wound. She winds each layer of cloth around her leg, stopping every few minutes to take a deep breath. She knows it will not hold, and she searches through the drawers, praying for a needle and thread, but finds nothing. After resting for a moment, she pulls herself back to the ledge overlooking the bedroom. At the bottom she sees a dark pacing shadow.

EARLIER THAT AFTERNOON, the lion had awakened to find the cage door open with no sign of the dreaded human with the whip in his hand. For years it had been at the mercy of the sharp leather that fell against its flanks. It associated humans with a hot pain that cut through its body. It left the cage and began to wander through the garden, first cautiously and then with a certain prowess, indulging in the power of its freedom. It heard a melody coming from the house and it followed the noise in through the open courtyard doors.

Meena Begum was the first human it saw in its newly emancipated state. Unwilling to relinquish its unexpected freedom, it gave into its first instinct and attacked.

MEENA BEGUM PUSHES the ceiling cover over the opening and limps to the dormer window. She throws it open, thrusts her head out, and shouts as loud as she can for help. But it is futile; the hill is too high and the garret window is located on a steep roof between a dome and a turret. The only living things that hear her are the seagulls that swoop around the roof with their own incessant cries. Still, she stands for a long time screaming out the window and banging her fists on the tiles of the slanted roof.

The baby begins to cry.

Meena Begum is at a loss at what to do. Even without the beast below it is impossible to get down without the ladder. She hushes the child to sleep and tries to think clearly. For a moment she wonders how the creature entered the house, but the pain in her leg drives her to focus on the priority of escaping. She knows she is losing too much blood. It stains everything: the floorboards, the window, even the child is covered in crimson. She feeds Hassan from her breast and sings him songs. He has calmed down and seems unperturbed by the change of environment, curiously crawling around the attic to inspect boxes.

Meanwhile, Meena Begum changes her blood-soaked rags with trembling hands. She limps to the writing table and climbs on. She is overcome by a great thirst. She looks out the dormer window at a tiny patch of sea visible through the glass.

Her face is pale against the moonlight.

Through all this the djinn has been sick with fear.

When the family left and the incense stopped burning, the djinn was free to wander the house as far and deep as it pleased. It carried the rain everywhere; rooms pooled and flooded, flowers crept up walls, and the air carried a deep whispering green. The djinn followed Meena Begum wherever she went; it watched her scrub and beat the laundry and hang it to dry, it watched her buy vegetables and talk to the fishermen about their lives. It squatted beside her as she scaled fish in the courtyard and listened as she read poetry in the library and sang songs at the sea. It did not care much for the man's child but it could bear its existence for her.

Earlier that afternoon, while Meena Begum was cooking in the kitchen, it had been swaying gently in the dining room with its eyes closed, listening to her voice over the music as she busied herself with pots. The rain falling around it stopped unexpectedly and it opened its eyes. It saw the shadow crouching in the courtyard.

Immediately it fled to Meena Begum and tried to warn her. It wailed next to her and pulled at her apron and knocked over the cellar of salt but she did not notice. It grabbed her and shook her by the shoulders but she continued with her cooking, too absorbed to notice the small flutters around her.

When Meena Begum left to go upstairs to check on the baby, the djinn wailed in frustration. Then it went to the dining room and waited. When the animal stepped over the threshold and entered the house, the djinn approached it and hissed. It whispered in its tongue for the animal to leave, to be gone, to get far from this house.

But the lion was not of the animals the djinn had known when it walked the earth. The world was newer now and animals had forgotten the language of djinns; they had lost their wildness, had changed too much to know the world as they once did. The lion ignored the djinn, slunk its shoulders down, and prowled through the house toward the source of the sound.

The djinn went to the woman returning downstairs. It tried one last time to warn her; it begged her to listen, and for a moment, she paused, as if she had heard. But then she continued on her way and there was nothing to be done but watch the terror unfold.

Now the djinn watches Meena Begum change her bloody rags and hold the baby close in her shaking hands. It sways to the songs she sings to the child in her broken voice. When she tells stories, it leans in close and listens, waiting to hear what will happen next.

When she cries, it creeps close, rubs its face against hers. It tries to take her hands in its own.

By late evening Meena Begum is very weak. She is pale and feverish and murmurs incomprehensibly to herself. Occasionally her thoughts are jumbled and she cannot remember where she is.

She knows she has little time to act.

She climbs onto the desk, pushes herself out the window, and crawls out between the gap onto the gable. A cool breeze ruffles her sari. The sky is watchful. She steps out onto the roof tiles with her bare feet. She clutches the drainpipe and inches along the gable as she searches for the jutting edge of tiles to grab on to.

The djinn at the window watches, gnawing at its fingers.

As she searches in the dark for a new tile to grab, her right foot, slippery with blood, suddenly gives way and she begins to slide jaggedly down to the edge of the roof's overhang.

Meena Begum screams and the whole world rushes past as she slips; the sky, the stars, and the sea run alongside her. As she slides, she grabs wildly in the air, but her hands find nothing. She sees the end approach quickly, makes one final attempt at scrabbling for something to hold on to, and her hands finally catch the edge of a tile. She grasps it tightly, despite it cutting into her hand, and is jerked back as the world stops falling. She clings. Her breath is ragged. She takes a deep breath and stays like this until she has enough energy to pull herself up. Then she climbs, holding on to the tiles.

The djinn climbs next to her on the roof, whispering words of encouragement.

Shaking with exhaustion, she reaches the garret window and falls back inside. She picks up her pen and writes weakly on a page in her diary, in faint scratches. Then she lies back on the armchair, pale and trembling like a leaf.

In her feverish and weak state, with her soul hovering between this world and the next, she picks up the sleeping bundle.

She bends her head low and begins to whisper in Tamil.

She tells the baby about where she grew up and the river than ran through her village. She tells him about the fish, how they moved fatly in her hands. About the white Memsaab and her red lips and rough hands that shook her awake from her dreams on that big soft bed. How her shoes were left behind. She tells the baby that her mother washed clothes in the river, and that one day there had been a green snake, as green as the skin of an unripe mango, that skimmed through the water, and Amma had screamed and Raju Uncle from the house down the road had killed it with an ax and burned its body so that no other snakes would return seeking revenge.

She tells him about the monsoon rains in her village, the way the skies grew dark and heavy and how the clouds were like cotton balls dripping water. She tells him about the way the earth turned to mud and the children ran out to play despite their mothers' angry shouts. She tells him that when it rained, even though the houses became wet inside and the river rose high enough to wash away small goats, the rains were the best thing about her childhood.

But mainly she tells it about the river, the way the light shimmered on its surface like glass. She says that the day she was born her mother had felt pains at the river, and before the midwife could arrive her mother had given birth to her at the banks with the other women raising their dupattas to shield her. They said she swam out of her mother like a fish. They named her Meena for the precious blue stone that resembled the eyes of the katla fish. She tells the baby about the boat she built out of sticks and palm leaves to take her to Delhi and how she had traveled for nearly an hour before it sank and she had to swim to shore. She tells him about how the women and she bathed early in the morning and the way they ran away laughing, wringing their hair and slipping on clothes when someone came to warn them that the men were on the way for their baths.

The end always returns to the beginning; the circle always seeks to be whole, and so when the end comes for Meena Begum, she is remembering the river and the way it runs through the village like a person, like a friend with a laughing face and open arms. She can hear the sound of rain and the way it fills the river like a drumbeat as it carries away twenty-one grams of soul.

The djinn beside her weeps with empty eyes.

It is the indomitable reign of Grand Ammi extending from over the sea that uncovers the fate of Meena Begum.

Pappu follows his order strictly. He watches Meena Begum, makes any excuse to return to the house, and has already informed Grand Ammi by telegram that he has seen Meena Begum using the Bohemian crystal, the fine china, *and* the Dutch tablecloths. What's more, he says, she is spending a lot of time with the fishermen at the rocks.

At a tearoom in town the next day it is Pappu who hears a drunken fisherman talking about seeing a big cat walking along the shore at dawn. He laughs with everyone else when they tease the raving man for having a toddy too much the night before.

He sips his masala chai and wraps his leftover samosas in a greasy twist of newspaper. But a nagging feeling overcomes him that he can't quite shake. He finishes his tea quickly and climbs up the hill. Slightly out of breath, he knocks at the front door, and when no one answers he goes around the back and finds the courtyard doors open. The wind has blown in leaves, which now scatter around the kitchen, which is filled with the smell of burned crabs. He follows the sound of ticking to the dining room and pulls the needle off the gramophone's record. He goes upstairs calling out for the new madam and finally enters her room. He surveys the broken mirror, then props up a fallen ladder and climbs into the attic.

He finds Meena Begum sitting on the armchair. Her skin is pale and her eyes are closed. In her stiff arms she holds a wrapped blanket.

Inside it, something moves.

Six

A,

Do not mourn me for I am with you always.

Seven

The opening of the attic has unhinged the djinn.

The girl has stirred up too much from the past and now it is restless, full of longing and ache.

Its world is already so unsteady—everything has been crumbling for so many years. Even so, it found a way to exist, to keep from breaking completely: If it stays still in small dark places and keeps quiet, the grief can be contained, its great sadness can be reined.

Still there are times when the heaviness becomes too much, and then it roams the house searching for her, searching for the sound of her voice. It wanders into the passages, opening trunks and throwing aside objects. It looks into cups and under floorboards. It runs its fingers over the wallpaper feeling for sound bubbling below the surface.

In its deepest grief the house begins to fall apart; the rafters tremble, the walls begin to crack. Blood runs from the ceiling, dripping through the floorboards and filling the passages until everything is swimming in red. There are screams in its ears that it cannot block out and a taste of metal at the back of its throat. It can see Meena Begum at her end, dying that painful death. It can see its futile attempts to save her. Useless fool it had been! It closes it eyes as the house around collapses; beams fall, windows explode with blood, doors burst open carrying rivers of gore, and walls melt to reveal bare bones.

In such fits of great despair it begins to change shape. It turns into the loss itself, into the form of what has gone. The transformation is exhausting, and for months after it carries remnants of the change; her nails adorn its fingers, her shoulders push through its body, and even when it returns to itself, it cannot shake the limp of her mangled leg.

When it is in its most intense state of change, when it can no longer control what is happening, its form abruptly materializes in the world of men once more and it can briefly be seen by humans. Once, the previous year, when the djinn had been feeling particularly distraught about the dead woman, it climbed out from its wardrobe to escape the heaviness. It stumbled through the house searching for her voice, unaware that in its deep despair it was shifting between shapes, caught in her form, until it heard a bloodcurdling scream and in terror it turned to find one of the old women at the bottom of the stairs, pointing.

It fled.

Now when it wanders the house it tries to stick to the shadows, lingers in the corners, confines its sorrow to quiet places like the pockets of old suits.

ONE AFTERNOON in the secret room in the reflection of the dressing table's mirror, Sana looks up to find her sister on the bed watching her.

"What are you doing here? I thought you didn't like it here," says Sana, closing the lipstick she is examining.

"I don't," says her sister, rubbing her arms and looking around. "But everyone is here and I didn't want to be alone."

"Everyone?" Sana raises an eyebrow and looks around.

Her sister turns to look at the djinn who looks at her morosely then limps away.

"Yes."

IT IS WHILE THE DJINN is full of sorrow one day, confined to the corner of the study, wearing the dead woman's hands that it cannot seem to shake off, that it finally meets the sister. It has sensed for a long time her uneasy presence in the house but it has ignored it the way it always ignores the presences of other things unrelated to its grief.

It snarls and hisses when it feels her close but is too consumed to react.

She bends down over it, crouched in the shadows. It hides the dead woman's hands from her, tucks them under its feet. Turns away. It shakes, fighting complete transformation. Its eyelashes deepen.

"What is happening to you, O Djinn? Why, you are almost human," the sister says. "I have never seen such a thing."

The djinn snarls and she steps backward. She observes the rippling skin and contorting body.

"Is this the grief?"

The djinn turns away.

"I know what you feel, O Djinn."

Despite its state, the djinn turns to look at her. Its fish eyes shiver.

"I too am forgotten. I too walk this place in misery. Yet what is our sin? To love?"

The djinn turns to her and listens. It stops shaking.

"Why are you choosing to exist like this? You have a choice to leave. You can find your kind. You can walk the world again. You are not trapped here like me."

The djinn shakes its head. It is trapped. Her voice is somewhere here. It must find it. It has searched the courtyard and the rooms; it has searched between the books and behind the curtains. It has grown tired but it will not leave until it is found.

"You are being foolish," she says, shaking her head.

The djinn snarls, snaps its teeth.

"There is nothing here," the sister says, backing away. "You are searching for something you will never find."

The djinn hisses. Tugs restlessly at the dead woman's hair on its head.

"I'm the only one here," says Sana as she straightens the objects on the dressing table.

"Oh dear, you're so stupid sometimes," her sister says as she walks around the room. "You can't possibly think such old places are empty? Something always gets left behind." She picks up a gilded frame that holds a photo of Akbar and Meena Begum.

"Put that down," says Sana quietly.

"I knew you were morbid, but don't you think this is all a bit much?" her sister says, ignoring her and gesturing at the room. "Always cleaning this woman's room, reading her diaries, trying on her things." She saunters over to the dressing table, studying the photo in her hands. She puts the frame down on the table. "I worry about you, little sister. Surely this can't be healthy." A smile plays on her face. "The last thing we need is you going *crazy*." She begins to pace the room again. "You know what I think? I think you're trying to replace our mother with this woman. I think you're *trying to find a new mother*."

Sana turns from her. "Get out."

"You shouldn't try to replace our mother. It would hurt her feelings," her sister continues. "She did have feelings, you know. She saw me for a moment before she left this world. You should have seen her face—she was horrified. She never knew I was always there." She comes close to Sana and lowers herself to her ear and whispers, "Do you know what she said to me just before she left?"

When Sana does not reply, she continues. "'Come with me.' That's what she said. She wanted *me* to come with her. She finally saw the daughter she should have had and she knew in an instant I was the one who was supposed to be with her. Oh Sana, imagine, we hated her so much but she didn't hate us—turns out she just hated *you*."

Sana looks down at the dressing table and replies, "You change what she says every time so why should I believe you now?"

Her sister looks at her with a hurt expression. "Because this time I'm telling the truth."

"When have you cared about Mother or her feelings?" Sana retorts.

"I know what it's like to be forgotten, to be replaced." Her sister picks up the gold tube of lipstick and ignores Sana's plea to leave it alone. She twists the cylinder and smashes the red pigment to her mouth; it stands out garishly on her pale skin, like a slash in her face. She puts her lips together and smacks. "We would do this when we were little, do you remember? Steal into Mother's room and try on her makeup? I always looked better than you."

Sana shakes her head. "I don't remember. Go away."

"You can't make me do anything."

"You're *dead*."

"Not quite." Her sister turns to the djinn and says conversationally, "She doesn't understand anything. She thinks things can only be alive or dead and that there's nothing in between. She's always been simple-minded. I don't know how *she* got a life to live and I didn't."

The djinn doesn't respond but climbs into the cradle and peers out from within. It searches beneath the covers, runs its fingers down the sides.

"Who are you talking to?" asks Sana.

Her sister turns to her. "I told you—there's something here from before. It knew your beloved woman as well. It even slept beside her. It says that she sang songs to the baby in that cradle. It says her voice was like the sound of a thousand stars singing."

Sana moves closer to her sister and looks around warily.

"You're lying," she says uncertainly.

Her sister shrugs.

After a moment, Sana asks quietly, "What else—what else does it say?"

Her sister looks at her and smiles.

"It says you should leave this room."

Sana looks around and sees nothing. "Why?" she asks.

"It says you don't want to know the ending of this story."

Sana reaches the last entry in the diary; she finds nothing but a rust-stained farewell to Akbar. She turns the rest of the pages urgently, but they are blank. She returns to the attic and opens boxes, searches folders, and skims books, trying to find some clue as to what happened. She empties drawers, scatters papers, and furiously digs through trunks.

She feels deserted.

The woman she has been getting to know, someone who has become a *friend*, someone who opened her life to her, is gone. What happened to the couple who were one shape, not two? The pair who said that only God could part them?

She sits in bed at night, twisting her sheets until finally she sees the shadow of her sister appear at the bay window. She hurries to her, grabs her by her shoulders, and shakes her.

"You must ask it! Ask the thing in the room what happened! Please," she begs.

Her sister pulls away. "*Now* you want favors? After you've pushed me away, year upon year? I told you—you only want me when you need something. You *selfish* little girl," her sister spits. She turns her back to Sana.

"Please. Please, *sister*," pleads Sana.

Her sister turns; a smirk cuts her face in the moonlight.

"I can't tell you." Her sister turns to the shadow of the djinn in the corner of the room, then continues. "It won't say what happened. It refuses to talk about it."

The djinn moans and slips into Sana's cupboard. It pulls the door shut behind it. It regrets revealing the room in the roof. It regrets the pain it has invited by exposing itself to the mouth of the monster. It has not found the peace it hoped to. Its limbs burn all the time now; hair pours from its skull, its face shivers and shudders, caught between two forms.

Her sister moves close to her and says in a low voice, "Everyone abandons you. Even the dead woman didn't care enough to finish her story to you. I'm the *only* one who cares. I'm the only one who has been there for you. Can't you see that?"

Sana pushes at her sister. "Go away," she says halfheartedly as she stumbles toward her bed.

Sana feels as if she has lost something important. Meena Begum was the whole she aspired to. She was supposed to be the missing piece to something she had lost. And now, unexpectedly, when she finally opened her heart to something, to someone, she has been abandoned. Again.

Her sister is right.

The loss of everything is too much.

Her ends feel sharp enough to cut.

She puts her hands to her face and sobs. When her sister approaches her, she lifts her head angrily.

"Don't," she says.

SANA SHUTS UP the secret room.

She avoids the passage in the east wing. She stops asking questions. Everyone is right, she thinks—it is better to mind your own business. It is better not to seek answers.

It is better to be quiet.

Months pass and she begins to do what they all do: forget. She throws out the lipstick, discards the poems, and packs away the diaries at the back of her cupboard. She stops going to the sea. She feels more alone that she has ever felt. It grows in her like a long shadow.

Her sister says less, watches more, waits for her to unravel on her own.

Sana learns to be silent again; the words collect in her mouth; they hesitate before the threshold; they look this way and that before crossing the street. She barely acknowledges the compliments Razia Bibi gives her nearly round rotis. She withdraws, gathering her edges to herself. There are no great secrets. The world is not going to change. Everything is painful if you allow yourself to feel.

She reels her words back in. They thrash, small and silver, beating themselves against the floor until they lay limp.

The light at the eaves flutters and dies down.

And the house, satisfied that it has finally managed to tame the wily newcomer, groans in satisfaction and eases its aching limbs.

Eight

To celebrate one year living at Akbar Manzil, Bilal Malek has a tea party.

He bakes a giant fruitcake, Fancy brings cupcakes with sunken centers and Pinky provides two cans of beans. Even Razia Bibi begrudgingly provides samosas, placing them away from the rest of the food as if to avoid contamination.

They crowd in Zuleikha's circular room, drink tea, and eat slices of cake on paper plates.

It is Doctor who has convinced Zuleikha to let them have it here. He wants to hear her play the piano, he says. He knows it is a request she cannot refuse because she never refuses him and so he never asks for anything. Until now.

She sits miserably at her bench, tapping one knee restlessly.

"I only came because I wanted to see what her place looks like," whispers Razia Bibi to Sana. "I heard so many things, that she has a huge walk-in closet *and* a balcony with a jacuzzi. But hmph! Nothing to see here," she says, crossing her arms.

Sana does not respond and Razia Bibi tuts.

"You still have nothing to say?"

Although none of them have said anything they have all noticed the change in the girl. She does not visit them. She has stopped asking questions. She can no longer be found poking around in the passages or in the garden. She does not appear anymore with her notebook, her questions about love. She goes straight to her room, seemingly no longer interested in anything.

She is lacking something but they do not know what.

Fancy brings her freshly cut roses from the garden. Pinky lends her a copy of *Dil To Pagal Hai*. Razia Bibi lies and says her cooking is improving. But she does not notice, barely acknowledges them. Something is happening inside her.

Something is closing.

So today for the sake of the child they are not as hard with one another. Razia Bibi only insults Bilal's cake once. Pinky tries to make conversation, asking the others about the weather. Bilal compliments Zuleikha on her Gothic décor, which she responds to with a long hard glare, and he hurries off to talk to Pinky about the weather.

They all move awkwardly around one another with half-eaten cupcakes and almost sigh in relief when Doctor announces that it's time for the main event.

Zuleikha groans and turns to her piano.

"Only because it's you, Doctor," she says through gritted teeth.

"I know," says Doctor pleasantly.

Zuleikha begins a small, slow piece and Razia Bibi yawns pointedly. Pinky examines the inside of a cupcake. At first, the notes seem stilted, as if lazy and unsure how to move; they plod along, almost reluctantly. Then Zuleikha's fingers begin to dance over the piano keys, picking up pace. It is as if the music has seen something in the distance and is jogging toward it with a hand outreached. The notes fall faster like they are racing across a field toward a break in some fence. They run and run and the music leaps off the keys into the air, where it spreads open like a bird in flight.

It hovers.

Sana looks up.

Inside her, something flutters.

Zuleikha plays the music and the world outside becomes nothing. Perhaps it is the unexpected letter from across the sea, perhaps it is the girl and the way her light has gone out so quickly, or perhaps it is a growing desperation that has been building in her, but Zuleikha plays with wild abandon, the pieces of her heart the score to which she composes. The edge is approaching; she can see it, she circles the lip, she can hear the roar of water, feel the spray on her face. A pounding fills her head and then she is over, she is falling, where the world has no memory, no pain, and nothing has to make sense.

Fancy sighs in her handkerchief. "Isn't it beautiful?" she murmurs. "I've never heard her play like this before."

Pinky next to her, nods. "Pinky has never heard such a thing."

RAZIA BIBI CLUTCHES the arms of her chair, feeling as if she is being pulled by something. She resists, distracts herself with inspecting the ragged drapes, the view of the ocean beyond. But the music calls to her, a note so tender sweeping her off her feet, and before she can gather herself, she is blinking her eyes in the blinding light of the hospital. She looks down and she is carrying her tiny son. She is exhausted. She is *so* tired of it all, of marriage, of men, of hopes and dreams, but here in her arms is proof that life can still surprise you.

BILAL SITS QUIETLY on the edge of the bed. In his palm is the small, slim hand of his wife. She smells like the outside, like the wind and the grass. Sweethearts pepper her hem.

The music rises.

In Sana's chest, a small box rattles.

The music grows, swelling with each note, filling them up with everything lost until it suddenly stops and waits—as if breathing, as if holding on to something. Then suddenly it lets go and they all crash to the floor as if they have been thrown from a great height. They hold their heads, dazed.

Zuleikha drops her hands. Her heart hammers in her chest.

Everyone is silent.

It is Pinky who raises her small hands together and begins to clap first.

THE PARTY ENDS QUICKLY after that, everyone finding excuses to leave, to escape the histories that have suddenly risen to fill the room. After, Bilal dispatches Sana to take leftover cake to everyone in the house. She is carrying a plate to Fancy when she passes the east wing and hears a faint rustle in its depths. Despite herself, she stops and turns to look down the passage. When she hears nothing more, she moves to leave, but then a distant creak breaks the silence. She peers through the clutter and makes out a faint light at the end of the hall.

She puts the plate down on a dresser and enters the passage, making her way to the end, where she can see a light under the door.

She turns the handle and enters.

A FIGURE IS SITTING on the bed.

Sana goes forward hesitantly. As she approaches, she recognizes Doctor. He is looking down at something in his hands, and as Sana nears, she sees it is a paper flower in his palm.

He looks up as she comes in and breaks into a gentle smile.

"Ah . . . so it *was* you," he says as she enters the room. "I wondered who it could be. Who could have opened this room that has not been opened in so long, and then I thought to myself, only Sana could have done this. I searched for months when I came here, you know. Looked in every place I thought the key could be. Eventually I gave up; I took it as a sign that it was never meant to be opened again. And to be honest, I think I was glad," he says. "Whenever I passed this wing, I always stopped and wondered." He pauses. "I've been thinking more and more about this room. Then today, after Zuleikha played that piece, I couldn't help myself and I came here. And lo and behold, I found that things were cleared from outside, the room was unlocked and cleaned. I almost thought I was dreaming."

He looks down at his hands and says, "She used to make these, you know. She was very good at it. She even made one for me but I never accepted it." He sighs and looks around. Then he places a hand on the cradle. "The baby was beautiful. A boy with curly hair. He hardly ever cried."

Sana's heart beats hard in her chest. She holds on to the doorknob briefly, then comes forward.

"You knew him?"

Doctor looks around the room and a spasm runs through his face.

Sana moves closer.

"I thought I forgot . . . I thought it was all forgotten. But—" and suddenly he seems to laugh. "What is *really* forgotten, tell me?" His voice goes low. "Now it's open. You've opened it and I'm sitting here—and it's too much. I remember too much of what I thought I had forgotten." Doctor looks up. "I grew up in this house. I haven't told anyone that. My grandmother used to call me 'Laddoo' and pull my cheeks until they hurt." He smiles and puts a hand to his cheek absentmindedly.

Sana steadies herself, feeling as if she might fall.

"I know it's hard to believe but this house was grand once. Abba came from India as a businessman and built it. He was a wealthy man with some crazy ideas, but he was a good father. We had more than enough servants, more than enough rooms, and a garden full of exotic creatures. It was an exciting place for a boy to grow up in. I played all sorts of games here; I knew every hiding place and *many* secrets. It's how I knew my parents were not happy together." He pauses. "One—one day my father came home and said he was getting married again. My mother was angry. It was a hard time for everyone. But you know, looking back . . . I'd never seen my father happier. We didn't see that then. We only saw darkness and misery at the time. The other woman—she was a worker in the factory—she moved here to this house. This room actually." He waves a hand in the air. Then he points to the cot. "Their baby slept there." He stops suddenly then. Puts a hand to his mouth. Too afraid to go on, and Sana is too afraid to ask.

After a moment, he takes a breath then continues.

"You must understand—my family were not happy about the baby. My mother became sick and my sister convinced me that our stepmother was a witch and that my half brother was a devil. So . . . I hated them both. I tell myself . . . most days I tell myself I was too small to remember, but I remember. We were not good children. We did things that were wrong. Even at that age I knew. People say I didn't. But I knew. But . . . there was worse to come." He pushes his fist to his mouth, unable to continue, looking fearfully into the crib. Finally, after taking a breath and closing his eyes, he continues. "I saw her, you know. I saw her talking to that bad man in the stables. I was hiding behind the water trough. I thought it was a game. I thought she had come looking for me, so I kept still. But she wasn't looking for me. She was looking for someone else." His voice turns bitter. "She didn't know I was there and she called for that man, and when he came she went close to him and she spoke to him and," here he begins to whisper, "*I heard what she told him.* And I didn't tell anyone.

"Even when we came back and she swore"—his voice starts to build again—"she swore to everyone on her father's life that she had nothing to do with it, I knew."

Doctor raises his voice, startling the house, sending the bats fluttering. "*I knew!*" he wept.

Nine

The sound of rumbling breaks through the sky and Akbar wakes up suddenly from a nap. He is drenched in sweat.

"It's just thunder," says Jahanara Begum nearby.

He nods and sits up. Then he walks to the windows and looks through the jali at the rain falling outside.

The journey is not going exactly according to Jahanara Begum's plans. When they first arrived in their village and heard the news of her father's "miraculous" recovery, Akbar immediately started talk of their return. It took persuading by both her family and his to convince Akbar to stay longer.

"We haven't seen our family in so long, beta," Grand Ammi complains. "The children must learn about their heritage. Rivayat is very important in this family—they must know where they come from."

Akbar agrees with that. He wants his children to see that this too is their life. He wants them to respect their culture and take pride in it. He takes them to his family's farms in the village, to the mud huts of workers, and makes them eat dhal chawal with them. He takes them through the dusty streets filled with cattle and people and tells them not to forget that this too is home. That the tastes and the smells and the sounds are in their blood. He takes them for long walks through the open lands, passing buffaloes and cows and shrines with small stones that mark the place where great saints are buried.

He tells them to look for the Signs and to follow them to the ends of the earth.

In a stream near a paddy field one morning, he bathes with his young son and points out to him the slippery dark body of a carp. He catches it between his fingers, where it struggles wildly before shooting out of his hands. His son lets out a rare laugh when the fish slips out, swimming through the field like an eel.

The boy has been quieter than usual since he arrived in India and he eats less. His worried grandmother tries to feed him mixtures of turmeric and ginger to flush out any sickness. She says it is the evil eye of relatives, and she prepares him a taweez wrapped in black cloth for protection. She keeps putting a palm to his forehead to check his temperature but he pushes her insistent hands away.

Soraya Bibi in the meantime has already established herself as the leader of her village cousins, and she relishes in having a group of young people to command and torment. She makes them plait her hair into pigtails, orders them to drop carnations wherever she walks, and has them pretend that she is Princess Soraya of Gujarat who has finally returned home from her journey around the world.

Akbar wanders the streets of his childhood and remembers his past. He walks through the loud and bustling markets with his son on his shoulders. He recalls running through these lanes as a young boy, with the world sweeping by as he passed stalls of watermelons and mangoes, baskets of turmeric and green chilies, and rolls of jute and cotton, leaping away from his laughing cousins as they chased after him, their fingers outstretched behind.

Jahanara Begum spends her days being fussed over by her family. She tells everyone about how exciting Africa is, about her mansion by the sea and her servants who are at her beck and call. She lies across cushions in her ancestral home, and while the maids braid her hair, she tells relatives that you would think the locals would all be savages but the British had done a decent job of taming them. Sure, they were lazy and dirty, but it was surprising how quickly they could be domesticated. Why, her head gardener was a local Zulu and he grew the most darling tea roses she'd ever seen.

She throws dinner parties to show off her husband and children. When a distant relative at the house mentions hearing something about a second wife, she flashes her violet eyes at them and says it's just rumors. Wicked rumors ignited by people jealous of her and Akbar's love.

She has her body scrubbed with turmeric every day and bathes in a bath of rose petals, has carnations threaded into her hair, applies the most beautiful pink and purple hues to her eyelids. She wears heavy jhumkas studded with jewels in her ears and has henna applied on her hands and feet like a new bride. When Akbar does not seem to notice, she grows angry. She paints her lips a furious red, her eyelids a darker shade of purple, and stains her skin with saffron stamens. She bathes in pure buffalo milk, scrubs her skin with sea salt until it is raw, and pushes back her cuticles until they bleed.

As a last desperate measure she secretly visits an aamil in the village skilled in the dark art of bringing back lost lovers. He gives her a silver amulet to wear around her neck and a small bottle of brown liquid that she is to put in Akbar's tea. She slips in the mixture with her ruined fingers and bats her purple eyelids at him, but he neither grows closer nor stops talking about returning home. When Akbar reminds her that she must start packing for their return journey, she throws the amulet out the window and breaks the bottle in frustration.

"You are disgusting," she hisses at her reflection in the winged mirrors of her trousseau. "I *loathe* you. Can't you do a simple thing? How *pathetic*!" She laughs manically at her reflection as her fever returns. "And now, after everything, you have to go back. Back to where you thought you would *never* have to return. You have to face what you've done." She stops, then looks down at her ruined nails and then back to her reflection with its wide violet eyes. "*But what have you done?* Why, you haven't done anything at all. You have nothing to do with what happens there. Whatever happens is fate and you can do nothing about fate."

She moves close to her reflection. "Listen to me—go back to that wretched house because you have to. Because as much as you *hate* him for this humiliation, it will be a bigger humiliation if you stay here. They are *watching*. They are waiting for you to fall, these jealous wretches! Don't give them the satisfaction."

THEIR RETURN TO the African continent holds a marked difference to their journey away from it. Grand Ammi and Jahanara Begum are quiet—the latter sulking and the former resigned to her fate to follow her son across the world. Jahanara Begum spends her days in the cabin; she misses the dinners and the dances and she speaks little. When she does emerge from her cabin, she is always a little disheveled, her lipstick smeared or her hair out of place.

Some of the passengers hear her screaming at herself inside her cabin and they wonder if she is unwell.

They receive the news on the ship over telegram.

Meena Begum was buried in the town cemetery six days before the SS *Takliwa* can reach its final destination. Her parents, a number of servants, and some of the fishermen attend her funeral. Daisy carries Hassan, jogging him on her hip when he cries.

Later, when she looks back on it, Grand Ammi says she had never seen her son look so stricken. It was as if someone cut open his face and revealed everything inside, she says. It had only been for a moment, for a flash of a second, because he had immediately composed himself and laughed.

It is a joke, a cruel joke being played by Meena Begum herself to punish him for leaving for so long, he says when he hears. She is probably standing with the telegraph conductor telling him what to write and they are both laughing together. This is how they play with each other, he explains. This is their idea of taking jokes too far. Oh, she nearly had him with this one. It is a good one for sure, he says to Jahanara Begum, who herself turns pale at the news.

He sends back a telegram saying he would get her back soon enough in a few days. For the rest of the journey he turns jovial, joking outlandishly with other passengers and talking boisterously. He pulls Jahanara Begum out of her cabin and tells her to sing for the people. When she refuses, he asks her to dance. He swings her around the deck and sways by himself when she leaves. He laughs loudly and unnecessarily and puffs on his pipe with more vigor. He stands at the stern of the ship at night and looks to the south. She is waiting for him, he says. She is standing at the beach at the bottom of the cliff waiting for his return, like she promised. He remains like this the entire trip. Grand Ammi says to leave him be, not to push the issue. She says people deal with grief in different ways and he will eventually have to face the truth.

Akbar arrives at the house joyfully calling out for Meena Begum. He ignores the ashen-faced servants lined up at the entrance and runs out to the cliffs, down the stairs to the alcove below. He searches among the rocks, calling out until he becomes frantic. He says the joke is over, that she should stop hiding. This isn't funny anymore, she should stop this right now, *right now*! He shouts into the wind as it whips his hair. Come out, he yells. He searches frantically while the family and servants watch from above. His fingers turn bloody as he scrabbles across the rocks.

When the only reply he gets is surf against stone, he looks into the sea and groans as if someone has punched him.

"No," he says.

He sits down and curls his arms around his knees.

He rocks himself, sobbing into the sound of the water. Grand Ammi at the top of the cliff makes everyone leave and then goes down.

She holds him.

Ten

With seemingly innocuous but carefully inserted prompts from Jahanara Begum, this is what they deduce: Iqbal Babu, the proud and bitter lion handler who harbored a hatred for his master that all the servants could attest to, finally lashed out. First there was his public humiliation when Akbar had stopped him from beating the lion, and then there was the talk of Akbar searching for a replacement. Unable to bear sinking to new lows, Iqbal Babu inflicted revenge in a way that he knew would pierce his master most: he unleashed the beast on the house with only the master's young wife and child inside. Then he disappeared. The police believed it too and promised a search but warned that he was probably already far away.

W<small>HO WOULD HAVE THOUGHT</small> him *that* crazy? the horrified servants say among themselves. Who would have thought he had such a devious mind? They shudder and hold their chests and wring their dishcloths in anguish.

Grand Ammi says little throughout this, but she looks strangely at Jahanara Begum after this: with a mixture of horror and respect.

ALL THIS FALLS on deaf ears with Akbar. He hears little of what anyone says to him. In the bloody garret he finds Meena Begum's farewell note and weeps. He shuts the room up, announcing no one is to enter. He lies on her bed below and stares at the ceiling, refusing to come out, barely eating. When the maids bring Hassan in, he carries him but soon passes the child back and asks them to leave. When he stops communicating with anyone, Grand Ammi takes over the running of the factory. Jahanara Begum sees little of her husband; occasionally she finds him in the garden sitting among the cages that he has emptied in a fit of sorrow one night.

One by one, he had opened their cages and lets the parrots, canaries, doves, and cockatiels take flight. As they sprung from their confines into the night sky, Akbar, almost delusional with grief, had begun to recite Iqbal's "The Bird's Lament" in Urdu, his voice rising through the darkness:

> *Spring has arrived, and budding flowers are laughing,*
> *On my misfortune in this dark house I am wailing*
> *To whom shall I tell my tale of misery, O God?*
> *I fear lest I die in this cage with this woe!*

By the end his voice was croaking, and he wandered the pathways aimlessly opening whatever cage he found. He let out the monkeys who screeched and raced for the trees, and he chased out the zebras and horses, but held back the Arabian stallion that Meena Begum was fond of.

Soon all the other animals leave except the giraffe, which wanders from window to window, and the peacocks, which strut through the gardens crying mournfully.

Eventually he is hardly seen at all. He begins to take long walks along the ocean. He leaves at sunrise and returns at night, sunburned and blistered. He stops bathing and his beard grows wild. He loses weight and turns dark in the sun. When the servants catch glimpses of him, they barely recognize him.

When he returns at night, his mother tries to talk sense into him. It has been *months*, she says, he can't continue like this. Look at how thin he has become, she cries. A terrible thing happened but he has to go on, she says.

But how? There are no Signs, he says. The Signs are gone. Nothing makes sense. Everywhere he looks she is there; he doesn't know where to look without seeing her, without feeling ashamed of the way she met her end.

Soon Akbar begins to talk to Meena Begum as if she is there. He whispers to her about how sorry he is, how he wishes it hadn't ended the way it did. He tells her stories about his life, things he hasn't yet had a chance to tell her in their brief two years together. His mother hears him talk about Egypt and the things he has seen and done there. He speaks about a rare kind of fish he had eaten in the Far East, a fish so red and delicate it seemed as if one was consuming rose petals. He takes out his books and opens them earnestly to his favorite passages to read to her, speaking fervently about the prose until he stops, suddenly aware of himself, and then he places his face in his hands, exhausted.

Sometimes, Jahanara Begum sees him sitting with his older son on the rocks below the cliff, speaking earnestly. When she questions Laddoo later about what his father said to him, he says nothing.

ONE DAY GRAND AMMI BURSTS into Jahanara Begum's chambers to say that Akbar had not returned home the night before. She says that she has looked through the entire house but there is no sign of him. They go into the garden and search the aviaries, the cages, and the stables, and then they go along the beach and comb the shore. Later they realize the stallion is missing. They call for the police.

They have been waiting for two days when they hear the news.

A fisherman at the lagoon says that he was sitting in his boat in the shallow waters late one night, trying to get a head start on the sardine rush, when he saw a man arrive on a white horse on the shore.

It's hard to miss a sight as grand as that, says the fishermen as he sits at the kitchen table at Akbar Manzil, his hat resting on his knobbly knees.

He says the man watched the sea for a while and then jumped off the horse and started to walk into the ocean. With his clothes and all, says the fisherman. He would have said something but he thought he should mind his own business. The man waded in to his chest and then he stopped. He just stood there looking out at the water, and the fisherman could hardly see him anymore in the darkness. When the man began to swim out to sea, the fisherman called out to him, but he didn't seem to hear. The last he saw was the man's head bobbing in and out of the water. The fisherman says he took his boat out, tried to reach the man as fast as he could, but when he reached the spot and called out, he couldn't see anyone anymore.

There was no doubt in his mind about what happened to the man.

No one can survive those currents, especially at night, he says.

Eleven

"My grandmother was aghast. She didn't handle it well at all. That wasn't how she raised her son. He was supposed to be a fighter like her, and the fact that he had just given up—given up on life, yes, but more especially *given up on her*—was too much to bear," says Doctor.

"I still remember it like it was yesterday," he murmurs. "There was a storm outside and it was raining. I was six years old. I was already in my pajamas and I was sitting on the carpet with my plastic army men lined up on the floor. It was France's finest against the might of the Austro-Hungarian army and it was turning out be a bloody battle. The wind was howling outside and the windows were shaking. I remember because I was pretending that the thunder was bombs falling down on the French army.

"I could hear noises downstairs, doors shutting and people shouting. I was just getting France to advance along the lines when my mother burst into my room and told me to start packing. Daisy and the other maids were following her, and she was telling them what to take and what not. Leave all the toys, she said. It was finally over; we could go home now, she told me. I was confused, because I thought we *were* home. She was throwing clothing into trunks and marching through the house barking instructions, said we were leaving this bloody place on the very next ship out. I remember standing at my door, wondering who she was—she looked so wild. Her hair was a mess and her makeup was running.

"Then my sister was by me and she was shaking me and asking me if I heard what Ammi had said, that I had to start packing everything *now*. That we were leaving the next day. Daisy was already in my room, packing my clothes hurriedly.

"I left my room and went into my father's library and sat on his chair and watched the storm from the dome. A few days before, my father had called me. He had told me that if anything were to happen to him, I would be the man of the house. He'd said I had to look after my mother and my siblings, that I had to be brave. He said I should follow my feelings, but more importantly I should follow the Signs. They would lead me where I was supposed to go, which was a better place than where I wanted to go.

"People were running up and down the stairs in the house. I picked up my father's favorite book, *The Masnavi*, and took it to my room, where I pushed it into the trunk Daisy was packing. I didn't know where we were going or for how long but I knew that everything was changing. That everything had changed since the day I heard my mother talking in the stables. My mother returned to my room, screaming that I needed to get dressed *now* and that I needed to help. When I asked her what she'd meant when she said 'going home' she stopped suddenly and looked at me hard.

"'This is not home,' she said. *'This is hell.'*

"My mother couldn't stay another minute in the house. She said it was cursed with the dead woman, that she could hear things at night, objects moving and something crying. She said sometimes she could even *see* the dead woman.

"Through all this my grandmother stayed in her room. When she had received the news that her son had left the world, the steel inside her broke. She changed that night. She remained in her room as my mother swept through the house, quiet, almost unable to move. She could barely even speak. Finally, my mother went to her, said we couldn't stay any longer.

"Think about the shame, she told my grandmother. What would everyone say when they came to know about what happened to Akbar? It was only a matter of time before the story spread, and it was not something they could hush up and quell, not like they had before. 'First that horrific death that we only just managed to keep out of the papers and now this. We won't be able to face anyone, Ma. Especially you, *especially* you—the head of the house! People will talk,' she told my grandmother. 'How you have failed as a mother. We have to go, now. And if you don't come with me, I swear, I am going without you. Come hell or high water, I will be on that ship out tomorrow morning.'

"And my grandmother—she just nodded and agreed. In fact, after that, she listened to everything my mother said. I don't think she knew how to think for herself after her son was gone. She aged in a night; her hair turned white, she became frail, she started to stoop. She took up walking with a cane. We didn't know it because she seemed so strong but she had really only kept going because of him.

"My mother could never truly escape that house, not after what she'd done. She thought she could, but her demons followed. Even years later she could never sleep with the lights switched off. Her dreams were filled with her secrets and her guilt. I heard the things she muttered in her sleep. Sometimes she cried, and once I even heard her say the other woman's name. She never showed it, though . . . she played her part until the end. I think it was putting everything into that part that killed her. Her heart gave out; it was just too exhausted to go on. I was a twenty-five-year-old intern in Ireland when I got the news."

He sighs then. Takes a deep breath before plunging back into the forgotten story.

The house shivers.

"The servants were asked to leave immediately. They packed up their things as quickly as they could. The cook was crying so much—how he loved my grandmother. By dawn they were lining up outside with our luggage. The sky was still pink. My brother was sent to live with his mother's parents. That was my mother's decision—she didn't want any reminder of the past. I remember seeing them take him away, and I knew I was never going to see him again. I wanted to run up and grab his hand and touch him for one last time, but I couldn't move. It was cold that morning, and as we rode away in the car, I looked back at the house disappearing behind me through the rear window and I remember thinking furiously that *I must not forget*. That whole ride to the harbor I had my eyes closed trying to burn the image of the house in my mind."

SANA LETS OUT a small breath when Doctor finishes. She looks at him in wonder, trying to see the little boy she had read about.

The house is quiet.

Eventually Sana says, "She kept diaries. The woman from this room. I found them in the attic. She wrote about you."

Doctor turns to look at her in wonder. "Me?"

"She said she never blamed you for anything. That you were too young to know better."

"She wrote that?"

Sana nods.

Doctor drops his head.

After a moment, Sana asks, "Did you ever see him again—your brother?"

Doctor clears his throat. "Yes. Nineteen years later. I returned after my mother died. Everything I knew had changed: the house, the people, and even the country. South Africa was a different place then—World War Two had ended and apartheid was in full swing. It wasn't a place I wanted to be in, but my father haunted me; I had to go back. I hadn't honored any of his wishes, you see. I hadn't followed any Signs, if I had even seen any, and I hadn't looked after my mother or my siblings. I never replied to my mother's letters after I left India and my sister and I never got on. After she got married, I hardly kept in touch. She knows I live here but she doesn't understand why I would call this place home. She thinks I'm crazy. Maybe I am . . . Anyway, I returned for a few days back then and wandered the city, but I was too afraid to go to the house. I found the cook, Pappu, so much older by then; he told me where to find my brother. He lived with his grandparents in a simple tin house on the south coast. He was standing outside when I went. He looked like both of them; her flashing eyes, his cleft chin. I discovered years later that my grandmother had made arrangements for him to get some money." Doctor laughs softly. "I didn't know the old woman had it in her, but she must have felt some guilt. In any case she did better than my mother . . ." Doctor sighs. "He was a good boy. You should have seen the way he treated his grandparents. My father would have been proud of him. *She* . . . she would have been proud of him."

"You didn't talk to him?"

"I didn't know what to say. What do you say to someone who doesn't know you exist? How do you explain to him that you've thought of him every single day? How do you tell him you're ashamed of the past, ashamed of time gone by, ashamed of how you behaved—all things he can't remember?" He shakes his head. "He became a lawyer. A good one. He has a practice that's involved in human rights—he helps with immigrants especially. I see him in the papers sometimes. He has a small house near the sea farther down from here, has a family; they all seem happy. I don't know what his grandparents told him about his parents but I don't think it was the truth. Why should he know about the past if it will hurt him? What right do I have to burden him with something like that? Why should I hurt someone who has done nothing to me? Why should I hurt him *even more?*"

THE DJINN WAITS A HUNDRED YEARS

THE DJINN STANDS at the door listening. It has watched Meena Begum's son grow up in this city. Once a year it would leave the house and make its way down the coast to see her son. It watched him turn from tottering toddler into a passionate young man, become sturdy and strong like Akbar and defiant and full of fire like Meena Begum. It watched him fall in love and marry and become a father of three. It watched him build a home.

It watched her son grow old.

Sometimes it goes down to the town and sits at her grave. It listens to the sound of hawkers calling and taxis speeding past outside the rusted railings of the graveyard. It remembers the first time it saw her on the beach all those years ago, how it followed the sound of stars and never stopped.

It brings her jasmine.

"AND THEN I LEFT. I went back to Ireland and worked. Soon after, I went to the refugee camps and forgot everything. When my wife died in Kenya, I knew it was time to finally come back," says Doctor. "It looked like things were going to change in South Africa and I always knew I would have to return one day. The house was damaged and almost worthless. It was a burden to the city, and it was not difficult to convince the municipality to sell it to me. And here I am, to live out the end of my days."

In the dim light of the setting sun, Sana places a hand on Doctor's back and pats him gently.

He closes his eyes, remembering the frightened small boy who sat in this room once, listening to his stepmother sing a song to the baby in her arms.

Twelve

It is Fancy who receives the Sign.

Two weeks before it happens, she dreams that she is sitting at her dressing table in the kitchen when she hears bangs outside. She peers through her curtains and sees the sky filled with fireworks—bright colors bursting over the sea.

"Look outside," she says turning to Sana, who appears beside her. "Look at the lights."

Sana isn't listening. She is watching something moving in the corner of the darkened kitchen. It moves stiffly forward, and slowly a girl, white-skinned and bony, crawls out of the shadows. She moves into the light and Fancy sees that she has no face; there are no features on her smooth skin. Sana whimpers and stumbles backward, fleeing the room. Fancy runs after her, shouting her name, but somehow finds herself walking in the dark passage alone, going toward a set of stairs that lead to a tower. She climbs spiral stairs that seem to never end, and when she reaches the door at the top, she finds not a room but open air. She is outside on a watchtower, the entire sky and sea spread before her. The city is smoking and ruined. The fireworks are still exploding, fountains of red and yellow bursting open. It is so dazzling she has to shut her eyes, and when she opens them again, she cannot see anymore. She blinks and blinks, reaching her hands out in front of her, but sees only blackness. In a panic she runs around crying for help until, in her blindness, she falls over the edge of the tower.

She wakes up with a start.

If she knew how to recognize a Sign, she would have known what this was. But Fancy was never taught about such things as Signs and so she gently pushes it away and goes about her business.

So she does not understand that something is coming for them all.

The night it happens, Pinky is sitting in her pantry watching *Dilwale Dulhania Le Jayenge* while eating from a can of beans. It's her favorite film, and she still finds herself gasping when Simran's father releases her to run after the train with Raj in it. She puts her spoon down for a moment to listen when she hears the stairs outside the kitchen creak; when she hears nothing else, she returns to her food and turns the volume louder. As she becomes engrossed in the film again, the screen with the embracing pair suddenly goes black and the lights go off. Pinky swears loudly in Tamil as she feels around for her candles nearby and lights a match. She goes into the kitchen to leave her dishes but stops and stands still for a moment. Something feels different about the darkness tonight. It is heavier somehow. Even the bats in the kitchen are not scurrying about. For once in her life, Pinky feels a little afraid, and she hurries back to her room at the end of the kitchen and pulls her pantry door firmly shut.

THAT NIGHT ZULEIKHA is sitting on the rocks, smoking.

She is thinking about the way the edge felt, how it thrummed against her fingertips. How close she has come to it after so long. The last time must have been in her youth. She had been sitting in a recital hall somewhere in Sweden and the crowd was on their feet applauding her performance. Her music was still spread in the air above the crowd, still ringing in their memory. A shimmering sky of a thousand lamps. She had never felt so bright, so full of life and wanting.

Afterward, as they made their way to the car waiting for them, moving through crowds of people and photographers, her mother had grabbed her, held her close, and said she had never been more proud. Just as she was about to step into the car, a reporter thrust a microphone in her face and shouted, "Miss Rasool, can you tell us what's next for you?"

And laughing, the laughter of one who cannot see what is waiting just around the corner, she replied, "Everything!"

On the beach, a dog barks and Zuleikha looks up suddenly, the memory caught in the air for a moment like a gleaming thread before it snaps and pulls her back to reality. She shakes her head and looks down at the cigarette that is burning her fingertips.

She flings it out to sea.

BILAL IS READING a recipe book by candlelight.

He runs his finger under the ingredients for a red fish curry. He says the words "curry leaves" several times to himself in a low voice. He imagines how it will cook. The burned tinge of frying garlic, the hiss of mustard seeds as it hits the oil, the way the turmeric spreads across the vagaar in hot yellow streaks.

He closes his eyes and remembers *her* scent, that particular smell of bittersweet sweat after a walk. It changed toward the end; a twist of chemical lemon, the antiseptic of never-ending hospital corridors.

He falls asleep with the recipe book on his chest, his glasses still perched on his nose.

THAT NIGHT FANCY is sitting in bed pulling off her rings and rubbing cream into her hands. She combs out her fine hair as she gets ready for bed. She tells Mr. Patel good night and blows him a kiss. She switches off the lamp.

She closes her eyes and her history returns unbidden.

She remembers the preparations for her wedding day, the lights and the sounds of the night before. The feel of cold henna on her hands and feet. The laughter of small cousins running up the stairs, the sound of music playing as someone opens the door to her room. The background blur of voices and laughter, someone asking for the window to be shut because the cold air will make the bride sick and don't they know she has henna on her hands? And then someone is pushing burfee in her mouth and one of the little nieces comes forward shyly to whisper in her ear.

"Are you in *love*? Are you in love with him?"

And the shrill embarrassed laughter of the child as she steps away from her back to the other little girls, fascinated with things like love and marriage. And her brothers, her big brothers looking down at her, their little sister, going away, going to be married, and suddenly there is a lump in her throat and she is crying and she doesn't know it, until an old aunt comes forward and places a rough hand on her cheek and tells her,

"It gets better. It gets better."

THAT NIGHT RAZIA BIBI rubs Deep Heat into her aching wrists after making fourteen dozen samosas. As she falls asleep, she remembers a time when her family went to the beach, a rare treat from her husband, who had been in a good mood. Ziyaad was seven and he was asking his father for money to buy ice cream. His father refused. She had taken out five rand from the small purse she keeps tucked in her bra and gave it to him despite her husband berating her that she was spoiling him and wasting money. She remembers the moment her son returns, holding a large cone with the soft serve running down his fingers as he tries to lick the huge ice cream. He was smiling with such a big grin that even her husband began to laugh.

It is one of those rare moments she stores away.

Bottles of light on a dusty shelf.

Doctor is sitting on the veranda watching the sea. He fidgets distractedly; he looks out at the ocean, overcome by a restlessness that has been building since his visit to his stepmother's room. History seems to tighten itself around him like a noose, and suddenly overcome by an unknowable longing, he stands up and reaches for his cane.

He limps up the stairs. As he climbs, a light begins to spread around him; the Persian carpets burst to life in rich color, the flowers on the wallpaper twist and bloom, he can hear the clatter of dishes and voices in the kitchen. Daylight streams in through the stained-glass windows and there is his mother passing him on the stairs with her long silky hair, violet eyes, and cold face. There is Grand Ammi below, marching through the foyer, throwing her silver dupatta over her shoulder as the servants follow. Through the stained-glass window he can see the fountain gushing water from the stone lion's mouth while Iqbal Babu wanders the courtyard, pulling his mustache and glancing at the upper windows. Doctor reaches a hand to the glass but immediately the scene falls away, the light fades, the colors turn gray, and the house goes dark. He blinks and shakes his head as he holds the balustrade. Then he continues up toward the last room in the east wing.

He is breathing heavily.

The room is bathed in pale moonlight, and the light catches moths that flutter delicately in the air. He can see his stepmother sitting at the bed nursing the baby. She looks at him as he passes and smiles gently before turning back to the babe. He walks toward the ladder. The room watches as he puts his cane down and begins the slow and stiff ascent up the ladder into the attic. When he reaches the top, he pulls himself through the hatch and the attic seems to swallow him up, like a mouth pulling in something with its tongue.

He wipes his face with a handkerchief. He cannot explain it but it feels like this is where he is supposed to be.

The circle feels full; the ends pull close.

He lights a candle, and in the dim light it feels like everything—the sloping ceiling, the dormers, the ragged rafters, and the writing desk—are all staring at him with accusatory stares. It feels as if they have been waiting for him all his life. He goes to the desk and runs his fingers over the surface. He sits down and closes his eyes. Instantly he is a boy again, pink-cheeked, dark-eyed, with sticky laddoo stuffed in his pockets as he cycles through the garden past fluttering birds and screaming monkeys. He remembers sitting in a washing basket, the smell of freshly washed sheets, listening to the muffled noises in the world above him.

He remembers how his father folded tobacco into his wooden pipe and read poetry to them. He remembers how his father's face would light up for a second as he held it close to the pipe when he struck a match. He remembers his grandmother and the way she walked with a stiff spine and chin held high, shouting orders to someone somewhere. He remembers how she aged so quickly, almost overnight; how her hair turned white, her skin shriveled, and how like a branch in winter she dried up, until one day, they found her dead, lying in bed with her hands clasped in her lap as if she had simply willed herself to death.

Suddenly the scent of jasmine overwhelms Doctor. He closes his eyes. In that moment, for a clear second he can hear the Bembe song from the refugee camp playing.

His head falls forward and except for the sputter of the candle next to him, all is silent.

Thirteen

That night somewhere in the future Sana's soul is roaming.

It hovers over a moment when she is a young woman in small heels crossing the street with twin boys at her side. She walks along the road until she reaches the sandy edge of the beach. There a man waits for her. The little boys run up to him and grab his legs as he reaches over and kisses her on the mouth.

Against the light she and the man appear as one with no ends or beginnings.

The soul hovers over the scene, watching with warmth.

Then the image begins to shake and shudder.

As it falls to pieces, the soul reluctantly rushes back to its summoning body.

SANA OPENS HER EYES and finds herself choking.

The room is hazy with smoke and the house is filled with a rumbling. She jumps out of bed and runs to the kitchen where her father lies asleep. She shakes him.

"Wake up. Wake up. Something is wrong." She pulls at him urgently.

Her father, groggy at first, rubs his eyes and then pulls on the glasses that have fallen to his chest. He looks at the smoke gathering along the edges of the room. He stands up quickly.

"What happened?" he asks.

"I don't know."

They rush toward the apartment door and throw it open. The passage is thick with smoke.

"Fire, there's a fire in the house," he says, shutting the door as they begin to cough. "We need to get out!"

Her father looks around desperately. He instructs Sana to bring blankets from the rooms as he runs to the tap and wets two dishcloths under the water. She returns carrying the blankets and he hands her one of the wet cloths and instructs her to hold it to her mouth, as he does the same. When he opens the front door again, she shouts, "Wait!" and runs back to her room. She returns with a small shoebox under her arm.

They wrap themselves in the blankets and enter the passage.

THEY NAVIGATE THEMSELVES PURELY by memory, running their fingers over walls, turning right and left until eventually they arrive at the top of the stairs. The reach of the fire is clear here and they can sense the flames now; already areas of the ceiling are burning and crashing to the floor. The rumble gets louder.

The wallpaper melts like candle wax running in garish streams down the hallways as flames tear through the house. Stumbling in their blankets behind each other, almost blind from the smoke, they rush down the stairs. There is a terrific crack and Sana screams as a burning beam crashes in front of her. She tumbles down the steps and loses her wet cloth. She begins to cough, unable to see or hear as the blaze engulfs her.

She looks for her father but cannot see anything in the red-hot hue.

She steps. Stumbles. Calls out. Unable to figure out whether she is walking *toward* the fire or away. She has no direction. The world teeters.

She bends down and crouches.

She feels in the heat of the flames a figure approach. She looks up and sees the shape of her sister before her.

"Help me," she says as the heat blasts her face.

Her sister bends down to her level. "*Help you?*" She takes Sana's face in hers and smiles. "Why would I help you, little sister? Look around. The end is here. Don't fight it."

Sana blinks, trying to see her sister in the bright light.

Her sister pinches her face tighter. "Now we can be together. Don't you see?" She looks reverently at the destruction around them.

Sana pulls her face out of her grasp and stumbles backward on her blanket. Her face is red with the heat. "I don't *want* to be with you!" she spits. "Don't you understand? I've never wanted to be with you! I *loathe* you. Just because you didn't get to live a life doesn't mean I don't get to. You think I'm the weak one? But you're the one afraid to see what's on the other side. *You're* the one scared to be by yourself."

"You *stupid little girl*." Her sister seethes. "You should be thanking me! You would never have made it *this* long, if not for me."

"No!" Sana cries. "*You're* the one who needs *me*. I never needed you. So go!" Sana is panting. "Leave!"

Her sister looks at her in surprise, the fire playing wildly across her gray eyes. Then she screams and suddenly lunges at Sana, digging her nails into her face, her scalp, wherever she can reach.

Sana falls back as her sister's body hits her. She grapples with her, grabbing at her wrists and trying to kick her off. Her sister wraps her hands around Sana's throat and presses against her windpipe as she straddles her. She leans forward and leers eagerly as Sana chokes. Sana attempts to pull her hands off but it's futile, her eyesight turns dim at the edges, and for a fleeting moment she is back in the bathtub after her mother's funeral, splashing, trying to get air into her lungs.

No, she thinks, even as her world fades, turning to black. She thinks of her father, searching for his lost love in every wayward stream. Of Meena Begum in the attic, fighting against every lost drop of blood, writing her last words to Akbar. She is strong too, she thinks. And—*I want to live.* She pushes herself forward suddenly and with a deep breath throws her sister off.

Her sister lands with a thud and struggles up slowly, scowling.

"Fine! It doesn't matter anyway," she yells. "Look around you." She turns to the fire raging around them. "It's going to happen anyway. There's no escape. The last of your little life is going to be so slow and so painful, you will *wish* I had done it for you." She steps back. "Let's see how you feel when you die all alone. Let's see how brave you are then." She turns away. "I'll see you on the other side, sister," she hisses as she walks into the flames and disappears.

Sana sits on the floor and screams.

THE DJINN IS WATCHING from a corner.

Just as it had watched as Doctor's head fell forward, the candle in his hand tipping over to cast flames down the writing desk. It had slipped mournfully to the woman's room below and begun to weep for her, for her song like the stars. Wherever her voice was hiding, it would burn away; there would be nothing left to find anymore.

The attic above turned into a burning inferno, and the djinn watched as the fire crept down and spread over the house. It followed the flames that licked the rooms, wailing and carrying the dead woman's face.

Down the stairs it went, drawn by shouting below, and there it found the two girls wrestling in the blaze. It watched the dead one leave.

Now the abandoned girl lies on the floor, gasping. Death is so near; it is almost upon her. Its fiery hands are already on her throat, choking her.

The djinn watches as she burns.

Fourteen

In the flames Sana makes out the blurry outline of a woman watching her. She's dressed in a sari, with deep eyes and long hair. Sana lifts her head and blinks.

It is Meena Begum.

The lights at the eaves flutter wildly.

Sana lifts a hand and reaches to her.

THE DJINN WATCHES the girl extend her hand toward it. It hesitates, coming out of the shadows, considering her outstretched fingers. Slowly, it brings its own to hers. They touch gently.

The girl is dying. But she is not dead. It can feel her heart still beating, faint as a whisper. The woman in the attic, its beloved, had been like this—almost at her end, barely breathing, it could already see the light fleeing her eyes. Her pulse was just a murmur, but still she had kept trying to breathe, to talk to the baby, to resist. It remembers how death had finally come, rising out of nothing, and how long she had held against its pull, until finally she had to let go. Oh, how it wept.

THE DJINN WAITS A HUNDRED YEARS

The girl looks at the djinn as if waiting. It sees in her eyes the eyes of the woman, and even though it knows that it is its own tormented reflection, it is overwhelmed. The djinn removes its hand from hers. It drops its head for a moment, then turns to the right and peers into the smoke.

It raises a twisted arm and points in the direction of something in the distance.

Fifteen

Sana can barely move, but she tries, crawling in the direction that Meena Begum points, Meena Begum who is already leaving, turning away, back deeper into the house, as if this were the only reason she had come. Sana drags herself though the thick smoke. She fights the fumes, coughing as she manages to make it to a passage where the smoke is less heavy. In the haze ahead, she can see a door. She makes her way to it, pulls at the door handle, and falls against the frame. Here the smoke eases a little, the unbearable heat lessens. Her eyes sting less; shapes become clearer. She tries to get a breath in and feels something loosen slightly in her chest.

She makes her way to the back of the dining room and tugs at the blanket, wrapping an end around her fist. She punches the glass through the lower dining room windows again and again. When the entire pane is smashed, she hoists herself through, her legs scraping through jagged edges. She tumbles outside, and as she rolls onto the grass, she sees in the distance her father running toward her.

She sucks in the fresh night air.

"Oh, thank God, thank God," her father is saying over and over.

"Give her some space to breathe," someone else is saying.

Hands below her head.

"Is she okay?"

Sana opens her eyes. The world begins to make sense again. Trees. The night sky. Her father before her. Zuleikha next to him, covered in soot. Pinky, wringing her hands. On the driveway near the entrance, Razia Bibi is yelling at Fancy. The shorter woman is wailing.

"Thank God," Bilal is muttering. "I couldn't see you when I came out—you were right behind me and then you weren't. I was just going back in when we heard the glass break."

"I'm okay," Sana croaks.

Bilal turns to Zuleikha.

"Is everyone out?" he asks.

Zuleikha turns to look at the burning building, her eyes wide. "I—I was down by the water when I smelled the smoke. By the time I came up there was already so much fire. Pinky came out first—then the two women. I went in for Doctor but I couldn't find him in his room. I promise I looked everywhere! His room is the closest to the entrance—he should have come out first. I couldn't breathe . . . I just came out now . . ." she falters. "I don't know—I don't know."

"Do you think he's still inside?" asks Bilal, standing now with his hands on his knees as he gasps for breath.

"I looked in his bedroom and his bathroom. I kept calling out for him. Where would he be at this hour, except in his room?" asks Zuleikha.

At this point Razia Bibi starts shouting, "She's gone crazy, someone stop her, *she's gone crazy*!" Razia Bibi is holding on to a struggling Fancy, who is squirming, trying to break the hold the other woman has on her wrists.

"Don't be stupid, Fancy! It will be suicide!" Razia Bibi shouts as the others make their way toward the wrestling women. "The bird! The bloody bird! She wants to go back inside for it!" Razia Bibi yells to them.

"You don't understand. You've never understood! You've never understood what he means to me. He's like my child, Razia, my child! *Don't you understand?!*" she yells as she pushes against Razia Bibi.

Razia Bibi lets her go.

"Okay. Okay. Fine then! If you want to save that stupid bird, then we'll save it. But don't think for a moment that you're going to stand a chance in there with those stupid lungs of yours. We all know I have nothing to lose—even my own child has forgotten me. I'll go."

Before anyone can say or do anything, Razia Bibi in a surprisingly swift movement pushes Fancy to one side and takes off toward the house.

Fancy yells for her to stop, but Razia Bibi moves fast. Already her thin figure is disappearing through the doorway.

Fancy makes to go after her but Zuleikha reaches out and grabs her. "Don't be a fool!" she hisses. "We don't need another death!"

They all stand there in shock, not knowing what to do until Fancy sits down suddenly and breaks into a wail. "She's going to die and it's my fault. I'm going to lose both of them. Why did she go?!" Sana moves close to the old woman and puts an arm around her. Fancy sobs into her shoulder. Pinky watches aghast.

Charred flakes of ash flutter around them.

Soon the sound of sirens fills the town below.

Then Fancy stands up, exclaiming in shock, pointing to the door as a figure emerges from the entrance carrying something. It's Razia Bibi. She is walking unsteadily, carrying a cage. Fancy rushes up to meet her, crying as she holds on to the other woman.

"You foolish woman! You pagli! *What were you thinking?*"

Razia Bibi is coughing, her face dark with soot, but she manages to croak out, "Well, I'm younger than you, you stupid. You wouldn't have made it!" she gasps before she collapses into another coughing fit.

The fire engine's wail cuts through the air as the vehicle makes its way up the hill. Sana sits on the grass watching the frame of the house collapse as the flames leap higher. She stares at the entrance, hoping Doctor will appear.

She closes her eyes. She knows, like everyone else does, that he is gone, that even as they watch, he is part of the smoke rising in the air. She turns and pushes her face into her father's chest as he wraps an arm around her.

Fancy's sobs begin to fill the air.

A group of paramedics make their way across the grass with blankets and stretchers.

Firefighters unroll hoses.

Sixteen

Akbar Manzil burns like a wick under the night sky.

The fire spreads quickly, everything suddenly surrendering itself in exhaustion. The house screams in agony as its limbs begin to first contort, then bend and break. Like pins pulled out of a puppet, each section holds together briefly for a second and then collapses. The rafters crash to the kitchen floor, the bats flutter through the smoke, and the moths turn to cinder.

THE DJINN STANDS in the ruins of the house watching it fall apart. There is a burning quality to its form now, like the shimmering lilt of a photo as it catches alight.

Its time for walking is over. Change has been building and now it is here, the final pieces falling into place.

The djinn watches the fire grow and waits, wearing the dead woman's face.

It does not flee its fate.

THE FLAMES POUR FROM the rafters and soon Akbar Manzil is a fiery pit. The windows burst open and shatter into the night. The envelope in Zuleikha's room curls at the edges and catches alight, the perfume bottles on Fancy's dressing table shatter, and Doctor's videotapes melt into a running black plastic stream. The djinn is engulfed and it begins to burn like a matchstick, growing small and dark and twisted until all that remains is a fine ash.

The paper flowers turn to dust.

THE FIREFIGHTERS LEAVE AT DAWN, and the last embers go out as a gentle rain begins to fall. The house hisses as its ashy remains turn muddy and water drips from the burned beams. It lies gasping for breath, clawing the earth and clutching at its injuries. Finally, with a rattle in its throat, it takes a deep breath and falls apart.

The carcass stands smoking, an open wound on the hill.

Seventeen

In the morning they gather together with their umbrellas, blankets, and bandages, rummaging through the mess, trying to salvage what they can.

Fancy supports Razia Bibi as she limps through the debris and pulls out warped pots and pans. Sana, with a blanket wrapped around her shoulders, picks through the objects, recognizing little of the remains.

PREETI HAS COME and is standing by her car. She calls out to Razia Bibi, handing her a cell phone. Razia Bibi talks then she hands the phone back, her eyes full when she speaks.

"He's coming home. He's taking the next flight back." She pulls the end of her scarf to dab her eyes quickly.

At the back of the garden, Sana finds Fancy sitting with Mr. Patel, surveying the damaged plots. She gestures to the dead roses when she sees Sana and says, "The smoke."

"I'm sorry," says Sana, taking the seat on the wall next to her. She studies the little green bird in the cage, who looks ruffled but alert. "I know how hard you worked on this garden."

Fancy nods. "It was beautiful, wasn't it?"

Sana looks out at the plot. "Yes."

Fancy touches a burned bush with her fingers. "They'll grow back, you'll see. They're hardier than we think." She stands slowly. She turns to Sana, reaches out, and gently tucks her hair behind an ear.

"You need to cut your hair, baby. You're hiding such a lovely chin."

Then she picks up the cage and walks out of the garden toward Preeti's car.

Sana lifts a hand to her ear.

She hesitates.

A mist rolls up the hill. It hovers over everything delicately. It wanders through the wreckage, wading through smoking books and cracked bathtubs, peering into pipes. It wallows in a small teacup. Crouches before a porcelain doll.

Swirls around the feet of someone who is crying in the courtyard.

"Pinky?"

Pinky looks up at Sana from the apron she is sobbing in.

"First time Pinky is crying for something that happened in real life. She didn't think there was anything to cry about in this life. But Doctor, he was a good man. He was always nice to Pinky. He-he didn't even mind that she didn't clean his room anymore."

She sniffs and wipes her nose on her smoky apron.

"What will you do now?" Sana asks softly.

"What do you mean what Pinky will do now?" Pinky says suddenly, fiercely. She drops her apron and stands up straight. "Pinky is not a loser. Pinky is a winner. Shah Rukh Khan says we must always try to stand up, even if someone kicks us down. I will find a new house to clean and a new pantry to live in and life will go on."

An old man with white hair and dark eyes emerges from the crowd that has gathered with their phones and cameras outside the taped-off area. He pushes past the people as he makes his way toward the front of the house.

"Look!" Pinky exclaims suddenly, as she stands on her toes and points. "Look! *It's Doctor!* He's alive! He survived!" she yelps. But her look of joy turns quickly to confusion and then dismay when he comes closer and she realizes it is not him. It is someone who *looks* like Doctor, except his eyes are different and he walks in clear wide strokes.

Sana studies him carefully and then gasps in astonishment. "I think I know who that is," she says to Pinky, rushing forward across the wet flagstones.

She meets him just as he approaches the opening of the courtyard. He has more hair than Doctor and he has dark lashes, giving him a softer face. He puts down his umbrella and gives it a little shake before closing it.

"Excuse me . . ." he begins. "I'm sorry to trouble but I just had to come see for myself. I heard about what happened. Such terrible news. Do you live here?"

"Yes," she says. "There are a few of us who are—were—tenants here." She studies him openly. "Are you . . ." She pauses, then continues, "Sorry, but who are you?"

"Oh, where are my manners? I'm sorry. My name is Hassan Ali. I have a law practice in town, although now I'm mostly retired. I'm sorry to hear about what happened to your home. It's really a terrible thing," he says as he looks at the smoking house. "Do they know how it started?"

When he says his name, Sana feels something inside her chest, a small shifting. Hassan Ali. Meena Begum's child, saved so many years ago in this very house. Meena Begum, who had not abandoned her. Who had saved *her* in her moment of need. Who had shown her that she was not a forgotten thing in the world. And now her child, an old man, was standing before her. Sana finds her eyes fill with tears.

She manages to reply, "No, not yet. Although they suspect it was something in the upper rooms."

"You see," he starts suddenly, "I know this is horrible timing but . . . I don't know how to explain this very well. I received a letter a few weeks ago. From a man who lives here—a Mr. Khan—he sent me a letter and he told me the strangest thing. It didn't make any sense. I didn't believe it so I ignored it. I thought it must surely be a joke or something. I'm sorry—I'm afraid I'm not making any sense. Forgive me."

"No. I understand," says Sana gravely. "The man who lived here, the man who sent you that letter—he said he was your brother, right?"

He turns to her, his eyes widening.

"Your half brother, actually. We called him Doctor," continues Sana. "And he told me that he had a younger brother named Hassan Ali. Your mother's name was Meena Begum and she lived in this house too. Whatever he wrote to you—I'm sure it's all true."

The man reaches out slightly as if to steady himself on something.

"I'm sorry," Sana says. "This must be a lot."

"How—how do you know that? How can it be true? My grandparents—they said—my father and mother died in a car accident. I mean I always suspected the story wasn't the whole truth but I just thought it was painful for them to talk about. When I got that letter, I didn't believe it. I've been thinking about what to do about it—I was still thinking about it and—and then I heard there was a big fire here. You could see the smoke for miles. Everyone was talking about it—they said no one got hurt but the house was destroyed. I didn't even think about it—I just grabbed my coat and I had to come see."

He falters, then says, "Is he—around? This Doctor fellow. Can I speak to him?"

Sana turns away suddenly, overcome. "You've got the wrong information, I'm afraid. Not everyone got out. Someone was still inside."

The old man's face falls as understanding dawns. "No—no, you see . . ." he starts. "I still have to *meet* him. I still have to talk to him about this. I just got that letter." The man straightens, his face aghast. "I didn't even know I might have a brother until a few weeks ago. I don't understand."

"Why don't we sit?" Sana says, pointing to the low crumbling stone wall in the garden. They make their way to the cliff edge and settle on the rocky surface. Sana looks down at the alcove and remembers how Meena Begum wrote about tucking her baby into a basket and putting him on the sand near the rocks. She thinks about how Meena Begum waited below with a lamp, searching the dark sea for Akbar. How her last moments had been used trying to save her child. She looks up at the old man next to her and it seems wonderous, how the history that had evaded her for so long was uncurling and revealing itself to her now, like a flower finally blooming.

"I don't have all the answers," she says to him. "I only know that your mother lived here until her death. She wrote about her life in her diaries. I found them, and then later, Doctor told me the rest of the story. He spoke about you—he said he thought about you a lot." Sana looks out at the smoking heap of the house. "I'm glad he decided to tell you."

"Why didn't he tell me all this before? Why did he only say anything now?" says Hassan Ali mournfully.

"I think he was afraid to. He said he didn't want to hurt you."

Hassan Ali rubs a hand tiredly over his face. "It's all so strange and unbelievable."

"Wait here a moment," says Sana. She goes to her father's Isuzu in the driveway and returns to the old man. "I saved these, because they helped me. I hope they help you too," she says as she hands him a box. He takes it from her and pulls the lid off. Inside are the diaries.

"She was an amazing woman," Sana says quietly. "She was the kind of mother I *wish* I had." She looks down. "She showed me how to be brave. She helped me face my fears."

The old man takes the box carefully. His eyes shine as he puts his hand in hers, clasps it, and nods. There is a small wind beginning up over the water. It ruffles his hair. He thanks Sana with a sad smile, tells her to come and visit him and his family. Then he pulls himself up, tucks the box under his arm, and walks away from the house.

Despite the warnings not to enter the property, Zuleikha makes her way to her room. The stone steps are darkened but firm as she climbs them. In the charred remains of her room, she looks through her ruined objects. She runs her hands over her desk, pausing over a scorched patch where a pile of ash remains. She examines it briefly and turns away.

She walks to her piano and runs her fingers over its husk, and to her surprise one of the keys still makes a *plink* sound. A small smile begins at her lips.

Sunlight breaks through the clouds and streams in through burned sections of the ravaged walls. She is drawn to the edge and she looks out of the building. She lights a cigarette.

The sea spreads before her like a brilliant mirror.

Eighteen

Sana turns to her father, who is sitting farther down the stone wall, sorting through boxes of their burned possessions.

"You're wet," she says.

He looks at himself as if noticing it for the first time. He adjusts his glasses.

She sits next to him. "You know when we first came here you said you thought she would like this place?"

He nods.

Sana looks at the house. "I didn't agree. I thought she would have said it was too old and dirty. But now, now I think, maybe you were right, maybe she would have said it had *character*."

Her father looks at the house too. "Do you know why your mother wanted us to move by the sea?"

Sana looks at him, then shakes her head.

"She knew you were afraid of water. She said it was her fault somehow. She told me girls couldn't have weaknesses, that the moment they did, someone would take advantage. A girl has to be strong if she's going to survive this world, she said. She made me promise I would take you to live by the sea, so that every day when you looked out at the water you would become a little more brave."

Sana shakes her head in disbelief. "No. She hated me."

Her father turns to her. "I know you didn't always have the best relationship, you and your mother, but she didn't hate you." He pauses. "She was a strange one. I know we don't talk much about her, but it was difficult for her, you know. She wasn't like us. Sometimes, I feel that she was like a wild flower in the veld and I picked her up and tried to put her in a vase. She found it hard to . . . exist. But she tried for a long time—for you, for me. I know she didn't show it always, but she loved us in her own way. We just didn't always understand."

Sana looks out to the water. It shimmers. She feels her edges pull and soften, like sea glass at the shore. A knot within her loosens and the secret box in her chest clicks and opens.

She turns to her father. She can see that he is more solid than she ever gave him credit for. He is a man who has loved deeply, loves deeply still, and she can see now that a person can be more whole with broken parts.

Her father digs through the cardboard box on his lap and pulls out a mangled metal rectangle that Sana recognizes as the camera she had found in the east wing. He holds it up for her to see. "Love comes in all forms, even ones we don't always recognize," he says, studying the irregular shape.

Sana smiles at him. She reaches out and gently pulls off his rain-speckled glasses. She wipes them carefully on her shirt until they are dry.

The light in the sky brightens.

"Where will we go now?" she asks as she places his glasses back on. "Another place by the sea?"

He looks into the distance. "No. I think we're ready for somewhere else."

Sana looks up at the sky; the clouds are gone, the sun is shining.

She knows it is a Sign.

Acknowledgments

All praise is due to God, the most gracious, the most merciful.

I'm grateful to so many for getting me here.

My agent, Julia Kardon who, on reading the first draft, which was like a house itself with too many rooms filled with too much furniture, shone her light through its dark depths and said, "I see a way." Thank you for staying to explore, for helping me clean up until this house flooded with light. You were the first to believe in me. My gratitude to you and the team at HG Literary.

My editor at Viking, Nidhi Pugalia, I don't how I got so lucky to have you with me on this journey. There was no one else in the world for this book; we spoke the same language and you knew this story and loved these characters better than me. Thank you for saving the sweethearts. I trusted you every step of the way and this story would not be what it is without you.

Soumeya Roberts for her tireless work on getting this novel into other countries and Ellen Goff for always keeping the gears running so smoothly. My UK agent, Caspian Dennis, for his advice and keen eye. My UK publishing team, Juliet Mabey and Polly Hatfield at Oneworld Publications and Andrea Nattrass at Pan Macmillan South Africa, for their edits and for being such joyous beings to work with.

The incredible team at Oneworld who has helped put this together: Mark Rusher, Lucy Cooper, Kate Appleton, Mary Hawkins, Julian Ball,

ACKNOWLEDGMENTS

Francesca Dawes, Paul Nash, Laura Mcfarlane, Anne Bihan, Hayley Warnham and Ben Summers.

The residencies and fellowships that housed and fed me while I worked. My gratitude to DW Gibson and the staff at Art Omi where I worked on the beginning of this novel in the Catskills. The Swatch Art Peace Hotel in Shanghai, where I worked on the middle of this novel in a big strange city that swallowed me up when I needed it to. Kima Jones and LaToya Watkins at Jack Jones Literary Arts, which allowed me to work on the end of this novel in the New Mexican desert, where I learned so much from so many. I am immensely grateful for these places where writers, especially ones from Africa, are given the space and opportunity to learn and connect with a literary world we do not often have access to.

Jenna Wortham, who was incredibly generous with advice and friendships and without whom this novel would not have happened. Khadija Patel, Sarona Reddy, and Aneesa Lockhat, my constant cheerleaders who have been there for me during the best and worst times. Jeremy Tiang, for the constant generosity. My friends who were early readers, who waded through pieces that I now realize were embarrassingly unfinished, I am grateful for your patience and kindness. My family: my brothers, my nieces, my nephews, and especially my sisters Saadiya and Zakkiya; thank you for supporting me.

Zahida, the best big sister, thank you for being my first reader, my ardent supporter, the one who holds me together. If you were not busy trying to help every person you meet, if you were not as selfless as you are, I know you would have written your own novel by now. This is your book as much as it is mine.

My parents, Goolam and Fawzi, for being patient and believing me when I said I was going to finish this story. I know I have not conformed to many things you expected, but you have loved me as I am. Thank you for giving me the time and space to write and for letting me be the haddi in your kebab. I am all that I am because of your love and duas.

Shubnum Khan is a South African author and artist. Her first novel, *Onion Tears* (2011) was shortlisted for the Penguin Prize for African Writing and the University of Johannesburg Debut Fiction Prize. Her writing has also appeared in the *New York Times*, *McSweeney's*, *HuffPost*, *Oprah Magazine*, *The Sunday Times*, *Marie Claire*, and others. She has a degree in Media Studies and a Masters in English from the University of KwaZulu-Natal. Her essay collection, *How I Accidentally Became a Stock Photo*, was published in South Africa and India in 2021. *The Djinn Waits a Hundred Years* is her debut novel in the UK.